Captive

VALERIE MICHAELS

iUniverse, Inc.
Bloomington

Captive

iUniverse books may be ordered through booksellers or by contacting:

iUniverse
1663 Liberty Drive
Bloomington, IN 47403
www.iuniverse.com
1-800-Authors (1-800-288-4677)

ISBN: 978-1-4620-1491-0 (sc)
ISBN: 978-1-4620-1492-7 (e)

Printed in the United States of America

iUniverse rev. date: 9/19/2011

Prologue August 1944

A LOUD GROAN OF PLEASURE LEAPT FROM *ObersturmbannFührer* Helmut Franz's throat as his favorite mistress brushed her soft lips against his lower abdomen. Her shoulder-length blonde hair made a small curtain over his hips, its softness sending flashes of heat through his body.

Monique Michaud pulled back, smiling as she slid her index finger under his foreskin. As soon as she caressed the tip, fire burned though him and he became stretched to the breaking point in expectation of her warmth. A fine sheen of sweat broke out over his body as he humped up his hips in encouragement. The slender curves of her hips and buttocks enticed him and her lush breasts drew his attention, inviting him to take their tips into his mouth. Once she created this fog of pleasure, there would be no turning back.

"Monsieur Frank," Monique cooed, her husky French accent sending chills of pleasure over his skin. "You are blessed with such a *queue magnifique.*"

Helmut urged her onto her knees facing his feet so her mouth was only inches away from his length. His mouth watered in anticipation as he eyed the pale blonde stubble that covered her womanly folds. Unable to help himself, he urged her downward and slowly brushed his tongue over her honeyed warmth and breathed in her musky scent.

As Monique closed her mouth around him and took him fully inside the recesses, grunts of pleasure rumbled in his diaphragm. He slid his fingers through the silky strands of her hair and pressed down her head in encouragement.

She was a much more rousing lover than the young and still innocent Therese Bauer. Therese's high, firm breasts and slender hips were very appealing, although her aversion to his touch had begun to grow weary nearly from the beginning of their relationship three years ago. Although he had caressed all the points that caused his other women to squirm with pleasure, she had merely lain there with tears streaming down her pale cheeks. When he had thrust deep into her tight heat, she had released a cry; not from excitement as with the others, but as if he had not given her a choice in their coupling. He brushed aside his thoughts and concentrated on the eager object of his intentions.

When he trailed the tip of his tongue over her warmth, she tightly grasped his hips and bucked hers as her climax began to build. "Oui, Frank," she moaned hotly as she released him from the warmth of her mouth. "*Oui!*"

Unable to stand it any longer, Helmut shoved her onto her back and widely parted her thighs. He rose on his knees between them and rammed himself inside her. He grasped the headboard and leaned his chest against her breasts as he began to pound away within her. Pleasurable fire spread over his body when she wrapped her legs around his hips and brushed her taut nipples against his as they moved together. Deep, passionate grunts erupted from his diaphragm and it didn't take long for his climax to build. As he drifted off into pleasurable oblivion a moment later, pain sliced into his chest and numbed his left arm if it were a razor.

„*Mein Herz!*" he tried to shout. Before he could force out the words, his throat clinched as another pain ripped through him and an eerie coldness crossed his chest. He collapsed onto his lover as an eerie blackness enveloped him. Almost immediately, he drifted into nothingness.

Chapter One

S COLONEL KARL HEINRICH, OF THE original *Schutzstaffel* bodyguard unit, sat with *der Führer*, his longtime friend, in the lavish conference room at the Berghof in Berchtesgaden, Germany. The room was much too overdone for his tastes. The rich decor with its Bavarian tile floors, rustic paneled walls, tapestried furniture and marble fireplace were extravagant and very beautiful. Lina would have described it as an antique shop in training. The best part was the view from the picturesque rectangular window, which showed a tremendous view of the Untersberg Mountain range. It was lightly tipped with snow even during the midsummer season. The decor seemed more akin to royalty than a government official. Heinrich remained in one of the comfortable chairs as his friend rose to his feet.

Adolf paced, a menacing figure even in dark shoes and casual navy suit with gold buttons, which complemented his homely features as well as they could. In comparison, the black uniform Heinrich wore fit his husky frame well and the darkness was a perfect contrast to his whitening blonde hair and pale blue eyes. The uniform had been designed for the purpose of intimidation and he had found that it virtually always had that effect. Even with their supporters, Heinrich usually caught a hint of fear in their eyes. Only his beautiful, young wife had failed to be wary of his presence and it had been her undoing.

The year had been 1938. Lina had been sixteen years younger than he, with platinum blonde hair, violet blue eyes and a voluptuously ripe body. He had been released on leave and had come home to find her in bed with her lover hovering over her. Heinrich had been unable to utter a word, rage soaring through him at the sight. Without giving either of them a warning, he had shot several slugs into the younger man's back. The force had knocked him to the bed and instantly killed him. A hysterical and bloody Lina had attempted to scramble out from under his body, pleading for her life and her husband's forgiveness.

Heinrich had stalked over to her, grabbed a handful of her waist-length tresses and yanked her off the bed. He had slammed her against the nearest wall and pressed the muzzle of his pistol against her abdomen. Silent, he had pulled the trigger.

Shock and terror had registered in the depths of his wife's eyes. "I love you, Karl," she had whispered tightly, forcing back a scream at the searing pain of her injury. "I am so sorry."

"So am I, Lina," he had returned. "However, it is unfortunate that I could not allow you to live after your betrayal."

When a bloodcurdling scream erupted from her, he brought up the muzzle of his gun and pressed it against the middle of her forehead. Again he pulled the trigger, ignoring the blood and brain matter that splattered onto the wall behind her. When he released her, she slid silently to the thick carpeting, smearing the mixture down the wall with her. "I love you too, Lina," he had said truthfully.

Once the shock of what he had done had soared through him, he had pointed the gun to his temple with the intention of ending his own life. It was then that he realized he had not been at fault, so he had called and reported the incident. As expected, few questions had been asked. The deaths had officially been ruled a murder/suicide and he had been cleared of any charges.

Heinrich shoved away the memory and returned his attention to his friend and leader. Adolf had always been a high-strung, charismatic individual, who reminded Heinrich of a thin human walrus with his boxy, fluffy mustache and with a mind bordering on insanity. Karl had accompanied him during the *Putsch* in Munich, although unlike his friend, he had emerged unscathed. He agreed with many of his friend's ideals. However, as far as his method, Heinrich would have found a much more subtle approach. Although they had been friends for years, he would not voice his opinions on such matters unless directly questioned.

Der Führer paced, deep in thought, with one arm across his waist to support his elbow and his chin resting on top of his clinched fist. Then he gripped the back of the dark-green sofa with both hands and stared over at him. "I am relaying this to you in confidence, *mein Freund*," he said. "You must tell no one what we have discussed."

Intrigued, Heinrich raised a whitening blonde eyebrow. "Of course," he promised.

Adolf nodded with a smirk, satisfied at the answer. "The Allies are coming closer to our initiative," he said. "It is necessary to replace our camp *Kommandants* with more dispensable factions. Now that Herr Franz is dead, it makes this particular transition much easier." He straightened and released the sofa to grip his hands behind his back. Since Claus von Stauffenberg's attempt on his life less than a month ago, he had been constantly on edge, only trusting a few to be near him and Heinrich was lucky to be one of them. "However, I loathe to admit I am at a loss on whom to choose as a replacement in his case."

Heinrich fought the urge to allow a smile of satisfaction from curving his lips. Rarely did his friend admit that he was at a loss for anything. "That is understandable," he agreed.

Adolf raised an eyebrow, another smirk turning in the corners of his lips. "However, you do have someone in mind?" he asked.

"May I be frank with you, *mein Freund*?" Heinrich asked. At a nod of approval, he continued. "As a matter of fact, there is someone who would be an expendable substitute. There is a young man under Rommel's command, who is quite the *pacifist*," he revealed, using the word as if he believed it to be a blasphemous curse.

Captain Lord Derek von Vetter had been under the field marshal's command in North Africa and was now at the Atlantic Wall. Karl questioned his loyalties, as well as those of the commanding officer, whom he was sure was aware of the plot against their leader's life and he would pay dearly because of it. He smiled at the possibilities.

Derek was very handsome with chestnut-brown hair and green eyes, well known for his unbending sense of humor. He had been in command of the Radio Interceptions and Communications Unit while in North Africa. His fluency in English had been indispensable, especially since the English spoke of everything over the airwaves, including their shoe sizes and the latest gossip about the King. Heinrich suspected there was a strong humanitarian streak in him, although the younger man kept this well hidden. He wondered how long it would take to break such spirit.

"Derek von Vetter is a mere captain; however, I believe we can influence his decision by a promotion in rank. If that does not accomplish what we wish, we may use his grandmother, Sabrina, and her companion, Miriam, against him."

Curiosity flashed in his friend's pale blue eyes. "How will utilizing such a threat accomplish what we desire?" he asked calmly.

Heinrich smiled. "Lady Sabrina's companion is a *Jüdin*," he was pleased to relate. "Her true name is Miriam Ephram."

They were both aware that Lady Sabrina's father had been the Thirteenth Marquess of Fairhaven in England until his death only a year after Derek was born. Sabrina had married Andreas von Vetter for love, although her father had disapproved, but he had allowed the marriage since the young man had been descended from Prussian nobility. There was another reason why Karl had suggested the captain would be the perfect substitution, although he kept that to himself. He was well aware the younger man had been his wife's first lover and that they had had a relationship for two years before Heinrich had married her. He planned to use that against von Vetter at the right time. As it was, if Derek's bloodlines were not so impeccable, with the noble line of his family reaching back to Henry VIII's reign, he would have the young man tossed from his profession.

Red rage crept up Adolf's neck and into his face, making his homely features even uglier. "Her papers show her to be a Maria Ehrmann!" he snapped.

Heinrich nodded, understanding his friend's anger. If von Vetter were willing to risk his life by obtaining fraudulent identification papers for her, who knew how many other Jews the young man had hidden. Such resistance from a commissioned military officer, no matter how passive, was a direct threat to the New Order.

"That is true, sir," he agreed. "As I am sure you would approve, we were able to arrest his contact, but now we must find a way to deal with the young captain. Convincing him to replace Helmut may be just the thing."

His friend gave a sharp nod. "As of Monday, October second of this year, *Major* Lord Derek von Vetter, Fifteenth Marquess Fairhaven, will be assigned as *Kommandant* of Murrbrück, I will not sacrifice any more high-ranking officers for the task. If he does not behave according to the Reich's ideals and methods, he will become incarcerated himself without the benefit of a court-martial and be labeled a criminal. Then you will personally see to it that he does not live to see the end of the war."

Heinrich was unable to keep a smile of satisfaction from curving his lips, glad his leader agreed with his thoughts. If he did not do as requested, the handsome and virile Derek will wish he had never been born. "Is there anything else you wish to discuss?" he asked.

A smile brightened Adolf's homely features. "You will report your updates to me," he ordered. "Young von Vetter is never to know we are in touch."

Heinrich nodded in understanding. He raised an eyebrow at his friend, wanting to turn the subject to more pleasant matters. "And how is your lovely Eva?" he asked brightly.

Chapter Two

"*MEIN GOTT*, ELIZABETH," WILHELM VOLKER PLEADED, his usually dull blue eyes bright with tears of worry. "I am afraid something has happened to Zarah and I do not know where to turn."

Elizabeth Kelley looked directly back into his eyes, her heart tightening with sympathy. She had been actively hiding her friend, Zarah Levy, since the SS had come looking for her several weeks ago. She had mistakenly assumed this was a fluke, but now she refused to tell anyone that Zarah was still there. "I'm sorry, Wil, but I have not seen or heard from her for the last couple of weeks," she lied. "I am worried about her myself." Although Wil and Zarah had been seeing each other for more than a year, Elizabeth couldn't risk allowing him to know where she was. Their lives depended on her not revealing the secret.

Wil ran a shaky hand through the top of his short, blonde hair and then brought it down to rest it on the arm of the chair. With his fair skin and hair, he seemed washed out against the dark, mint-green chair. A cloth sofa of the same color sat at an angle on the chair's left side. The paisley rug that laid on the hardwood floor was mixed with shades of blue, maroon and black, along with the green that matched the ensemble. "If you hear anything at all, even something trivial, would you let me know?" he asked.

Elizabeth reached from the matching chair at the sofa's right and rested a gentle hand on her friend's sinewy forearm. She gave him a reassuring smile. "Of course I would, Wil," she lied. "I promise."

He made an attempt to smile, although his eyes quickly filled with tears. "If anything has happened to her, I think I would want to die," he said, his voice cracking with emotion. His shoulders shook and he buried his head in his hands to cry.

Her eyes quickly filled with sympathetic tears at Wil's pain and she worriedly bit her bottom lip. She had been debating whether to tell him where his beloved was, although now she had made her decision, since she had no reason to believe that his breakdown was anything but genuine. "If you swear on your life not to reveal what I am about to tell you, I will let you know where Zarah is."

Wil's head shot up at the news and he wiped the tears from his cheeks with his fingertips. "Oh, you don't have any idea what that would mean to me," he said with heavy relief in his voice.

Elizabeth smiled as her heart lifted. It wouldn't hurt telling Wil that his girlfriend was still there. He wouldn't harm Zarah for the world. "I guess I'm just a romantic at heart," she teased. She rose to her feet and motioned for him to follow her. She led him from the living room, past the small guest room and up the hardwood stairs to the top floor.

As they came to her bedroom, Wil glanced in her direction. "Is she upstairs?" he asked uncertainly.

"Yes."

The room had originally been intended to be a storage room, but she had turned it into her bedroom because of its large size. She headed toward the dresser on the left. Since it wasn't that tall or heavy, she was able to tug it aside and reveal the attic-sized space behind it. Although the door was rather small, a person could squeeze through it and into the rooms behind.

With Wil following her, Elizabeth passed through the small door and around the corner of another wall. It was similar to the walk-in attic of her parents' house in the States, although this resembled another bedroom instead of a cubbyhole.

Zarah sat on the small bed, reading an old issue of a popular magazine. The casual, short-sleeved, emerald top and black slacks were a lovely contrast to her dark-blonde hair. A tiny lamp sat on the table next to her and it gave decent enough lighting for her to read. "Just one minute, Elizabeth," she said. "Let me finish the paragraph."

"You might want to finish that later. Wil is here to see you."

At Elizabeth's words, her friend's head shot up. When her gaze landed on Wil, a light of surprise and happiness flashed in her dark-blue eyes. She burst into happy tears and shot off the bed, dropping the issue to the floor in the process. "Wil," she cried as she launched herself into his arms.

He grasped her around her waist and spun her around, his face bright with his smile. "I have missed you so much, Zarah," he said into her hair. *„Ich liebe dich."* I love you.

At the loving embrace, Elizabeth decided she had done the right thing in letting Wil know where Zarah was. Smiling, she turned and left the room.

Later that night, she tightly grasped her pillow and breathed a deep sigh of annoyance, irritated that she couldn't sleep because of the thoughts of seemingly everything that ran through her mind. She often had this problem when she went to bed too early, but she hadn't wanted to stay up any later since she had stayed up past midnight the last two nights. Good thing she was on vacation from the clothing store nearby, where she was a salesclerk or she would have been no good to anybody.

She couldn't help but remember what her mother had told her to do when she couldn't sleep as a child. "Just pretend your mind is a blank page," she told herself as she forced her thoughts from her mind. "It will refocus your mind. If that doesn't work, breathe deeply with your diaphragm and through your nose instead of your mouth. It will relax you enough to where you will fall asleep."

It took several attempts to push away the thoughts, although it seemed only a few moments had passed when an odd pounding echoed in the recesses of her mind. It was muffled, as if she were hearing it in her sleep, so she ignored it at first. Unfortunately, it didn't take long for her to realize she wasn't dreaming and that the pounding was coming from someone at the front door. As she snapped fully awake, her heart and body jerked in fright.

Zarah poked her head out of her room with her hair mussed about her cheeks and her eyes filled with sleep. "What's going on?" she asked, her sleepiness heavy in her voice.

When the pounding became so hard that Elizabeth was afraid that whoever it was would damage the door, she gulped as the color drained from her face. Her heartbeat raced and her nerves tightened as the truth of the matter slammed through her. Only the SS and the Gestapo came during the middle of the night and the people taken away were never seen or heard from again. *It couldn't possibly be them,* she tried to reassure herself. *They would just be bursting into the house, so stop overreacting.* Logic disregarded that when a rush of fear lit through her as the pounding became more insistent. "Go back into your room," she whispered furiously to Zarah. "Now."

Zarah nodded and shot back into her room. Elizabeth dragged herself from the bed and made her way over to the dresser. She groaned as she tugged it back in front of the room to block it, her sleepiness making it seem even heavier. She took deep, slow breaths in an unsuccessful attempt to calm her screaming nerves, but she couldn't keep a shudder of dread from rushing through her. Not bothering with a robe, she quickly rushed out of the room and down the stairs.

Just as she turned on the main light, the front door slammed back against the wall and a squeal of fright leaped from her throat. She jumped out of the way as the man she knew as Wilhelm barged into the room with two SS men in tow. Wil's black leather jacket made a perfect contrast to his pale hair and the brown of his slacks fit to his thighs. Black jackboots ended just below his knees, adding further menace to his appearance.

Before she could ask him what was happening, one of the men grabbed a handful of her hair and slammed her down onto the floor. It was all she could do not to cry out as a lick of pain flashed through her neck and the roughness of the carpeting scraped against a cheek. She could barely breathe when he rammed a knee into her back and held her in place. He took a thin, black tie wrap from his belt loop and roughly tied her wrists behind her.

Elizabeth was so stunned that the thought to fight didn't even enter her mind, but when the sight of Wil's copper Gestapo badge caught her attention, the cold fingers of dread slid down her spine and tears sprang into her eyes. Even without an official uniform, the badge was unmistakable. She would never have believed that a friend of hers and the boyfriend of her closest friend could turn out to be Gestapo. How could she have been so stupid? Now both women would pay dearly for her mistake. "What's going on, Wil?" she asked. She wanted to cry out when the man who had tied her up pressed down on her head to keep her in place.

"Where is Zarah?" Wil snarled, his eyes showing no emotion. "Do not lie to me. Is she still in the hidden room?"

Elizabeth crinkled her eyebrows, as if confused by his demand. "I don't know what you're talking about," she lied.

Ignoring her evasion, Wilhelm turned to one of the two officers. "Uli! Upstairs, behind the dresser!" he snapped.

„Ja, mein Herr," Uli returned just as sharply.

Wil turned to the other officer. "Klaus, make sure she does not move," he ordered.

Elizabeth ignored the tightness of the wrap as Klaus pulled it even more taut, but she shuddered violently as the dresser crashed to the floor. As chills rushed through her, she fought to suppress a whimper of fear when Zarah screamed in terror. She flinched at the crack of Uli's palm at it connected with her friend's cheek.

„Schweig, Jüdin Hure!" Uli bellowed. Silence, Jewish whore!

Zarah was silent for a moment, but then wailed loudly. She and Uli descended the short flight of stairs soon afterward.

When Elizabeth saw the pain of betrayal in her friend's eyes as she stared directly at Wil, the tears she had been holding back began to stream down her cheeks. It was all she could do to hold the whimper in her throat. *Dear God, Elizabeth. What have you done?*

"You evil traitor!" Zarah screamed at the man she believed had loved her. "I hope you fry in hell along with all your bastard friends!"

Elizabeth could do nothing but watch as Wilhelm stepped over to Zarah and raised his hand in the air. He brought it down in an arc and slammed the back of it across her cheek. When she cried out, he raised his hand again and repeated the process. She made an attempt push Klaus off her to defend her friend and she cried out when he slammed her back down onto the paisley rug.

Her breath seemed to rush from her lungs, causing them to tighten painfully. *„Hurensohn!"* she forced out as tears welled in her eyes, her heart beating wild and hard from terror and rage. Son of a bitch!

Klaus grabbed hold of her hair and yanked up her head. She sucked in her breath when he raised his hand. The next thing she knew, the back of his hand connected loudly with her cheek. As the stinging began to spread through her, the officer sneered. "If you do that again, I will kill you," he warned.

As Elizabeth's emotions numbed, Uli watched, with a smirk of amusement turning in the corners of his lips.

Wilhelm laughed, apparently amused by the emotional reactions of the two females and his officer's threat. He turned his full attention back to Zarah and sneered. "Dirty *Jüdin*," he spat in contempt.

"*Nazi Arschloch*," Elizabeth tried to shout as new rage and the horror of the situation enveloped her. Nazi asshole! This man had pretended as if Zarah was the love of his life and now treated her as if she meant less than nothing.

Klaus pressed her head down as if with a vice, the action hurting her neck more than her cheek. "Shut your damn mouth, *Jude-liebhaber!*" he shouted into her ear, the loudness numbing her eardrum and making her heart and body jump. "I will not tell you again."

She glanced at her friend, tears springing to her eyes as she noted the emotional pain full on her friend's features. Zarah's screams had dwindled to whimpers, but she shook so hard and her cheeks were so pale that Elizabeth expected her to collapse at any time.

"Now that you ladies have calmed yourselves," Wilhelm growled, "you will be going with us."

Uli chuckled, shoving a teary-faced Zarah out the door and into the night.

"You will follow me, woman," Klaus demanded in nearly accentless English.

Elizabeth defiantly raised her chin as he grabbed the inside of an elbow and yanked her off the floor. Her head swam as she rose to her feet. She wouldn't have been surprised if she weren't able to move very well the next day, since the muscles in her thighs, stomach and arms had already tightened. "I will not," she snapped.

Wilhelm gave her a cold smile. "Yes, Elizabeth," he corrected. "You will not need a suitcase. Come as you are." He shrugged. "You are lucky, my dear. If anyone else had denied me, they would be dead. Remember my compassion in this instance."

"But..." she protested. Although the days were still relatively warm, the nights had become chilly and all she had on were her blue flannel pajamas. She wasn't able to grab a pair of shoes or slippers, so there was no doubt she would be leaving without a coat.

"You have been hiding a *Jüdin*, Elizabeth. You are lucky I do not kill you for it now," he said with another cold smile. "*Move!*"

Her heartbeat slammed against her ribs at Wil's shout. When Klaus nearly dragged her out the door, she had no choice but to allow him to push her toward the awaiting car. Wilhelm walked behind her as well, pushing her between her shoulder blades to make sure she continued moving. He urged her inside the black staff car and slid into the backseat beside her. Klaus started the engine and soon pulled away from the curb.

Her heartbeat shot up in anger and disgust when Wil slid his hand between her legs and cupped her. She angrily shrugged away his hand. "Keep your filthy hands off me!" she snapped.

With deliberate calmness, he pulled his pistol from his holster and pressed the muzzle hard against her temple. His action briefly stopped her heart and her head swam, as she was sure she would pass out. "*Nein*, Elizabeth," he said as he switched the pistol to his left hand. With the right, he yanked open her pajama top. She had to tighten her throat muscles to keep from releasing a gasp of shock.

Klaus, who had been watching every now and then in the rearview mirror, grinned in appreciation of her bared breasts.

Wilhelm laughed and dropped his gaze to her nipples, which were tight from the chill of the night air. She had to force herself to relax so the shivers gripping her body didn't take control of her. She had hoped the men would close the windows, but there was no way she would ask them to do so. They would just laugh if she admitted how cold she was. "Nice tits," Wilhelm leered. The driver burst out laughing in agreement.

He squeezed the underside of a breast and slid his thumb over the nipple. Elizabeth's face flamed at the deliberately intimate touch and her stomach rolled with revulsion.

Wil slid his hand away from her breast to the other, cupping the upper swell. "Too bad you have hidden away your Jewish friend," he sneered in English as he brought his face close to hers. "With breasts as lovely as yours, I would have enjoyed taking you as my lover."

Elizabeth fought to ignore his hands on her. "Well geez, Wil," she snapped in English, her tone deliberately sarcastic. "It certainly breaks my heart to know you don't want me anymore."

Wil grasped a handful of her long hair and yanked back her head. His action shot a flash of pain through her neck and she was barely able to hold back a cry. "Open your big mouth again, Elizabeth, and I will expose more than just your breasts," he snarled. "Do you understand me or shall I strip the nightclothes from your body and take you to your destination naked?"

Horror rushed to the marrow of her bones at the graphic picture her mind conjured. She would find out what true humiliation was like and she had no doubt that he would do exactly as he had threatened. Although she was tempted to pop open her mouth, she nodded in understanding.

"Now keep your mouth shut."

As the kilometers dragged by, her best friend's terror continued to replay itself in her mind. The man who had claimed to love her had taken her away and God only knew what would happen. Elizabeth had trusted Wil as surely as she had trusted Zarah, so she would always be responsible for what happened to her. The worst part of her ordeal would be her guilt about turning in her friend and it didn't matter that it had been unintentional. She would never forgive herself. She turned her head to the side and rested it against the backseat. She was unable to keep the tears from falling.

Chapter Three

A FEW KILOMETERS AWAY, ULI TURNED THE staff car down a gravel road with tall trees on both sides that led to a public *parkplatz,* where he stopped by a lamppost. Although the electricity had been turned off due to the blackouts, there was sufficient light for them to see with the near full moon. He turned off the engine and switched his attention to the woman beside him, flashing her a grin as he slid an arm around her shoulders.

Smiling in return, Zarah reached up and fluffed her hair into shape with her fingers. "Well, Uli," she drawled. "How did I do?"

Ulrich Hardtmann chuckled warmly. „*Wunderbar,* Louisa," he said, his deep voice full of satisfaction. "If I did not know you, I would have believed you really were hysterical. You are a terrific actress."

Louisa could not help but chuckle. „*Vielen Dank,* Uli," she said. She made a point to remind herself to thank her friends for their delayed entry into the house since it had helped her finish preparing for their arrival. Making her face pale had been easy. She had buried it in cold water until it was numb and had forced up some phony tears a few moments later. She was amazed at how easy it had been to fool the young woman, who had believed her to be a friend.

Elizabeth had believed her to be a Jew for over a year and she had surprised herself at the finesse, with which she had pulled off the scheme. A few carefully chosen words and false memories were all she had needed to convince the other woman she was a Jew. With a sickeningly sweet disposition added, the plan could not have worked better. She had no remorse or sorrow for what she had done. She had done what was needed for the benefit of the Third Reich, no matter how trivial. If Elizabeth had been willing to hide a friend she believed to be a Jew, who knew how many others she would conceal.

Uli released the buttons of her silky green pajama top and eased one shoulder back to bare a breast. He dropped his gaze to her and cupped her in his hand. "How lovely it is to touch you in this way again," he groaned as he ran his fingertips around the outer curve. When he brushed it over her nipple, heat rushed between her thighs. "I hope it has not been too stressful for you to endure Wilhelm's lovemaking."

A shiver of desire rushed through her as she recalled their times together. She *had* enjoyed them, although she preferred Uli's company in general. "Not too stressful," she chuckled.

Uli eased her top back off her shoulders and onto the seat behind her. "I am sure he enjoyed himself with you also, Louisa." His expression turned more serious as he raised an eyebrow. "Are you sure you do not prefer him over me?"

As much as she had enjoyed Wilhelm as her lover, he was not the most intelligent man she had ever known. She narrowed her eyes, but allowed a teasing smile to curve her lips. „*Nein*," she said. "Would I be with you now if that were the case?"

Uli chuckled, the action brightening his flat gray eyes. He would be a very handsome man if he smiled more. "I suppose you would not," he agreed.

She gave a nonchalant wave of her hand, wanting to change the subject to more important matters. "Enough of that," she tossed away. "Did I do well on my assignment?"

He bent his head and kissed her lingeringly. A shiver of desire rushed through her when he trailed his lips down the curve of her neck to a breast. When he replaced his finger with the tip of his tongue, a flash of heat rushed through her. She withheld a hot groan when he lifted his head and gazed deep into her eyes. "Yes, you did," he grinned. "And Elizabeth never suspected you are Gestapo?"

Louisa laughed. "No, she did not," she drawled. Now that the other woman was on her way to Murrbrück work camp, she would take the house as well as the property inside for herself. Besides, it had been her home as well for over a year.

She lifted her bottom off the seat and tugged her pajama slacks

Valerie Michaels

past her hips. Once naked, she rose to her knees in anticipation of Uli's lovemaking. The chilliness of the early morning heightened her sexual arousal and her nipples became sensitive as new desire flowed through her.

Uli sat back against the driver's door and released the buttons on his slacks. He did not usually wear a uniform, but she enjoyed how the black material brought out the blonde highlights in his pale-brown hair. He freed his erection from the material and grasped her hands in his to pull her astride him.

Louisa smiled brightly at her lover as she impaled herself on his swollen rod. "The fool will go to her grave believing I am Zarah Levy and that I am *Jüdin*," she said with complete satisfaction.

Chapter Four

ELIZABETH HAD BEEN SO PREOCCUPIED WITH thoughts of the evening that she didn't realize Klaus had pulled up to the train station. If these were normal circumstances, she wouldn't have lifted an eyebrow at the number of people boarding the trains, even at this hour. These were far from normal circumstances, especially with the various uniformed men forcing crowds of men and women onto the railroad cars, which looked as if they should be hauling cattle instead of human beings. Her heart took a nosedive, partially drawing her from her trance.

Some of the people were fully dressed, although many wore only their nightclothes, as did she. A few carried small suitcases and satchels, but most had nothing but the clothes they wore. Expressions of dread and worry had etched lines of anxiety into their faces. A small number seemed unmoved, but Elizabeth was sure they felt as she did, as if they were in a waking nightmare. It didn't matter how cold the air was or that the only natural light radiated from the waxing moon. She seemed to float as if she were only there in her mind, part of her wondering if this were really happening. She wanted to pinch herself back to reality, although logic told her it had to be a dream.

Elizabeth eyed the numerous trains stopped on the tracks and the soldiers, who carried Lugers, P38s and Mauser K98s. They watched everyone and everything, neither their eyes nor their faces giving away any thought or emotion. Various types of dogs walked with them; Belgian Malinois, German Shepherds, Rottweilers, with expressions as blank and unfeeling as their masters'. It was downright spooky.

"Do not stand there gaping like a fool," someone snapped from her right. "Out!"

She turned her attention to Wil as he eyed her with a sneer, but she refused to be intimidated any more than she already was. "Aren't you going to take me somewhere and interrogate me first?" she found herself snapping. "Isn't that what you people usually do?"

To her surprise, Wilhelm laughed. "We know all there is to know about you," he said.

Without acknowledging his comment, she numbly stepped from the black vehicle. The chill of the early morning air blew through her pajamas and to her bones, but she forced herself to put one foot in front of the other. A shiver of alarm rushed through her when Wil pressed his palm against her back and urged her along. It was all she could do to keep from sinking to the concrete and begging him to take her back home. Hot tears rushed into her eyes and she took a deep, shaky breath as she tried to calm her erratic heartbeat. Her mind still did not want to believe this could possibly be happening, but her heart said otherwise.

They crossed the walkway in less than a minute and once on the other side where passengers were being pushed onto the trains, Wil yanked on her upper arm to stop her. "Halt," he ordered, his hard tone indicating she better not even *consider* arguing.

Wil silently took a Swiss army knife from a small pouch on his belt and drew out the blade. He sliced through the ties wrapped around her wrists and then closed the knife before slipping it back into the pouch. Partial relief spread through her when he freed her hands from the restraints and she rubbed her wrists in an attempt to bring back the circulation and ward off the stiffness. Just as she was about to express her appreciation, a wail of desperation rang out.

A pretty, dark-haired woman attempted to yank her arm away from a guard with tears of panic streaming down her face. Elizabeth's heart sank to her toes as the empathic warmth of fear rushed through her. "Please let me go!" the woman begged. "You cannot do this!"

As soon as the guard slugged her hard across the jaw in answer, her knees buckled and she slumped in his arms. Elizabeth stood stunned as he shoved her onto the car as if she were a mere sack of potatoes, at a loss to understand how human beings could treat each other in such an abominable way. Knowing it had been happening for years and being numb from the ongoing anger was still not the same as when it happened in front of her. Even knowing she had been keeping her friend safe from harm was never going to be good enough.

"There is nothing you can do for her," Wil said, his voice filled with satisfaction and sick pleasure. "Besides, he has treated her quite... humanely."

Elizabeth glared at him with all her rage flashing in her eyes. How he could live with himself for taking pleasure from the scene? How could he have treated Zarah the way he did and not have any feelings of remorse? It was beyond her comprehension. "What's wrong with you people?" she snapped. "This is sick!"

Wil tightened his lips. "If you do not wish the same to happen to you, you will keep your damned mouth shut and do as I tell you," he warned. He eyed her partially opened top with a sneer and reached under the lapel to squeeze her breast in a vice grip. As she fought back the need to cry out in pain, he slowly drew his hand from her. "Fix your top or I will take you where you stand."

A shudder of loathing rushed through her at his touch and his words. She tightened the flannel over her breasts and tucked the ends into the bottoms. She wouldn't put it past him to turn his threat into reality.

They made their way to the closest car and once there, Wil shoved her through the open doors, nearly knocking her to the ground in the process. „*Tschüß,*" he said with a wave and smirk. Bye!

Elizabeth fought the urge to flip her middle finger into the air as she backed against the opposite wall of the cattle car. She took a quick glance around, eyeing the slats that doubled as crude windows. She wrinkled her nose as she tried to prevent herself from sneezing because of the slight filter of dust in the air. The musty scent of the wood penetrated her senses as she took a breath and she fought back hot tears as she waited for the inevitable. At least they would have some airflow when the car became overcrowded. If it weren't for what remained of the moon's lighting shining through, it would have been pitch black.

She was somewhat relieved when others came onboard, but her own lack of loneliness wasn't enough justification for them to go through what she was going through and what horrors she had no doubt Zarah was going through at this point as well. Nobody made eye contact, but even if they could have, it would have been pointless because of the near darkness.

It was as if very little time had gone by when the car was crammed full of people and the train began to move along at a sluggish pace. The dead silence sent a shiver along her spine. Several women were silently crying and an older man asked no one in particular why he was being taken away. The moonlight passed through the slats as the train continued to move, briefly shining on the side of a young man's swollen cheek. He seemed to be unconscious and Elizabeth assumed that the only reason he wasn't slumped on the floor was the lack of space.

She had heard rumors of people who were crammed into these cattle cars seriously injured and some even after they had died. Although most here seemed to be relatively healthy, a sick shudder rushed through her and nausea leaped in the pit of her stomach. *Gee, lucky us.* A hysterical chuckle rose at the derisive thought and she hiccupped to withhold it. Although tears burned behind her eyes, she found herself too numb to cry. Even with the slats, the air was stifling and heavy. She didn't know how those crammed in the middle ever had any air. Sweat covered her skin and her knees ached from the constant standing. Her body seemed heavy because of her lack of sleep and Klaus's treatment of her. She didn't know how she had the energy to stand.

The kilometers and the hours seemed to pass at a slow crawl. The darkness of the night had lightened and it gradually became morning, which had begun on the cooler side and had turned warmer. The air had become stifling again as the humidity rose. The lack of airflow emphasized the smell of the sweaty, filthy bodies and her stomach tightened with nausea. If she had eaten any food before her so-called arrest, she would not have been able to hold it down. As it was, her mouth tasted pasty, as if she had eaten a tube of glue and she expected the dry heaves to start any second. She would have given anything for a few swallows of water.

A white haze drifted into her vision as she became lightheaded and her knees weakened. Thankfully, someone grasped her arm to steady her and when her vision came back into focus, a tall, dark-haired woman in her mid-thirties gave her a sympathetic smile. "Are you all right?" she asked, with warmth filling her brown eyes.

Elizabeth nodded. "Yes, thank you for helping me," she said. "I would have fallen on you if you hadn't caught me."

"You're welcome," the woman said, holding out her hand. "I am Talia Strauss."

She shook Talia's hand in return. "I'm Elizabeth Kelley," she said.

Talia crinkled her eyebrows and curiosity filled her eyes. "Why are you here?" she asked, but then gave a humorless smile. "Besides the fact that some vicious men shoved you in here."

Emotional pain sliced through Elizabeth's heart and she took a deep, shaky breath to suppress her hysterical laughter. She envied the woman her sense of humor at such a traumatic time. "I was brought here by someone I believed was a friend," she found herself saying. "He turned out to be Gestapo and brought me here because I had been hiding my best friend, Zarah, from them."

A look of sympathy and understanding entered Talia's eyes at the information. "Zarah is a Jew, as I am?" she asked gently.

Tears rushed into Elizabeth's eyes and she nodded. "Yes," she said softly, her heart burning in memory of her friend. It had been easier to deal with her pain by not thinking about the situation, but Talia's question reminded her of the mixture of emotions that flowed through her. "God, I'm scared for her and it's all my fault." Tears began spilling down her cheeks as she related the story.

Zarah might now be dead for all she knew and she would always be responsible for what happened to her friend, since she had told a Nazi where she had been hiding her. It didn't matter whether or not she had known who he really was and she would have to live with that fact for the rest of her life, for however much longer that would be.

Talia's eyes filled with tears and she tucked her long hair behind her ears, her hands shaky from the movement. "I am so very sorry, dear," she said, her voice husky.

Here was this woman who herself was being taken away to God only knew where and her only concern was for someone else. "You know," Elizabeth started, her heart tightening. "In spite of the way Wil used me, I would do the same thing over again. I had to help my friend, no matter what."

"I just wish more people would do as you have done, Elizabeth. The world would be a much better place."

Before Elizabeth was able to let Talia know that she wished she could have done much more sooner, the train jerked to a stop. Her heartbeat shot up as panic began to set in. She swore, her voice shaky. Various reactions from crying to cursing sounded around the car.

Talia grasped her hands and squeezed them, her own terror at the situation showing full in her eyes. "Pray, Elizabeth," she urged. "That is all we can do."

Dread filled Elizabeth's eyes, along with hot tears, both tightening her heart. „*Wasser!*" a young male voice called. When what the soldier had said sank into Elizabeth's conscience, she and Talia took a long glance at each other. The people in the car with them burst out laughing with nearly hysterical relief and she nearly cried as her own relief spread through her. Everyone scrambled to the windows to get some of the liquid to relieve their hot, sweaty bodies. Elizabeth never thought she would be so happy to get something she usually expected without thinking about it.

She watched in anticipation as a soldier, who didn't look old enough to have a driver's license, pointed a water hose at their boxcar. As the water cascaded onto her and cooled her overheated skin, she stood still and closed her eyes. She opened her mouth in hopes of getting some of the liquid on her tongue to ease her thirst. It rained down on her face, immediately refreshing her.

After several swallows of the cool liquid, she moved back and allowed others to take her place. However short-lived the relief was, she was thankful for the small amount of the liquid she did receive. Several minutes later, the water was gone and the people stopped where they stood. New tears of apprehension rushed into her eyes as the train started moving again. The stop had merely postponed the inevitable. When someone squeezed her shoulder, she turned to see her new friend.

Talia smiled gently. "That was somewhat of a relief, yes?" she asked.

Elizabeth gave her a nervous smile. "Sort of," she said with a weary sigh. The water had been wonderful at first, but now the boxcar was more humid than ever. The flannel stuck to her skin and she rolled the sleeves up past her elbows in an attempt to cool herself. She gathered her long hair with her hands and held it on top of her head, but that still didn't stop the sweaty feeling from taking over her body. There was no way she could do so indefinitely, especially since her biceps screamed from pain after the men's abuse; however, it seemed to help for now.

"You are American?"

Elizabeth nodded, surprised that Talia had noticed. She wondered whether it was the intensity of the situation that caused her accent to come through her German. *Duh, Elizabeth. You also have an English surname.* "Yes, but I've lived much of my life here, so it's just as much home as the States," she said. "At least it used to be."

Her mother had died from ovarian cancer when Elizabeth was ten, but she still had fond memories of her. Soon after, her father, Daniel Kelley, had been sent to Germany on assignment with a well-known news network called the Unified Press Agency. He had taken her with him, but three years ago, he had returned to the States. She had been foolish enough to believe things couldn't get any worse, so she had chosen to stay. How wrong she had been. "My father begged me to go back home with him after Japan attacked Pearl Harbor, but I refused to," she said. "Besides, I wanted to do something for others and that opportunity arrived when I hid my friend. I just didn't realize how bad things would get."

Talia gave her a warm smile. "That is still very noble of you," she assured her.

"I just consider it doing the right thing. As you said earlier, I wish more people could do that. If so, all that has been happening in the world wouldn't be. I just wish I had done something sooner myself."

It seemed that their conversations were a catalyst, since others finally began speaking among themselves. It wasn't long after that that the train came to another stop. Elizabeth hoped they would be given more water, but logic told her they had arrived at their final destination. As the doors opened, one of the guards ordered everyone out. Since she and the others had been standing for several hours, her knees hurt more than ever, so much that she was afraid they would give out on her. Thankfully, however, she was able to remain on her feet. Once she had stepped from the train car, her aching knees became unsteady and she found herself stumbling. As her heartbeat shot up from the scare, she grabbed onto the doorjamb to keep from falling to the ground.

"Stay on your feet, red-haired bitch!" one of the guards snapped. "You are moving too slowly!"

Elizabeth wanted to scream at him what he could do with his comment, but he would probably shoot her as easily as he took a glance at her. She wobbled by him, keeping silent as her insides burned from the temptation to rail at him. As she forced herself to take one step after another, her friend caught up with her. Without a break in their strides, they exchanged a look of understanding.

"We will survive this, Elizabeth," Talia stated under her breath, apparently so the guards wouldn't hear her. "Have faith."

Along the walkway, Elizabeth unintentionally looked up. She noted the gray outer wall of the camp with the watchtowers of the same concrete and with electrified razor wire along the wall. She did not have to be told that they had arrived at their destination, as a shudder rushed through her. She compared the feeling to something dead running its icy finger down the inside of her spine. It was the creepiest feeling she had ever experienced and it seemed as if the gates of hell physically lay ahead. Her faith would be the only thing that would allow her to survive this ordeal.

Chapter Five

ELIZABETH SUPPRESSED A VIOLENT SHUDDER AS she and the others made their way through the guardroom and gate entrance that she later learned was called the *Jourhaus*, with the inscription *Arbeit macht frei* welded into the wrought iron. A hysterical laugh bubbled up in her throat at the deceptive phrase and she gulped to force it back down. The lie implied that if one worked hard, one would be released from the so-called prison. What a crock that was!

A dark-haired guard of about twenty-years-old made a scooping motion with his hand. "You are moving too slowly!" he bellowed. „*Schnell! Schnell!*"

Elizabeth, along with the others, quickened their pace, but the guard kept yelling at them to move faster. A blonde looked straight at her and allowed a smile to curve his lush lips, his golden brown eyes twinkling with laughter.

"Are you here for me, red?" he asked.

Her nerves flamed as her heartbeat shot off into a burst of cannon fire and her skin burned with anger. Who the hell did the bastard think he was kidding? It was all she could do not to snatch his rifle off his shoulder and smash the butt of it into his pretty face. Although it wouldn't do her or anyone else any good, it didn't wipe away the temptation.

"Did your lover send you here, sweetheart?" another asked in guttural English, his tone teasing.

At first, Elizabeth wondered why he assumed she understood English, but she figured he was only goading a reaction. As a childhood

25

friend had said to her, "No one will know you are not German until you open your mouth." The memory would have been funny in normal circumstances, but her cheeks warmed as a couple of other guards shouted similar comments at her. She forced herself to ignore them, although her insides continued to burn. She was sure it was the shock of the situation that kept her from losing her temper altogether.

"They will be plenty of trouble," Talia said with a mixture of fear and anger. "They are assuming from your red hair that you are not a Jew and because of this will not think twice about taking you by force."

Elizabeth's heart raced with panic as dread passed through her. *Great. That's all I need to hear.* Unfortunately, Talia was right and she would have to constantly be on alert. If the guards decided to force themselves on her, she wouldn't have any say in the matter. She had no doubt she would be living with constant fear of what might or might not happen. She had had enough of that as it was.

"They will try to play prisoners against one another, so do your best to remember that and not allow them to get away with it," Talia stated.

Elizabeth distanced herself from the words she would rather not have heard and turned her mind into a blank page. Once this ordeal was over and she survived, she would leave this country for good. There would be too many bad memories for her to remain.

She, Talia and a small group of new prisoners were led to the *appellplatz* for interrogation. There, the guards asked Elizabeth's name, where she was from and whether she had any illnesses or medical problems that would prevent her from working. The procedure was what she assumed it would be had she been arrested for a legitimate reason, but this method was all very systematic and very cold. Next, they herded her, along with many others, inside a building called the *Desinfectionskammern*, the word translating into "fumigation cubicles."

Once inside, another guard patted her down with his hands seemingly everywhere. When her pajama top gaped, pleasure flashed in his slate-gray eyes at the sight of the inside curves of her breasts. Disgust tightened her stomach when he reached under the lapel to squeeze them and then slid a hand under the waistband of her pajamas to cup her between her thighs. Her palm itched to slap the bastard across his face for touching her so intimately, but he would only hit her back, or worse, if she did. It was clear that he did so out of sheer enjoyment, not for a legitimate search.

"Strip down to just the skin on your bodies and no hiding anything from me, not even your privates," he commanded, his voice loud and clear. "No jewelry, nothing. If you do, I guarantee we will find it. After you have been shaved and given your identification number, you will be deloused. Once the sweat and filth have been removed from your body, you will be given your barrack and work assignments."

Shivering as if someone had pushed her into a cold river, Elizabeth stepped out of her pajama bottoms first, to keep her most private parts covered as long as she could. She pushed them down, along with her panties and then off, wanting nothing more than to curl into a ball and disappear. Tears gathered in her eyes, but she wouldn't give the guard the satisfaction of allowing them to run down her cheeks. She grasped the lapels of her top and stopped, but when he raised an eyebrow as if indicating that she had better continue, she tugged the top off her shoulders.

The guard slowly ran his gaze down her body and up again. She stiffened her legs in order to keep them from quaking, but it didn't seem to make a difference. Her lower lip began to quiver when a grin of approval curved his lips and she bit her bottom one to keep her sob from escaping. His direct attention cheapened her in ways she couldn't fathom and the only saving grace was the length of her hair that flowed softly to her waist. God only knew how much longer she would have the tresses to cover her. She glared at him, allowing the humiliation that raged through her to shine in her eyes, but he smirked as if her reaction were nothing more than an amusement. Most of the other captives had remained silent throughout the process, but she didn't know how long it would last.

"Why are you doing this?" one young woman with pale brown hair suddenly cried out in protest. "What have we ever done?"

Elizabeth's heart went out to the girl, who spoke with her fear full in her voice, since she had been wanting to demand a response to those questions herself. This made her worry even more about Zarah and heated panic rushed through her because of it. As she made a useless attempt to force it down by again trying deep and slow breaths, the nearest guard brought his rifle up and then sharply back down to ram the butt into the woman's stomach.

The silence in the room was as deafening as it had been on the train. Elizabeth's heart and stomach lurched in empathy as the blonde doubled over in pain and released a soft, whimpering wail.

"That was unnecessary, sir," one young man said in her defense. When another guard rammed the side of his weapon against the man's temple, he fell to the floor and pulled a bench onto his chest as he hit the hard wood.

"If any of you speaks another word without being directly questioned, I will shoot you on the spot," the guard warned loudly, his cerulean eyes sparking with amusement. "This is your only warning." When no one made a sound, a wide, triumphant grin curved his thin lips. "Now I will say it again, ladies and gentlemen, strip down to just the skin on your bodies. And no covering yourselves."

A few minutes later, the slender young woman in front of her, who was beautiful enough to be a fashion model, with long, brown hair and equally dark eyes, understandably attempted to hide herself by crossing her arms over her voluptuous breasts. The guard stormed up to her.

"What did I tell you not five minutes ago, young woman?" he demanded. "Were you not listening?" He grasped her by her wrists and roughly yanked down her arms. "When I said no covering yourself, that included your tits and your cunt. Keep your arms down or I will tie them behind your back."

Her bottom lip quivered and tears pooled in her dark eyes, but she kept her arms down as she had been ordered and did not react otherwise. Elizabeth doubted she could have been as brave if it had been she. She caught Talia's watery gaze and tears of dread filled her own eyes.

When a shadow caught her attention, she turned to see a tall, dark-haired man wander slowly into the room. The field gray of his uniform jacket brought out the green of his eyes and the darker slacks fit his thighs well. The black jackboots that ended just under his knees emphasized his manly calves. His blonde-highlighted hair was cut close to the scalp in military fashion and his eyes were flat as he observed the procedures. He appeared to be an inch or so over six feet tall and a few pounds short of two hundred. There wasn't an ounce of fat anywhere as far as she could see and he was tanned as if he had been spending much of his time outdoors.

When she noted the Afrika Korps cuff title showing, she knew her assumption was correct. He had obviously been transferred before the losses at Tunis or he would have been a prisoner of war along with the others. Under normal circumstances, Elizabeth would have considered him a very good-looking man, but she had to keep her guard up with him and the others. They were here to do everything but good and she had to remind herself not to forget it.

"This is your lucky day," the guard said with a laugh in his voice as he spoke to everyone and no one in particular. "The new *Kommandant* is here."

The *Kommandant's* insignia, with the unadorned, braided epaulet that indicated that he was a major, but he did not have that sick enjoyment in his eyes as the other guards had. If she hadn't known better, she would have believed him to be as shocked at the situation as the people being interned. He paled somewhat as an unknown emotion flashed in his eyes.

Elizabeth hardened her emotions, not trusting him an inch. His reaction could have been a trick, for all she knew. Wil had certainly had her fooled, with his tears and verbal worries. She wouldn't make that mistake again. God help her if she did.

Chapter Six

WHEN MAJOR LORD DEREK EDWIN VON Vetter entered the room, he took a quick glance over the crowd of people. His emotions numbed to the core when he saw the fear and uncertainty on their faces as well as in their eyes. He amazed himself by being able to keep his shock at the scene from showing, but by the grace of God, he managed.

He had lived through the scorching heat of the African desert during the day and the dramatic temperature drop at night when he was sure he would never stop shivering. The sandstorms made you believe you would choke to death, in spite of the fact that you covered your face and your body. The burning eyes, throat and lungs made you feel as if the dust had made a layer on top of each, so you were as afraid of being buried alive in the sand as being maimed or killed by enemy artillery. Even when compared to the combat itself, the camp situation was far worse. As a fact of war, you had to kill to keep from being killed, but that wasn't all true here. Murder, abuse and humiliation were meted out, merely because these people had beliefs and ideals different from those of their controllers. The physical problems healed quickly, but the emotional ones could scar you forever.

Some of the people were in the process of removing their clothing, but most had already done so. A couple of them were in the process of having their hair shaven from their heads and various other parts of their bodies. One of the victims was a young girl of about eighteen with tears running down her pale cheeks as her beautiful, dark auburn hair dropped to the floor. She said nothing and showed no other reaction besides the tears. She stared straight ahead in an apparent attempt to forget the horror of what was happening to her. His insides wrenched. If he had had any food in his stomach, he would have had to fight with all his being not to toss it.

The guard shaving showed no emotion in the depths of his slate-gray eyes or in his physical being. He completed everything in a cold-blooded, methodical manner as if these people meant less than nothing. Derek had not missed what he had said to the young woman when she did what any normal person would do and attempted to cover her breasts after she had been forced to strip.

How could he have been so bloody stupid? There were numerous rumors about these camps, but Derek hadn't known whether he should believe the horrific stories. Disgust and revulsion rushed through him when the truth of the matter whammed through him. Since he was now *Kommandant* of this camp, he deserved everything he would get after Germany lost the war. His "assignment" was more of a punishment, however, the Allies wouldn't see it that way and his command alone would be enough to condemn him.

He suddenly wanted to get rip-roaring drunk and let everyone return to their homes and their lives. Unfortunately, he couldn't do the latter. Instead, while he was here, he would do everything he could to resist the injustices that had been committed and make the prisoners' lives here as easy as possible. Even then, nothing could make up for the freedom that had been stolen from them. He would never forgive himself for not doing more sooner.

He ran his line of vision over a woman, who rested her hands on her ribs as if someone had slugged her and bit her bottom lip in an apparent attempt to keep it from quivering. He was sure that if she moved her hands away, her skin would reveal a bruise. His attention then went to a man, who had been slugged in the temple with some hard object, no doubt the butt of a guard's rifle. A bruise had already begun to form and blood had clotted on the small cut. He turned his attention to Erich, the guard who had snapped at the young woman for hiding her body from the others. „*Achtung!*" he roared.

The guard shot to attention as commanded, straightening his spine and pulling back his shoulders.

"What happened with these people, Erich?" Derek demanded.

Erich Kurtz stared straight ahead, his back still rigid and his eyebrows crinkled in uncertainty. "They were insubordinate and have been punished, *Herr Kommandant*," he replied without looking at him, his tone loud and imposing.

Derek did not attempt to curb the anger that raged through him. "Do not again arbitrarily harm another person in this camp, either physically or emotionally and curb your filthy tongue when the women are present," he ordered loudly. "If I hear of you treating anyone with anything other than respect, you will have to deal with me. When I am finished with you, you will wish your mother had never given birth to you. Do you understand me?"

„Ja, Herr Kommandant!"

"I want these two people you have abused taken to the infirmary so Doctor Weidenbach can check their injuries. I want them to take it easy for the day or for however long it takes for them to recover."

„Ja, Herr Major," Erich agreed, although his cerulean eyes shone bright with anger and resentment.

When Derek glanced at the young woman, she sent him a silent thank-you with her dark eyes. The man also nodded his thanks, although distrust showed fully in his eyes. Derek nodded to both in return and then turned his attention to the younger of the two women. "I apologize for my guard speaking to you in such a way, miss. It will not happen again." When she returned his attention with a cautious smile of thanks, he turned back to the guard. "Return to your duties," he snapped.

„Ja, mein Herr," came the curt reply, which was edged in belligerence. At this point, Derek didn't much give a damn. He again ran his gaze over the group and it rested on a young woman of about twenty-one. She was very beautiful, with flame-auburn hair that reached to her waist and large, emerald eyes that could have melted his soul. His heart tightened when he realized she was next to have her hair shorn. He found himself stopping beside the gray-eyed guard and staring down at him. "You will not shear her hair," he found himself stating.

The guard ignored him and turned on the shaver. Instead of using his service pistol, Derek snatched the rifle from the young guard next to him and placed the muzzle against the guard's head. "You will not shear her hair," he repeated.

Although nervous sweat showed on the guard's forehead, he silently brought the shaver close to her head. When Derek cocked the rifle, the sound reverberated throughout the room, which became silent as everyone's attention rested on him. He pointed the gun down between the younger man's legs. "If you shave one hair from her head or mar her flesh in any way, you will live the rest of your life as a eunuch," he vowed. "Do you understand me?" The threat was his last resort and he prayed he wouldn't have to make good on it.

The color drained from the guard's face and he immediately turned off the shaver „*Ja, Herr Kommandant,*" he said, his voice husky from apparent fear.

The woman gazed directly into Derek's eyes. "Do not give me special privileges, sir," she said. Although she spoke in fluent German, he could detect a faint American accent. "I stand with my people."

"Why are you here?" he asked, without acknowledging her statement. She thought of these people as her family and he respected her for it.

"She's..." a very young guard began.

Derek turned a cold gaze to him. „*Schweig!*" he barked. Silence! When the young man audibly snapped his mouth shut, he turned back to the woman. "Why are you here?"

"I have been put here for protecting a friend from your people, just as I would for anyone."

Nodding, he turned to another young guard with reddish-blonde hair. "When she is cleaned up and dressed, bring her to my quarters," he said for the other guards' benefit. He assumed *Kommandants* had a mistress or two who were captives and although he did not wish to speak with her for that purpose, he deliberately implied the opposite with his words.

„*Ja, mein Herr,*" the guard acknowledged.

Derek turned and walked out of the room. On the way back to his office, he decided he would inform his closest friend of his decision. Hans Lindberg was a leading member of a German Resistance group, which he and six other police officers who had been fired for being married to Jews had started. His grandmother was a minor member as well and had been allowing resistants to stay at his residence while he was away.

Hans had asked him several times to join his resistance group. Derek had said he would think about it, since he hadn't been fully aware of the extent of the atrocities in his country, even with the rumors and half-truths that were circulating. Now his decision was made and he would officially join. Kristal Müller was a waitress at the *gasthaus* near his residence and a member of that same group. Since she had offered to aid him before, he would contact her as soon as he could.

Derek had intended to inspect the rest of the camp after he had visited the processing rooms, but now it was something he wished to avoid. He hesitated to call these people prisoners, since the word implied that they had been brought to these places because they were criminals instead of victims. Their only "crimes" were being Jews, hiding Jews, having a different belief system from the Nazis or being homosexual. There were actual criminals, who had been sent to these camps, but they still did not deserve to be treated as if they were less than human.

As he stepped into the outer office, the uniformed secretary shot to his feet and greeted Derek with the now-required Nazi salute. Many people in his position were abductees of the Reich, but clearly and thankfully, that wasn't the case here. Manfred Rutger was slender, with dark-brown hair and gray eyes, appearing to be not much older than twenty. He was younger than Derek had expected, but young seemed to be common with the staff here. Withholding a snort of disgust and contempt at the young man's greeting, he ignored him and went straight into his office.

Once there, he plopped down in his chair and slammed his feet up onto the desktop. He crossed his legs at the ankles and released the loud snort he had previously withheld. "SS stands for Sacks of Shit," he snapped in his natural British English. "Protection Squadron, my ass. So who's going to protect us from these assholes?"

His grandmother and her companion had been close friends nearly from the moment they had met. Derek had found a resistant, who had had identification papers falsified for her in order to spare her from the atrocities to which her people were being subjected. His mind briefly went back to the moment he had been forced into this new assignment, when he had sat rigid in his chair. SS Colonel Karl Heinrich had paced in front him, the stark black of the uniform he proudly wore a perfect contrast to his whitening blonde hair and cold blue eyes. The colonel was a close friend of the *Führer's* and had been well before the notorious Beer Hall *Putsch* in Munich in 1923. He was a member of the original body guards, one of the few who retained the distinction and he was *Gauleiter* for the region as well.

Heinrich had married Derek's girlfriend, Lina Weimar, after knowing her for a month. It wasn't because of *who* she had married, but because she had never come to him and broken off their relationship. Although Derek had not been in love with her, she had deeply cut him. He had gotten on with his life and accepted his commission with the German Army, which was then referred to as the Reichsheer. Since he had been in military school since he was ten, the military was in his blood and was the only career, in which he could imagine himself.

He had read of Lina's death in '38 and his heart tightened with an emotional ache he had nearly forgotten as the colonel resumed his tirade. He knew full well that this Karl Heinrich was the same Karl Heinrich who had married Lina and whom had murdered her after he had supposedly discovered her with a lover. Although Lina had foolishly rushed into marriage with the Nazi, he doubted she would have been stupid enough to take a lover, considering who Karl was. And he doubted it was the murder/suicide the official story had claimed.

"It has come to my attention that your grandmother's companion is in reality a Jew by the name of Miriam Ephram," Heinrich had said. "Is that not correct, Captain?"

Derek's head had swum at the news and he had been sure he would pass out from the shock of his secret being discovered. He had trusted the contact who had given him the papers, believing he was only doing the right thing in helping hide Miriam's identity. It appeared he had made a grave error in judgment and she would pay dearly because of it. Although there was no denying the truth of the allegation, he had been unable to utter a word. It did not matter, since Heinrich had continued with his tirade.

"It is your choice on how you will enter the camp, Captain," the colonel had said, his tone as glacial as his posture. "Either as *Kommandant* or as a prisoner. If you choose not to become *Kommandant*, I will imprison you as well as your grandmother and her companion. You will be classified as a criminal and all three of you shall die there."

Derek had just kept his jaw from dropping as the shocking reality of the situation had raced through him. Numb, he had watched as Heinrich continued to pace.

"If you do plan to accept my offer, you will be rewarded with a promotion to the rank of major. If you continue your good service to the Third Reich, without question or divided loyalty, you will be rewarded most justly." He had stopped pacing and sent a hard, cold glance down at Derek, who hadn't bothered to conceal the anger that burned in his eyes. The other man had openly laughed, something that was a rarity.

The colonel had bent and rested a hand on each chair arm next to his wrists. "I see you are angry, *Major*," he had said with a smile, using Derek's proposed new rank, as if he had agreed to the change. "That is good and can be used to your advantage." He had then rested his hand on his shoulder and bent his head close to his ear. "Use it wisely, Derek."

Derek had remained still, although his rage at Heinrich's threats had continued to burn through him. The next thing he knew, Heinrich had trailed a hand down his chest and over his stomach to rest between his legs. He had barely managed to withhold a shudder of revulsion at the other man's touch.

"What is your answer?" Karl had asked in his ear as he slowly kneaded his phallus. "I remind you to choose wisely, because I would hate to see you lose what you are blessed with." After a final squeeze, he had removed his hand. "Your choice. Either you accept your assignment as *Kommandant* or become a prisoner along with your family. Which will it be?"

"The assignment, sir," Derek had said, his voice choked with an intense mixture of emotions. He did not have a choice. He could not deny the colonel at granny's and Miriam's expense. If it hadn't been for them, he would have risked becoming a prisoner. Anything would have been better than becoming the filthy vermin that allowed people to be murdered and tortured.

"Without question and without divided loyalty?"

"Without question and without divided loyalty," he had lied.

Derek shuddered and brought himself to the present. He had known even then that Heinrich's molestation was nothing more than a show of his power. It was a power that the colonel knew he had and he had used it to his advantage. He yanked his feet to the floor and rose from his chair. After making his way to the file cabinet, he pulled a bottle of Schnapps from a drawer and opened the lid. He tossed back his head and took a swig, grimacing at the strong taste. He couldn't stand the stuff, but it was the only liquor around. When the door to his office opened, a smug-looking guard walked inside and chuckled. He immediately recognized Sergeant Braun, the guard who had attempted to shave off the redhead's tresses.

"Having lusty thoughts for the lovely *Amerikanerin?*" Übel questioned as if they were friends, his slate-gray eyes bright with amusement.

Clearly, Derek's threat to emasculate him had only swayed him temporarily. There was no doubt, based on his insufferable attitude, that he would be trouble. Derek reminded himself to watch him. "Do you have a point to being here or did you just want to brighten my day?" he said, not bothering to conceal his sarcasm. He would have to speak with the secretary about not informing him of the sergeant's arrival.

"You *requested*," Übel said, emphasizing the second word with a sneer, "that I bring the *frau* to you when she was cleaned up. Rolf will be here with her in a moment."

Derek glared at the guard and slammed the bottle on top of the cabinet. „*Fein!*" he snapped. Fine! "Now get out."

„*Ja, Herr Kommandant,*" Übel grinned, obviously unfazed by Derek's anger. The guard snorted in apparent humor and raised his arm in the Nazi salute. „*Heil* Hitler," he barked. Smirking once more, he turned on his heel and stalked out of the room.

Derek curled his upper lip in disgust, raising his upturned fist and shooting his middle finger in the air. "*Heil* this, you pathological asshole," he snorted in English. "You and your bloody *Führer.*" Before he could stop himself, he smashed the Schnapps bottle against the wall, the glass breaking as loud as he expected, and watched as the liquid made a slow path down the wood. A moment later, Manfred burst into the room with worry showing on his features.

"Are you all right, sir?" he asked.

Derek glared at him before he bent down and picked up the shattered pieces of the bottle. "In the future, knock before you just barge into the room," he said as he tossed the shards in the trash. He would clean them up later. After a long silence, the secretary closed the door softly behind him.

In an attempt to calm himself, sat back down at his desk. He rested his feet on top and forced his attention to more pleasing thoughts. *The lovely Amerikanerin.* He had always had a weakness for women with long hair and the American was one of the most beautiful he had ever seen. It was her spirit that attracted him the most and that she had spoken her mind to him without fear. He was duly impressed. When Manfred knocked, he gave the young man permission to enter.

"The corporal is here with the prisoner, sir."

"Thank you, Manfred."

His heart slammed into his ribs in anticipation when Rolf Siedenstrang brought her into the office. The redhead had donned the atrocious blue-striped slacks and shirt that looked more like pajamas than real clothes, but somehow she even made them look elegant. The red chevron sewn onto the left side of the shirt and on the upper right thigh of her pant leg indicated that she was a political prisoner. She had been incarcerated for nothing more than doing the honorable thing, which was protecting a friend from an injustice. It was certainly no different than what he and his grandmother had done for Miriam.

The hard, wooden clogs made her feet appear larger their normal size. Her long, wet hair had been gathered at the back of her head, tightly secured with a green hair band. Her eyes flashed at him with hate and anger, and Derek knew he deserved every bit of both.

To his surprise, Rolf released several buttons on her shirt. It was apparent that it had been a requirement with the previous *Kommandant.* "That isn't necessary, Rolf," he said. "Dismissed."

Confusion lit Rolf's aqua eyes. „*Ja, mein Herr,*" he acknowledged with a nod. After a slight bow and without the salute, he turned and walked out the door.

When Derek returned his attention to the redhead, she rested her fists on her gently rounded hips and tapped her foot in annoyance. She glanced at the damp spot on the wall, where he had smashed the bottle against it, and then back at him. She raised an eyebrow in amusement. Derek couldn't help but grin as he tugged his feet off the desktop and rose to a standing position. He motioned at the chair in front of his desk with his hand. "Please, my dear," he said in English.

She hesitated, as surprise flashed in her eyes, but she raised her eyebrows and sat down. "So you speak English," she said with a sigh.

"Yes, I speak English."

"So how did you learn it?" she asked. "Even your accent is *la-di-da*."

When she rested her right forearm on the top of the back of the chair, the action brought the inside curves of a breast to his attention. He chuckled, suspecting the action was deliberate. "You are one gutsy broad," he said, this time using an American drawl.

"You even know some American slang," she mused. "Well, how about that."

He walked around to the front of his desk and sat in the adjacent chair. He crossed a leg and rested his chin in an upraised palm. "Yes," he said, returning to the British English he was used to speaking. "Even some American."

She crossed her legs at the knees and gently moved her right foot forward and backward. "So, from whom did you learn it?" she asked, her tone laced with belligerence. "Some prisoner before you murdered him or her?"

Derek inwardly cringed at the remark, but he couldn't say he blamed her for making it. He pulled away his hand and sat upright. "Believe it or not, my grandmother is English," he found himself relating. "My grandfather and mother were both German. My parents died when I was a small child and granny raised me since."

Andreas and Sabrina's son, Philipp, and his wife, Amalie, had taken a cruise aboard the "unsinkable" Titanic and they had the misfortune of going down on the ship only a couple of days after Derek had turned two. He had very few memories of them, so Sabrina was more of a mother to him than a grandmother.

"What, no '*grandmère*'?"

Derek laughed, since many of the German upper-class added French to their vocabulary, but his grandmother preferred to be called granny. "Granny would have a fit if I called her that," he said truthfully. "She has a low tolerance for snobbery, which has trickled down to me."

The redhead wiped the tiny smile from her face and raised an eyebrow. "So why did you bring me here, Major?" she asked.

He raised an eyebrow, surprised that she recognized his rank. "I am impressed that you know my rank," he said, expressing his thought.

She briefly nodded toward his left shoulder epaulet. "Your insignia gave it away," she told him.

"Of course," he said, but did not acknowledge her statement further.

"So how 'bout being a gentleman and answering my question? Am I to be your sexual slave while I'm here?"

Desire slammed into his gut at the sensual picture his mind conjured, but as tempting as she was, he would never force himself on her. "What's your name?" he asked, not trusting himself to answer her question.

"Elizabeth."

"A lovely name, Elizabeth. And your surname?"

"Kelley, with an e-y."

"Well, Elizabeth Kelley," he said with a smile. "What happens while you are here depends on you. I must do something with you and I have no desire to hurt you. Or anyone else, for that matter."

Elizabeth gave a doubtful snort. "Then why don't you set everyone free?" she asked. "What have any of these people ever done to you?"

Guilt raced through him at those questions and he had no good answer to them. "I cannot set everyone free, Elizabeth," he said truthfully, although that was exactly what he wanted to do. "Also, if I personally had wanted to hurt you or rape you, I would have done so already. You know that as well as I."

She pulled the corners of her lips into a semi-agreeing smile. "True," she said with a deep sigh.

"I am taking a grave risk in bringing you in here and suffice it to say, I did not have a choice in taking this assignment," he found himself saying. She could be a spy for all he knew, but he seriously doubted it.

"Do you really expect me to believe you?" she said.

"There are other people involved and I am not talking about the captives," he said, but then gave what he hoped to be a nonchalant wave of his hand. "But enough of that. I have already told you far too many things."

Elizabeth briefly crinkled her eyebrows at the word "captives", but the office door opened before he could say anything else. Without thinking, he grasped her hands and urged her to her feet along with him. He slid a hand to the back of her neck and an arm around her waist to tug her against his body.

When a small grunt burst from her lips, he took the opportunity to lower his head to hers. He shoved his tongue into her mouth and swiped it against hers in a wet, open-mouthed kiss. Although she did not respond, her body stiffened against him. He lifted his head and gazed into her soft eyes, his entire body burning red-hot at feeling her body against his. *Good God!*

"Excuse me, my lord," his secretary apologized. "Your grandmother is on the telephone."

"*Danke,* Manfred," Derek said without looking up from Elizabeth, his voice surprisingly normal. Her eyes were invitingly glazed, so he had no doubt her heart was beating as wildly as his.

„*Ja, mein Herr,*" the young man returned. A moment later, he backed out of the doorway and closed the door.

Derek released the still-entranced Elizabeth and urged her back down in her chair. He squatted in front of her and grasped her hands, nearly releasing a groan at their warmth and softness. "Will you excuse me for a moment, Elizabeth?" he asked gently.

Her only response was a nod.

He stood up and turned to face his desk, taking a deep breath before lifting the receiver from the phone's cradle. "Hallo, Granny," he said brightly into the mouthpiece.

"Hello, my darling," Sabrina returned, just as bright. "I called to tell you that Johannes phoned today to say hello and to see how you were doing."

The sound of his grandmother's voice never ceased to relieve him. At seventy-five, she was still healthy and energetic, with iron-gray hair that had once been a lovely shade of chestnut brown. Even then, she did not look anywhere near her age. She had been living in her own flat in his house fifteen kilometers from the camp since the military had requisitioned their estate house as a headquarters "to protect the nearby railways for benefit of the Reich", as they had claimed. After six months of staying with her unwanted guests, she had moved into his residence. Thankfully, one of the resistants was able to relay her new location to the others. Many had been staying there in the last couple of months and Hans had returned for the first time in two years. In any event, Derek hoped the estate still stood at the end of the war, especially since it had been in his father's family for generations.

Miriam was thirty-years-old and had worked for his grandmother since a few months before the *Kristallnacht,* when Nazis destroyed

Jewish property, arresting and murdering many Jews in an attempt to force their population out of society. There was no way that Derek would let anyone harm Miriam. Although he technically harbored a Jew and Colonel Heinrich had discovered this, he had no doubt that he had done the right thing. In any event, he and his grandmother had agreed to use the "Johannes" smokescreen for Hans when he stayed at the residence. "Thank you, Granny," he said warmly. "I will get in touch with him when I return home."

"I have the number written down. I'll see you later? I thought I would have Maria make us schnitzel for dinner," she added, using the alias for Miriam that they had agreed upon, since the phone could be tapped. "How would you like that?"

"You know that's my favorite," he said with a smile of regret, his conscience laced with the guilt of having decent food while the captives had little or nothing for dinner. He would correct that gross error as soon as possible. "I have to go, Granny. I'm in the middle of a meeting right now."

"I'll see you later then," his grandmother said with warmth in her voice. "Maria sends her regards."

"Give her my regards as well," he returned. „*Tschüß.*" He gently placed the receiver in its cradle and returned his attention to Elizabeth. He gave her a warm smile. "I apologize for the interruption, Elizabeth."

She sighed as though in sheer boredom, but by the soft look in her eyes, it was clear she was not. "You never did answer my question, Major," she snapped with bravado. "Am I to be your lover while I am here?"

"That is up to you," Derek teased.

"Sure it is," she scoffed. She still surprised him with her outspokenness and her fiery temper, for which the others wouldn't hesitate to harm her. He hoped that one day he could explain why he wasn't here by choice.

She defiantly raised her chin. "Would the people here be looked after if I agreed to become such?" he was surprised to hear her ask.

"Whether or not you choose to come to my bed is not a condition for the people here to be treated well."

"Surely you don't expect me to believe that, *my lord*," she said, emphasizing the title. "I believe that is what your secretary called you."

"I cannot say I blame you," he said. He was unable to keep from grinning at the fact that she had caught Manfred properly addressing him. She was sharp. "I also do not expect you to believe me when I say I will do everything I can for the people while they are here. You will see proof of that very soon."

"We will see, *my lord*. Won't we?"

"My first name is Derek, Elizabeth," he said.

She raised an auburn eyebrow. "But what if I don't want to call you Derek?" she challenged him.

"Then call me full of shit," he couldn't help but suggest. "It's your choice."

Elizabeth rose to her feet and narrowed her eyes. "I have a feeling you are not to be trusted, Major Lord Derek von Vetter, grandson of an Englishwoman," she snapped, with a hint of a chuckle in her tone.

"Then I will persist in attempting to change your mind," he vowed. "You will discover what a nice guy I am, I assure you."

"I will never believe that."

He withheld a smile at her determined words. "You will, sweetheart," he promised, not bothering to hold back the endearment. "I can guarantee it."

She cocked her head to the left. "Just for grins and chuckles, which rank are you?" she asked.

Derek crinkled his eyebrows, confused at the question. Weren't they just discussing that? "I'm sorry?" he asked.

"Since you are addressed as 'my lord,' you must be at least a viscount, but probably an earl. You may be higher, but I'm not much an expert on the subject. So what rank are you?"

He chuckled as a flush entered his cheeks. He was either called "'major," "sir" or until recently, "my lord" or "captain." He would have liked to be called by his first name for a change. "Does it matter?" he couldn't help but tease.

Elizabeth sighed, as if annoyed by his question. "Not particularly," she said. "Call it idle curiosity."

Derek found himself giving a gentlemanly bow. "Derek von Vetter, Marquess Fairhaven, Earl Thornley and Viscount Greene at your service," he said.

Elizabeth's eyes briefly widened, but she covered the reaction with a smirk. "Then I suppose it's time to take my leave of you, your lordship, three times over," she said. "Shall I curtsey on my way out?

He couldn't help but grin. *God, she's darling.* "That isn't necessary."

Chapter Seven

THE BARRACKS WERE AS OVERCROWDED AND filthy as Elizabeth had expected and the wooden bed, or shelf, as she would call it, would be too hard to sleep on. The thin blanket each of the women had would barely keep them warm at night when the cooler weather arrived. She had just stepped inside when one of the women joked that if the bed became too hard, they could always sleep outside on the concrete.

She had expected to be harassed and ridiculed for being in the *Kommandant's* office and was surprised that she wasn't. The others seemed to accept her so far, but if the major decided to pursue her, as he had implied, she didn't know how long it would last. *Just don't lure yourself into a false sense of security, Elizabeth.* She did not know what had driven her to speak her mind with him, considering his position. He could have killed her on the spot for even opening her mouth. She reminded herself to keep up her guard because his attitude might have been a trick to see how far she would go.

She was disgusted with herself for her physical response to his flirty charm. When he had kissed her so intimately, her heart had pounded wildly and it seemed as if lava had invaded her blood. It had taken every ounce of willpower she possessed not to wind her arms around his neck and give in to the sensations he had aroused in her body. *It's only physical desire,* she told herself. It would burn out soon enough. No matter what the reason, what kind of a person did that make her? How could she be so physically drawn to the man who was her captor?

At sixteen, she had given her virginity to an older man, who she had later found out was married. The very handsome Lukas Fuchs had taught her the first pleasures of making love and she had thought it was just that. She had also found out that it hadn't meant the same to him, since she had found out he was married. She had been heartbroken and her friends had become worried for her. With the exception of leaving the house for school, she had refused to go anywhere. A month later, Lukas had called upon her with excuses on his lush lips. She had slammed the door in his pretty face and ran back upstairs to her bedroom, tossing herself on the bed and bursting into tears. She had been sure her heart would break and that she would never find love again.

When her father had come home later and found her, she had explained what had happened. He had informed her that if Lukas returned, he would have him arrested. She knew that this wouldn't happen, since she was over the age of consent, but it had made her feel better to hear the words. "He's not worth your tears, Lizzie," her father had said, using the nickname she hated and he adored. The name gave her visions of Lizzie Borden, the woman who allegedly murdered her father and stepmother with an axe in April of 1892. "Find yourself a real man, someone who will treat you like a lady." He shrugged and winked. "Preferably someone with bucks."

At his last teasing statement, she couldn't help but laugh. She had decided right then that she was better off without Lukas.

Now she was in a horrid work camp and the sinfully handsome Major *Kommandant* had made his interest in her known. She insisted to herself that she couldn't trust him. No matter how much he flirted or made her laugh, he was bad news. She was a fool for even *considering* being attracted to him. A relationship with him would only make her life a larger hell than being a captive and the devastation she had gone through with Lukas would pale in comparison

The English titles surprised her the most. *Geez, Louise! Not just one, but three!* When he spoke German, there was no indication of an English accent, but when he spoke English, the accent was upper-class proper and all evidence of the German accent was gone. It didn't make him any safer that he was an English nobleman able to procure a commission in the German military. That alone made him untrustworthy.

Elizabeth and several other women had been assigned to the herb and flower garden. Their guard, Rolf Siedenstrang, was the young man who had escorted her to Derek's office. He didn't seem to fit in this type of environment, any more than most people. He seemed so innocent, especially after Derek had stopped him from unbuttoning her top. It was as if that type of reaction was rare. He was an inch or so under six feet, with a lanky but firmly muscular build, blonde hair with pale red highlights that one didn't notice until the sun shone on them. She suspected he had a somewhat rebellious streak, although she didn't know what caused her to think this. When her name sounded in the back of her mind, she forced herself from her thoughts.

Zsuzsanna Izsak raised a pale brown eyebrow, her eyes sparkling warmly. She appeared to be in her late twenties, with a slender yet curvy build. Although her hair had been a dark honey-blonde before her head had been shaved, Elizabeth could still see the remnants of the former color. "You were in the *Kommandant's* office for quite a while," she said. "Would you care to talk about it?"

Great. Here comes the third degree. "No," she said. "I would rather not talk about it."

When Zsuzsanna laughed, Elizabeth was glad to see that at least someone had a sense of humor about the whole thing. "Do not worry, Elizabeth," Zsuzsanna assured her. "You did not ask to come here any more than we did."

Elizabeth breathed a sigh of relief. "Thanks, I think," she said.

"It's no problem," her new friend said. After a brief pause, she raised an eyebrow. "He's rather gorgeous, isn't he?"

"I didn't notice," she lied. He was very charming as well, but not with the phony charm she had seen in many men. When one considered his noble upbringing, he was surprisingly not a bit as pretentious as she had expected someone like him to be. She expected more surprises from him in the future, but whether that was good or bad was yet to be determined.

When the other woman burst out laughing, a couple of the others briefly glanced their way. "No, of course not," she said in teasing doubt. "Neither have I."

A moment later, a shiver rushed over Elizabeth's spine as if someone were watching her and she snuck a glance over her shoulder as Derek walked slowly by. Although he didn't say a word, he nodded and smiled in greeting. A blanket of desire spread through her when she caught the teasing awareness in his eyes. *Stop it!* she chastised herself. The memory of his passionate kiss taunted her and she gnashed her teeth in an attempt to squelch her physical feelings.

"Good afternoon, ladies," he greeted them with a warm smile.

A couple of the women stopped what they were doing to gawk at him, but most ignored him, as expected. In any event, it was clear that such a greeting was nearly nonexistent since most captives did not react. Elizabeth could almost hear the silent, collective sighs of relief as he walked away.

"And you are immune to that charming and gorgeous man, you say?" Zsuzsanna teased.

"That's right," Elizabeth lied again.

"Sure," Zsuzsanna chuckled doubtfully. "I will leave that one alone."

Chapter Eight

OR THE NEXT TWO WEEKS, DEREK continued to make a point to walk by Elizabeth every day. His warm smiles and nods of greeting had made it clear he was still very much attracted to her. She had believed that when he had given her that kiss in front of his secretary, it was to cover up that he had only been speaking with her. No doubt it was typical for someone in his position to have a mistress who was incarcerated in the camp where he was in charge. She had no intention of allowing him any liberties nor would she allow him to see how attracted she was to him. *Damn him, the bastard!* Why did he have to be so damned sexy and such a damned flirt? *He's the Kommandant of a work camp, Elizabeth. Are you out of your mind?*

"I do believe you are about to smother that poor flower," someone seemed to tease.

Elizabeth turned to the voice as Talia smiled. *„Bitte?"* she asked, unsure whether she had understood correctly.

"That flower," her friend repeated.

When Elizabeth glanced down at the flower she had partially buried under the dirt and noticed that half of it sagged from the weight of the soil, she rolled her eyes. "It looks that way, doesn't it?" she sighed, making more of a statement than asking a question.

Talia took a glance at Derek as he walked away. "He has had his eye on you since the first time he saw you," she said as if Elizabeth hadn't noticed. Talia grasped her hand. "Has he forced himself on you, Elizabeth?"

"No, he has not," she said with a sigh. What was so ironic was that he wouldn't need to force himself on her at all. She had never been so drawn to any man in her entire life, even her first lover. She was a complete idiot for even *thinking* of being attracted to him.

Her friend nodded and raised an eyebrow. "I do have to admit, he is not what I had expected," she said with a gentle upturning of one side of her lips. "But if the others find out about the attraction you feel for him, they will feel betrayed and lash out at you. In their eyes, you will be a collaborator."

Elizabeth let go of her friend's hand and resumed her task of planting the reddish-orange flowers. She absently wondered how they would survive in the cold. It was still somewhat comfortable during the day, but that wouldn't last much longer. "I feel no attraction toward him," she lied. Her heart pounded as the opposite of her words screamed through every nerve of her body. She looked forward to seeing him, no matter how brief the time was, and she found herself missing his presence when she didn't.

Talia gave her a knowing chuckle. "Yes, you do, Elizabeth," she corrected. "I can see it is there even though the others apparently have not."

Except for Zsuzsanna, but it would be best to keep that information to herself. There was no telling how many of the others could see it. Talia rested a hand on her forearm, the action startling her. Elizabeth turned her attention back to Talia. "I'll be careful," she promised.

Her friend smiled at her with sympathy and the same flashed in her dark eyes. "Be sure you do or your life will be made hell," Talia reminded her. "If anything happens between the two of you, it may not only be the guards you will need to watch out for. I say this not as a warning, but because I care for you."

Tears stemming from an unknown emotion rushed into Elizabeth's eyes and she sighed with a heavy heart. If the others ever found out about her feelings for Derek, she would be a target of theirs as well. "Thank you for your concern, Talia," she said, not really wanting to hear it, even though it was true.

"Just remember that I will be here for you if you need to talk with someone."

A small smile tugged her lips. "Thank you," she said.

Chapter Nine

ELIZABETH HUNG THE LAST OF THE clothing on the line after the long afternoon of washing. There had been only a few pieces left, so she had offered to finish. Her hands were beyond dry and she wished she had some lotion to soothe away the rawness. In spite of the humidity, she was glad she had been able to move into the laundry room. She headed toward the door when someone entered the room. Her heart tightened but skipped a beat when Derek came to a standstill and flashed her a warm smile. He looked so wonderful in his uniform that her breath caught, tightening the knot between her breasts.

"Are you finished, Elizabeth?" he asked gently.

Her stunned heartbeat shot off into a barrage of gunfire and heat spread all the way to her marrow. "Y...yes," she stammered, her nerves jumping as fast as her heart was racing.

When Derek stepped toward her, it was all she could do not to move away. If he touched her, she wouldn't be able to say no. "Am I making you nervous, sweetheart?" he asked.

Although her bones melted at his endearment, she shook her head in denial. "N...no," she lied as her body screamed the opposite.

He continued to take slow, steady strides toward her and other than his boots clunking on the wooden floor, the only sound was her heartbeat pounding heavily in her ears. "No?" he asked with a bright light of awareness in his eyes.

She started to back away slowly, but the wall stopped her within a couple of steps.

Derek caught up to her and immediately grasped her hands to rub them between his. Her insides burned at his touch and she released a shaky sigh. "I will have to see about finding you some lotion for these lovely hands," he said softly. He wriggled his eyebrows. "I do have ways."

"Oh?" she asked, pretending nonchalance as a soft quiver rushed through her, not from fear or worry, but because of the warmth of his hands entwined with hers and the closeness of his body. When he bent his head toward hers, she was barely able to hold back a whimper of anticipation.

He stopped within a breath's distance and gazed into her eyes. "Yes," he said, his voice sensually soft. "To keep them as soft as the rest of your skin."

She unconsciously whispered his name and the next thing she knew, his tongue entwined with hers. She mated hers with his and released a whimper of wanting as new waves of fire swept through her body. Without realizing what she was doing, she released his hands and slid hers around the back of his neck. She tugged his head closer, urging him to deepen the already intimate kiss.

She didn't protest when he slid a hand up her abdomen and slowly trailed it up to close over a breast. He encircled her sensitive nipple through the material with the tip of his thumb and responding flames burned between her thighs. He released buttons on her top and then slid a hand inside. When he caressed the swollen nipple between his thumb and index finger, she peeled her mouth away and released a soft gasp. As he switched to her other breast and repeated the procedure, she leaned her head back against the wall. He pressed up against her so she was fully aware of the hardness of his body. He lowered his mouth to hers again, slithering his tongue inside and against hers.

Unable to help herself, she slid her fingers through his hair and pressed her breast into his palm. As soon as he slid his hand away from her breast and pulled it from the top, his action cooled her overheated skin. He trailed a hand under the hem of her shirt and upward over her abdomen and then back down again. A long heartbeat later, he eased the hand downward to between her thighs and slid his middle finger against the sensitive bud. As she humped against him, his continued caresses dampened her already burning warmth and her blood seemed to burn hotter.

The touch of Derek's tongue, lips and body brought out a craving, fiery passion she fought to control with everything she had. Her mind swirled as she began to float into the stars. As he peeled his lips and tongue away, their equally deep and labored breathing sounded in her ears.

He grasped her hand and urged it down to cover his stiffness. Unable to help herself, she gently squeezed him in her palm. "Now try to tell me you don't want me," he said with a heated groan.

That was the last comment he should have made and it was as if he had submerged her in a tub of freezing water. She shot away and quickly refastened the buttons he had undone. "God damn you!" she shouted in English, tears of rage at her weaknesses falling down her cheeks. She stepped back toward him and shoved him against the wall, surprising herself with her own strength. She raised her fists and slammed them against his chest. "You son of a bitch!"

He stood there stunned, neither saying a word nor reacting to her assault on him. If he had been anyone else, she would have been signing her own death warrant, but she didn't give a damn. She hauled off and slapped him with all her might across the face, but he still didn't react. A casually dressed Rolf walked in and paled as he stopped in his tracks. It appeared from his stunned reaction that he was sure Derek would kill her on the spot.

"I hate you, Derek von Vetter!" she screamed, not caring that the young guard was worried for her safety. She called Derek every foul name that came to mind as all of her emotions from the last few weeks came bursting forth. Shame lit through her when she accused him of being a traitor to both his countries, but she ignored the emotion.

Derek shook his head at the guard, silently indicating that he not worry. The young man, still stunned, gave a faint nod and walked from the room.

Elizabeth was barely able to calm herself as she stepped toward Derek with the intention of hitting him again. Out of sheer emotional exhaustion, she wrapped her arms around his shoulders and held him tightly to her, her heart seeming to race out of control. "Why can't I hate you, Derek?" she bawled into his uniform jacket. "Why do I let you affect me this way?"

He slid his arms around her shoulders and held her to him. "Go ahead, sweetheart," he urged gently, his voice shaking from his own emotions. "Let it out. It's all right with me."

"Damn you for making me feel this way about you," she continued, her heart still ferociously pounding. "Legally you're my captor and you own me, so how can I want you? I can't! I can't! I can't!" She realized from her reactions that she was in danger of falling in love with him, but there was no way she was going to let that happen. *But it's already too late, Elizabeth,* her conscience insisted. She wanted to scream at herself to shut up and stop it.

"You're the *Kommandant* of a work camp, Derek, where numerous people have been abused, starved and murdered. Even though you've stopped that here, how can I be such a goddamned horny slut wanting you the way I do and live with myself?" She pulled away, allowing the tears to make a trail down her cheeks. He watched with a mixture of emotions in his eyes, but did not bother defending himself against her words. "I want to be in your bed. I want you inside me. I want us to make love and be lovers, but I can't let those things happen. If I do, I'll lose what's left of my self-respect and hate both of us. There is no way in hell I will ever let you touch me again!"

She stalked across the gray-tiled room, knowing her last two comments were nothing but lies. She could feel him watching her with every fiber of her existence and she wanted to do nothing but beg him to take her back into the warmth of his arms. *God, Derek! Have I completely lost my mind? Why did I have to do something so stupid as fall in love with you?*

She had no doubt that if he hadn't said a word, she would now be letting him make love to her against the wall. If she had confessed her love for him, there would have been no denying him anything.

Chapter Ten

EREK RESTED HIS HEAD AGAINST THE back of the chair and propped his feet up on the desktop. He had made a habit of resting that way when the stress of the day got to him, which was every day that he had been at Murrbrück. Today, it was compounded. The pain and devastation in Elizabeth's lovely eyes and in her bearing ate at his insides as if his guilt for hurting her were a noxious disease. He knew he deserved every vile label she had slapped on him. As much as he planned to do for the captives here, he could never give them back their freedom or their lives. If he let them go, he would be placing their lives at risk of probable, if not certain, death.

In Auschwitz, in Poland, and many other death camps like it, the majority of those who entered were immediately put to death in the gas chambers by Zyklon B cyanide gas or worse. All this because some sociopath blamed certain individuals for all the problems of the world and planned to systematically eliminate them from the face of the earth. That so many others followed this insane scheme to the letter was beyond Derek's comprehension. Although Murrbrück and the other camps in Germany weren't "death camps," people had been murdered and starved while being forced to work as slave labor. Derek knew he was every bit as guilty of being a party to the atrocities as his superiors were. He didn't know which was more terrifying, living with the blame for what was happening or ending his own life.

His previous commander had been indirectly involved in the Bomb Plot to eliminate their leader. Rommel had been given the so-called "option of suicide" or his wife and son would have been executed along with him. As far as Derek was concerned, the Nazis had murdered him as if they had put a gun to his head and pulled the trigger. He had only this morning received word of the truth, which was the opposite of the public account that he had died from so-called complications of his war wounds. They were serious, yes, but hardly life-threatening.

Derek's friend Claus von Stauffenberg had fared no better. Because he had left the bomb at the scene to go off and end their leader's life, he had been executed by firing squad. Executions were often recorded and sent to the *Führer* for his personal viewing enjoyment. Derek took a shaky breath and squeezed his eyes shut to keep them from filling with tears of guilt and shame. *Damned bastards!* his mind yelled. How could they be such monsters and live with themselves? Had they no conscience at all?

When Elizabeth had slammed her fists against his chest and slapped him with all her might, he had stood there doing nothing and showing no reaction. Rolf had walked into the room in time just as she had hit and cursed at him and then had paled because of her actions. He had assumed the younger man believed he would kill her on the spot. With any other *Kommandant*, he would have been correct and she would have been shot dead before she finished her first sentence. But Derek refused to kill her or anyone else for speaking the truth.

He had sworn an oath to himself that he would do everything in his power to make sure that each captive, who came into Murrbrück left alive and it was past time to do more than just convince himself it needed to be done. If someone came down with a sickness or disease, he would find a way to save him or her if it was the last thing he did on this earth.

He had already spoken with Hans in order to find a way to supply the people in the camp and thankfully, he had pulled through. His friend had a supplies contact by the name of Kurt Dietrich, who he said was a master of disguises. Kurt had been able to obtain a variety of uniforms, from a low-ranking courier to a high-ranking member of the *Schutzstaffel*, commonly known as the SS. At least the captives would soon be able to sleep at night without worrying about freezing to death or being eaten alive by insects.

When a knock sounded on the door, Derek shook his head to

draw himself back to reality. „*Herein,*" he called out, giving the person permission to enter.

The door opened and Manfred stepped back to allow Rolf into the room. "You asked to see me, sir?" Rolf asked with uncertainty flashing in his eyes.

Derek gave Manny a nod of dismissal and then turned back to the guard. "Yes, I did." He waited for his secretary to close the door before he continued. "Come on in."

Rolf stepped closer, but remained on his feet. He was off duty, dressed in navy shorts and T-shirt, in spite of the cool day. "Yes, sir," he said with a question in the tone.

"At ease," Derek prompted as he tugged down his feet. He stood and walked around to the front of the desk and then leaned back against it.

Rolf relaxed his stance and clutched his hands behind his back. "Thank you, sir," he said with a nod.

"First off, do not fear for Elizabeth's safety. I do not wish to harm her or anyone else here. In fact, that is why I requested to speak with you. I am taking a grave risk in relaying this information to you and it is imperative that you not repeat anything we have discussed."

"Yes, sir."

Derek rose to his feet and slipped his Walther P-38 from his holster, holding the butt toward Rolf in offering. "I am compelled to change the inexcusable situation in this camp and if I lose my life in the process, then so be it," he said. "I have been blind far too long. So if you plan to turn me in to my superiors for my actions, go ahead and pull the trigger."

Rolf balked, but did not take the pistol from his fingers. "No, sir," he said, his voice tight. "I will not."

Derek narrowed his eyes in the pretense of anger. "Are you refusing a direct order from your commanding officer?" he snapped.

The younger man paled at the demand, but did not back away. "Yes, sir," he said. "I am."

Derek quickly turned the pistol around and pressed the muzzle against the guard's forehead. "Do you still refuse?" he snarled.

Rolf audibly gulped and a fine sheen of sweat broke out on his skin.

"Yes, sir," he sneered. "I refuse to kill you. So if you wish to shoot me for refusing your order, then do it now."

Derek chuckled and after a quick gun-slinging spin, slid the pistol back into its holster. "I give you my thanks, Rolf, and my respect," he said. "I do not wish to harm you."

A visibly shaken Rolf collapsed into a chair and allowed a crude curse to pass his lips. "Thank you, sir," he said, his tone shaky.

"I apologize for my actions, but I had to see whether I could trust you. Now I have no doubt I can, my friend."

Rolf did not smile, although a slight smirk tugged at the corners of his lips. "I will do what I can, sir," he offered.

"And Rolf?"

"Yes, sir?"

"You have my permission to call me Derek when it's just you and I."

"Thank you, sir. I mean Derek."

Derek realized that he had done right in choosing this young man as an ally and that he would be a good friend through the future years. He sat down in the chair adjacent to his friend and crossed a leg over the opposite knee. "Tell me whom I can trust and besides Übel and Erich, whom I cannot," he urged.

Rolf crinkled his eyebrows and rested his chin on his upraised fingers. "Fritz and Ulrich are the most sympathetic," he began. As expected, he said that Erich, Übel and most of the others lived up to the *Totenkopf* guards' brutal reputation. Rolf and the sympathetic guards were part of the *Ersatzgruppen*, the Reserve Army. It seemed that Rolf was what the Americans called a "homesteader", one who stayed at the same assignment for several years. He was surprised that even the Wehrmacht would put such polar opposite personalities in such proximity of one another, but then again logic did not necessarily come into play where the military was concerned.

Derek was surprised when Rolf told him that he was involved with a local off-camp resistance group and that he had begun his own within the camp. The young man's parents were members as well and they lived on a farm in a nearby small town. They frequently provided a safe haven for anyone who needed a place to stay, to sleep, eat or merely obtain a change of clothes.

When he was able to, Rolf frequently gave captives medicines to prevent future illnesses. He modestly stated that his influence was only minor and passive and that he did not deserve Derek's praise, since he could always do more for those who needed his help.

In exchange for the information, Derek told him about his contact with Hans and Kurt. He questioned Rolf about Manny and learned that his secretary was sympathetic to their cause as well. He breathed a sigh of relief, glad that his friend had given him the information. It would simplify things quite a bit.

Derek told him that if anyone, meaning Heinrich and the others, found out about what had been happening, he would give him a hand signal that he was in trouble. If that weren't possible and he managed to get free of the compound, he would have a message delivered to him to tell him where he was located.

"What about Elizabeth?" Rolf asked.

"I will take her with me, of course," Derek answered. There was no way he would leave her there. God only knew what they would do to her. If she were lucky, they would kill her outright.

"Are you in love with her?" he was surprised to hear Rolf ask.

Derek's heart softened and he allowed a slow smile to curve his lips. He had been asking himself the same question all afternoon, but he had denied it because of the swiftness of his feelings. Now sitting here, he could only come to one conclusion. The answer was yes. He was in love with her. "Yes, I am," he confessed.

Rolf grinned, his eyes warm. "I see," he said.

Derek raised an eyebrow. "Is there anyone you have your eye on, my friend?" he teased, holding back a chuckle at the cliché.

Rolf flushed, nodding as if picturing a young woman in his mind. "Possibly," he said with a slight smirk.

"What is her name?"

"She is Katrine, the young woman Erich snapped at when you came into the processing area."

Derek remembered the lovely brunette with the brown doe eyes, who had covered herself and received a crude reprimand from Erich Kurtz. "Yes," he said. "She is quite lovely."

Rolf chuckled and his cheeks briefly flashed bright pink. "She is," he agreed.

Derek couldn't help but grin. "If you two need to be alone sometime, let me know," he offered. "I'll see what I can do."

Still flushing, Rolf chuckled again. "Thank you, Derek," he said.

Chapter Eleven

I T HAD BEEN TWO WEEKS SINCE Elizabeth's outburst and it was now November. The day after the incident, Derek had surprised all the prisoners with thick pallets and pillows in each section of so-called beds. They would be a great comfort, since the colder weather had arrived. They still had thin blankets to cover them, but those were also being replaced with ones more capable of keeping people warm. He had given them heavier coats, along with gloves, scarves and heavier shoes, with thick socks to keep them comfortable during the long winter months. The captives were able to choose work they preferred and they were allowed to continue with their various religious practices, including taking off the various Sabbath days of rest. They had another day off in addition to that, allowing them free time for games and the like. For their own safety, the work had to be done, but it would keep their minds occupied and stifle boredom.

As much as Elizabeth and the others appreciated what Derek had done, they didn't realize what a feat it was to have supplied nearly three hundred people. Although their camp was very small when compared to others, Elizabeth was still impressed with his determination. In any event, she refused to admit it to him. She continued to work in the laundry area, preferring it to the chill of the outside. Each day was a continual reminder of the earlier incident, although the emotional pain of it had eased. From the corner of her left eye, she caught Derek watching her and checking up on the women's progress. Elizabeth had no doubt that he kept a close eye on her in an attempt to pull a response from her, but she pointedly avoided his gaze.

"I know she cannot ignore me forever, Rolf," Derek said loudly in English. Her heartbeat shot off at the words, since it was clear that she was the subject of their conversation. At least she was the only English-speaking person in the room besides him. Or Rolf, so it seemed.

"I am impressed with her efforts, sir," Rolf returned, speaking in English as well.

It was clear to Elizabeth that he was attracted to Katrine, who worked in the laundry as well, since he watched her with longing in his aqua eyes. She wondered if that was how Derek looked at her. It had startled her that the guard spoke English so well, albeit with a thick German accent, but she did not let on that she had noticed. He was surprisingly quite nice, but she had the suspicion he wasn't as naïve as he led others to believe.

"Isn't she darling?" Derek asked, drawing her attention back to him. She flushed, but continued with the uniform shirts she had been ironing.

"She is lovely, yes," Rolf agreed. The men walked off a moment later, chuckling between themselves.

A few days later, one of the sympathetic guards brought her a small holder of hand cream, that she assumed was Sabrina's due to the expensive label, but she returned it without acknowledging its receipt. Her heart leaped with guilt at refusing him, but she had to do so for her own peace of mind. She was about to pile a load of clothing into the tub when Rolf came into the room. When she gave him an uneasy smile, he nodded in return.

"*Herr Kommandant* wishes to speak with you, ma'am," Rolf stated, his voice flat.

"Tell him I'm busy. I have many things to do."

A momentary flush darkened his cheeks when Katrine and Dominique burst into girlish laughter, but he arched a reddish eyebrow. "He suspected you would say that," he stated. "He said if you did not come with me, he would have Übel bring you instead."

Elizabeth exaggerated a sigh of annoyance. "Then I guess I'd better go with a *jawohl* on my lips," she said, with deliberate irony. When a slight snort of laughter sounded in Rolf's throat, she raised an eyebrow. "It's okay to laugh, Rolf. I won't tell anyone."

A hint of a grin curved his lips, but it didn't go any further. After a knowing smile Katrine's way, he turned back to her. "Follow me, ma'am," he said without acknowledging her answer.

She exchanged a smirking glance with her friends and rose to her feet. She snatched her jacket from its hook and headed out the door. As she and Rolf stepped onto the concrete walkway, the crisp wind rushed over her, She shivered, sending him a questioning glance. "Did Derek tell you why he wanted to see me?" she asked.

He crinkled his eyebrows as if unsure how to answer her question. "How is it you Americans say?" he asked. "When he barks, I jump. I do not question a superior officer under any circumstances."

Elizabeth sighed and turned her attention back to the walkway, forcing herself to ignore the other captives' stares and raised eyebrows as they watched her and Rolf's progress.

As they arrived at the outer door of the office, Rolf held it open for her. She walked in, ignoring Manny as he gawked in her direction. Without waiting for the guard or knocking, she barged into Derek's office. "Okay, Vetter," she found herself snarling in English. "What's so damn important that you had to interrupt my work?"

Rolf coughed as he hid his shocked laughter. Derek was on the phone, but informed the person he would call right back. After hanging up, he rose to his feet and walked around his desk. He leaned against it and crossed his arms over his ribs. She flushed when he and Rolf shared a look of amused understanding. "I wanted to speak with you," he said without preamble. At his words, a grinning Rolf closed the office door and left them alone.

"So talk," Elizabeth prompted without attempting to be polite. Her rudeness was the only thing that kept her from bursting into tears. Derek looked so sensually appealing in his uniform slacks and khaki shirt that she wanted to toss herself into his arms and beg him to hold her. Her body nearly shook with the desire to do so, but she took a deep breath to force down her nerves. *Damn it! How can you affect me this way?*

Sorrow flashed in his eyes as he raised upright. "How are you doing, babe?" he asked.

His gentle endearment caused a flash of emotion to slam into her heart and hot tears to burn in her eyes. She was disgusted with herself for the reaction and that her bottom lip threatened to quiver. "I've missed you," she found herself confessing.

He stepped toward her and tugged her into his arms. "I've missed you, too," he returned. "It feels so good to hold you again, Elizabeth."

The warmth of his firm body and the steady beat of his heart engrained themselves into her being and gave her emotions permission to spill forth. Tears burned a path down her cheeks and a soft sob bubbled in her throat. He said nothing to her as she released her tears, just caressed the length of her hair. His touch was so soothing that she wanted nothing but melt into his warm body. She pulled back and wiped the remaining wetness from her eyes with the hem of her top. When she let go, she chuckled at the slight dampness she noted on his shoulder. "I did it again, didn't I?" she teased.

Derek grinned. "Don't worry about it," he said. "You can cry on my shoulder any time. Would you like to talk? It may make you feel better."

"All right," she found herself agreeing.

He urged her over to the black leather sofa and wrapped his arms around her shoulders to hold her against his chest. Unable to control the urge, she rested her head in the crook of his neck and wrapped her right arm around his waist. "You were brought here for hiding your friend, but that's all I know," he said. "Tell me more."

Elizabeth released a shaky breath, her heart pounding at the horrible memories. "Yes," she said. "Zarah had been my roommate for more than a year. She had been evading the SS for a long while, although she hadn't gone into formal hiding until they came looking for her at work. She had been dating a man named Wil for about a year and although he knew she was a Jew, he still cared deeply for her. Since she was terrified the government had caught up with her, I offered to hide her and swore I would never tell a living soul where she was. I had been able to keep the SS at bay, which was a surprise in itself, but then one day Wil had come by asking about her since he hadn't heard from her. I lied, telling him I hadn't heard from her either and would let him know if she returned. After he shed what I thought were legitimate tears, I confessed that she was upstairs in a hidden room. When they were reunited, I was sure I had done the right thing. That night, I had just nodded off when a loud banging on the front door jerked me out of my sleep. I told Zarah to stay hidden in her room while I went downstairs. Just before I opened the door, the so-called visitors came barging into the house. Come to find out, Wil is Gestapo and had brought a couple of black-shirts with him. He had used me to find out what had happened to her and it's all my fault that they arrested her."

As she relayed the rest of the scene to Derek, the entire thing replayed itself in her mind. The shock of discovering that Wil was a Nazi and the terror that had raged through her when he had taken away her friend. She had no clue as to where they had taken Zarah or whether she were even still alive.

"Wil hid nothing as he took me to the train station. He molested me …" she started, her voice briefly cracking. "He said if I had not been hiding a *Jüdin*, he would have taken me as his lover." The memory of his hands touching her breasts still caused a churning of disgust to stir in her stomach.

Derek slid his fingers through her hair, his touch relaxing her. "You are a strong woman, Elizabeth," he said gently. "If anyone can survive this, you will. And I'm sorry about your friend."

She continued to grasp him, but refused to hold her feelings back any longer. She breathed a deep sigh. "Thank you," she said. "Sometimes I wonder how I'll make it through the next day." She swallowed hard. "I'm surprised I have stood it this far without losing my mind."

"Why do you say that?"

She wondered whether he asked because he genuinely didn't know or whether he was allowing her to release her stuffed emotions and feelings. "We, others and I, were crammed into a boxcar and there was no room to move around or to sit. It was humid, but I was lucky enough to be able to stand by a crude window. Even then, it was almost unbearable. When we stopped, my heart almost did also. Thankfully, we were given water, but unfortunately by a young soldier holding a water hose."

She was glad Derek continued to listen without interrupting since she would have burst into tears. She had cried enough in the last few weeks. "I believed that was the most humiliating experience I had ever had in my life. I hate this phrase, but water was something I had always taken for granted. To be crammed into a train car to be sent to a place where they worked you to death or slowly tortured or starved you was something I was sure would never happen to anyone. I never thought human beings could do such things to each other and without a single thought to whether it was right or evil. Once we arrived, I knew immediately what this place was. It was as if something evil were running its frozen claw down the inside of my spine." She pulled back and gazed deep into Derek's eyes, hers filling with fresh tears. "It would have been hell if it weren't for you, Derek."

He pulled her back against him and squeezed her in a hug. "I wouldn't blame you if you did hate me, Elizabeth," he said into her hair. "When you called me every name you could think of, I had no doubt that I deserved every one of them. As much as I can do for the people here, I will never be able to give them back their lives and their freedom. Until I can, nothing else will be good enough."

She switched their positions so she could slide an arm back around his neck and snuggle into his comforting warmth. "You told me once that you weren't here by choice," she reminded him. "If you ever want to talk to me about it, I'll be listening."

He released his own shaky sigh. "I cannot tell you the whole story right now, but I am not the monster I appear to be," he said.

His guilt and sorrow sounded in his voice, both causing her heart to melt. "I know you're not a monster, Derek," she said in all honesty. "I have never believed that. You proved it when you helped Katrine and those others whom Erich abused that day."

"Thank you, sweetheart. It means the world to me to hear you say that."

She pulled back and gave him a warm smile, her heart again melting. *I love you, Derek.* Her heartbeat shot off at the thought. To keep from confessing her feelings for him, she bent her head and pressed slow, gentle kisses along his jawbone. The slight salty taste of his skin and the musky scent of his body caused her heart to pound wildly.

"Does this mean you wouldn't be opposed to sharing some passionate kisses every now and then?" he asked as she took his earlobe between her lips.

Elizabeth couldn't help but brush her tongue along the smooth skin of his ear, grinning when he gave a passionate shudder. "I wouldn't be opposed to it at all," she teased. She pulled her mouth away and gazed into his eyes. "I would like that very much."

Derek turned to her and gave her a lingering kiss on her lips, making them tingle with awareness. "I want to make love to you so badly, Elizabeth," he said with a groan. "I don't want you to ever feel I forced you into bed with me. We'll take it as slow as we possibly can."

Elizabeth's body melted in anticipation. "Until then?" she asked hopefully.

He bent his head and brushed his lips over hers. "We share as many kisses as we want," he said in between them.

Elizabeth slid her hands into his hair and tugged his head closer to invite deeper kisses. She opened her mouth in preparation for their mating tongues and when they touched, a groan of pleasure bubbled in her diaphragm. She pulled back and allowed a soft chuckle to pass her lips. "I like the sound of that," she said.

Derek grinned. "So do I." At their agreement, he lowered his head.

Chapter Twelve

T HE BUBBLY BLONDE WAITRESS FLASHED ÜBEL a flirty smile as she laid his second beer on the table in front of him and he returned a charming smile of his own. He had never had the pleasure of meeting her, since this was not a place he usually frequented. The majority of the building was a hotel, but the *gasthaus* was open to the public and one did not have to be a guest to order a meal. The decor was rather boring, with its golden-brown carpeting, pale wooden bench dining tables and tall windows, covered with pale-brown shudders, but the room was inviting in spite of that.

„*Danke*, Kristal," Übel said warmly.

„*Bitte*," Kristal returned with an invitation sparkling in the depths of her soft, blue eyes. Her blonde hair fell to the middle of her back in silky curls, the color reminding him of beams of moonlight. Her red-and-orange patterned uniform and white smock covered her from her waist to the hem of her ankle-length skirt. The puffy sleeves were gathered just above her elbows and the scooped neckline showed off the swells of her lush breasts. The material hugged her shapely hips, urging him to give into the temptation to take her to the nearest guestroom and ram into her lovely body.

"If there is anything else you need, please do not hesitate to ask," she said in apparent offering.

"I will do so," he promised. With another smile, she returned to her duties. Übel turned his attention from the lovely Kristal to the man sitting across from him.

Colonel Heinrich still wore his uniform and the stark black of the material contrasted with his whitening blonde hair and blue eyes. His face appeared somewhat gaunt because his cheekbones were so prominent, but his build was otherwise husky. Übel nearly laughed as he observed that the handful of other guests were uneasy and voided his and Heinrich's gazes altogether. He was glad Karl had suggested they meet at this particular *gasthaus*, since it was near the camp, and it appeared this was the correct decision. Watching the very cute waitress was an added incentive, although the hard bench was wearing thin, even with the added cushion.

"She is rather comely, yes?" Heinrich asked with a grin in his voice. It was rare that he smiled, but smiles sounded freely in his voice when something pleased him.

Übel chuckled as he took a quick glance at the young woman, the stiffness of his body reminding him of how she affected him. „*Ja*," he agreed. "Her smile is an invitation for me and I may have to take her up on her offer."

"She would be just right for a handsome man such as you," his friend teased. "I would say her bloodlines are quite free of taint, yes?"

Übel ginned, although he brushed away thoughts of Kristal. "Speaking of handsome," he said without answering his friend's question. "The prisoners are more readily accepting our new *Kommandant*, since he is treating them like employees instead of threats against our New Order and is giving them excessive amounts of supplies to aid their comfort."

A flash of anger burned in Heinrich's eyes, although Übel suspected this information didn't surprise him. „*Und?*" And?

"He allows them breaks and they can chose work for which they have a preference." He leaned forward and rested his forearm on the table. "Von Vetter has gone soft on a political prisoner, a lusty *Amerikanerin* by the name of Elizabeth Kelley. There is no doubt they are lovers, Karl. He is constantly panting after her. A few weeks ago, she blasphemed him and he did nothing to stop her. If he were any other commander, she would have not finished her first statement. He has also found allies in Rolf and a handful of the other guards. Erich, a few others and I have not seen everything he has done, since he has given us out-of-the-way duties."

"And his allies?"

Übel snorted as he leaned back in his seat. "They are being most *kind*," he said with a sneer on the last word. "Rolf is panting over a Polish dissident by the name of Katrine. She was interned for a public protest against the Reich with her sister, who was sent to Auschwitz for organizing that protest. It would be unlikely that she is still alive, but if she is as beautiful and sensual as Katrine, that is a strong possibility."

"They are of little significance," Heinrich said with a wave of a hand, seemingly disregarding them. "But since you have expressed an attraction to Katrine, take her, to keep control of Rolf and steer his loyalty from von Vetter." He gave a cold smile. "Watch the marquess and his American lover and report to me anything you see of importance. When it is the correct time, I will be taking over."

The last statement brought an unconscious smile to Übel's lips. When Heinrich came to take Derek's place, everything would be as it should. "Until then?" he asked.

"We will meet here one day each week and you will give me information on what changes von Vetter has made. Do not let anyone, including Erich, know you are doing so. When the time comes, I will serve his lordship with the proper punishment concerning his resistances; he and his American whore." Without further explanation, he slid from the seat and gave Übel a slight bow. "Until next time, my friend."

„*Tschüß*," Übel returned brightly.

Karl stopped by the waitress and slipped payment for their drinks into the neckline of her dress, causing a flush to cover her cheeks. With a warm grin in her direction, he walked out of the *gasthaus*.

Kristal discreetly tugged the money from between her lush breasts and opened the register to place it inside. Übel gave her another charming smile as she caught his eye. When he crooked his finger, she did not hesitate in coming over to his table.

"What can I get for you?" she asked with another smile.

He grasped her hand and tugged her down onto his lap. With the firm softness of her buttocks pressed against his already tight *Schwanz*, it tightened even more. "You," he stated. "Are you finished with your shift?"

"I am," he was pleased to hear her say. "Do you have something in mind?"

"I do," he said in his friendliest tone as he humped against her.

As she bit her bottom lip to force back a gasp, the look in her narrowed blue eyes hinted at further pleasures. He snatched the additional tip from the table and slid it between her breasts. When he deliberately brushed the tip of his index finger over an inside curve, a small groan sounded in her throat. „*Herr Braun*," she said, her tone high.

Übel chuckled and urged her off his lap. "My name is Übel," he said in offering. "Would you care to be alone?"

Kristal stepped to the nearby doorless armoire and snatched her coat from a hanger. He caught up with her and grasped her elbow as he led her outside. Once out of view of the main windows, he shoved her back against the building and bent his head. He plundered her mouth, shoving his tongue inside and rolling it around hers. She pressed her breasts against his chest and slid her arms around his neck as the heavy kiss continued. He slipped his hand under the neckline of the uniform dress and cupped a bare breast. When he lightly trailed his fingertips over her nipple, a cry erupted from her.

Übel wondered how the lovely American reacted when von Vetter was loving her. *No doubt as wildly as Kristal is thrashing now,* he thought with an internal smile. If the rumor of Elizabeth's outburst were true, there was no doubt, and he wanted to find out himself how passionate she could be. He couldn't help but notice her when she first came into the camp, as did several of the other guards. Her fiery hair fell to her waist and her green eyes reminded him of newly grown grass. He had enjoyed watching her strip and seeing the lush, yet gentle curve to her hips and the teardrop breasts. The silky thatch of auburn hair between her thighs had made him want to ram inside her. Too bad she had hidden her Jewish friend, he decided. Otherwise, von Vetter would have had some competition.

He drew his thoughts away from the sensual Elizabeth and drew up the hem of Kristal's skirt. He slid a hand over her shapely thigh and around to the back of her knee. When he lifted her leg and hooked it around his hip, he humped his hardness against her. At the already intense pleasure of her body against his, he peeled his lips and tongue away and gazed into the depths of her eyes. "Is your bed large enough for both of us?" he asked.

Kristal narrowed her eyes and dropped her gaze to his lips. "Yes,

Übel," she returned, her desire sounding in her voice. "My bed is large enough for both of us."

Übel grinned, having no doubt he would be hearing the word 'yes' quite often through the night.

Chapter Thirteen

"**B**UT WHAT DO I TELL THE gate guards, sir?" Wolfgang Kerr asked for the third time in less than two minutes.

Derek turned his attention from the papers and forms he had been trying to sign for the last several minutes and raised an eyebrow, annoyed at the guard's continued hesitation. "I do not care what you tell them," he snapped as he straightened. He quickly signed the form before him and handed it to the guard. "I want those supplies delivered to each and every person interned here. If they have a problem following my orders, they can come to me. *Capisce?*"

The young man straightened his back and audibly gulped, but took the form from Derek's fingers. "Yes, sir," he acknowledged.

"Dismissed."

Wolfgang raised his arm in the Nazi salute, pledging allegiance to their nefarious leader. The light of the room shone off his platinum hair as he headed toward the door.

Pardon me while I puke. Derek withheld his disgust and tossed his pen onto the desktop. "Fine," he said flatly, past giving a damn what these people thought. "Whatever."

The young man opened the door, but stepped back to allow someone else to enter. Derek breathed a silent sigh of relief when Elizabeth wandered into the room and smiled softly.

"Good afternoon, ma'am," Wolfgang greeted her. Without awaiting an acknowledgment, he closed the door behind him.

Derek stepped toward her and held out his hands, his insides melting when she entwined the warm softness of her hands with his.

"If I hear that goddamn salute one more time, I'm going to barf," he said in English.

Elizabeth chuckled as she cocked her head to the side. "Which one?" she teased.

Derek exaggerated German-accented English as he mimicked the guard. He didn't mean to blame his mood on him, but the young man was the ant on the picnic of his bad afternoon. He was amazed at how a handful of insignificant problems could ruin someone's day. Brushing aside his irritation, he took her into his arms and buried his face in her soft hair. "I'm so glad you're here, sweetheart," he groaned softly. "I knew you would make me feel better."

"Me, too," she agreed as she slid her arms around his neck.

The sensual warmth of her body and her feminine, musky scent penetrated his senses. He wanted to do nothing but melt in her arms. She pulled back and raised her head to gaze into his eyes. "God, I've missed you," he groaned. Making no effort to resist the temptation to kiss her, he bent his head. He eased his tongue inside to stroke over hers and groaned deeply at the softness of her mouth. A new flash of heat spread over his body as she responded in kind and his rod begged to be sheathed inside her waiting warmth.

He slid his hands from around her waist and grasped the cheeks of her buttocks to tug her against him, groaning as she humped back against him. He peeled his lips from hers and gazed into her eyes. His heart slammed into his ribcage when her gentle wanting showed within their depths. It was all he could do not to confess how much he loved her. He couldn't imagine his life without her. "I want so badly to make love to you," he groaned softly.

"I know."

His heart flipped and melted as he gazed deep into her eyes. "I need you, Elizabeth," he confessed, not bothering to keep his emotions from his voice. *I love you so much, babe.*

If the women in her barrack realized how far their relationship had progressed, they might see her as a collaborator and target her for ridicule or perhaps worse. There was no way he would allow that to happen. If it were at all possible, he would marry her and take her away from the camp. Unfortunately, the safest place for her was here.

Elizabeth slid her fingers through the back of his hair and gave him a soft, warm smile that softened his heart. "I need you, too, Derek," she said softly.

"Excuse me, sir?" someone asked cautiously from behind her, causing both of them to jerk in surprise.

Derek glanced over her shoulder and raised an eyebrow at his secretary, not realizing that Manny had opened the door. Sometimes, the young man was *too* efficient. "This is not a good time, Manny," he drawled.

A slight flush darkened Manny's cheeks as he cleared his throat. "I would not have bothered you, sir, but you told me that when the supply list arrived, you wanted to be informed of it immediately," he reminded him. "Your exact words were, 'When the list arrives, let me know, no matter what I am doing'."

Keep your mouth shut next time, you stupid get, Derek reprimanded himself with a roll of his eyes. "Leave it on the table there and I'll sign it later," he ordered. "I will be detained for a while, so take a break. A very long one."

Manny smirked, his lips tight, flushing somewhat as he tried to keep from laughing. "Yes, sir," he said, his voice choky.

"Knock next time, would you, Manny?" he asked before the secretary closed the door.

Manfred made a noise that sounded distinctly like a snort of laughter. "I did, sir," he explained with another smirk. "Several times." A heartbeat later, he closed the door behind him.

When Derek turned his attention back to Elizabeth, they burst out laughing. "Where were we before we were so rudely interrupted, my dear?" he asked.

Chapter Fourteen

ELIZABETH MADE NO PROTEST WHEN DEREK pulled her along with him as he walked backward toward his personal quarters. When a flush burned in her cheeks, he grinned. "Derek," she said with a sensual whine, as if he were teasing her.

He chuckled and wriggled his eyebrows in a leer. Once in the room that looked as if it belonged in a private residence, he urged her down onto the firm mattress of the dark oak, four-poster bed, with the navy-blue comforter that brought out the blue flecks in his eyes. She had nearly forgotten what it was like to lie on a regular bed, but it seemed even better with the man she loved on it with her.

"God, you're so beautiful, Elizabeth."

Her heart flipped at his words. "Thank you," she returned softly. "So are you."

Chuckling, Derek urged her onto her back and partially covered her with the warmth of his body. Flames of molten heat spread through her body when he released one button after another until he parted the lapels. When he eased back the material and cupped a breast, her nipples turned sensitive and a soft whimper leapt from with her. Unable to help herself, she arched her back and briefly closed her eyes as she released another whimper. He bent his head and at each slow exchange of their tongues, the flames grew hotter within her. When he dragged his mouth from hers and kissed a path from her jawbone to her ear and gently nipped at her lobe, a new shiver of pleasure rushed through her.

She found herself whispering his name as he released her ear and trailed his lips down the curve of her neck. As soon as he took a nipple into his mouth and suckled it, she leaned up into him. She slid her fingers though his hair, holding his head to her as mewls of pleasure bubbled in her throat. "I'm ready for you now, Derek," she whispered hotly. "Please."

When he pulled away from her for the moment, she gave another whimper, but this one was in protest. He chuckled. "Don't worry, sweetheart," he assured her. "I swear we will be together today."

"We better be," she said with a teasing groan. As soon as another sexy chuckle erupted from him, she exaggerated a pout. She sat up and eased her shirt off her shoulders, urging him to run his darkening gaze over her. After tossing the top onto the floor, she raised her hips and peeled off her slacks, her heartbeat skyrocketing as he eyed the length of her body. She slid her arms around his neck as he tugged her underneath him and bent his head. A lick of fire spread over her as their tongues entangled, fighting as if in a duel. She released the buttons of his uniform shirt, urging him to release a groan when she slipped her hands inside. She slid her hands up the warmth of his smooth chest and over his shoulders to ease his shirt off him. Her bones seemed to burn as he peeled his lips from hers and trailed kisses from her mouth down to the tips of her breasts. When he traced her sensitive nipples with the tip of his tongue, she groaned in abandonment and slid her fingers from his shoulders into his silky hair.

He slid a hand over her abdomen and between her thighs to part her lips, triggering a whimpering cry from her. She bucked against him as he lightly probed her heat with his middle finger. She unbuckled his belt and released the buttons on his slacks, easing her hands under the material and cupping the firmness of his buttocks. "I want you now," she whispered, as she reveled in the feel of his mouth on her skin. As he lifted his head and gazed deeply into her eyes, a groan of pleasure sounded in her throat. She trailed a hand around and cupped his hardness, urging him to press his silky length into her palm. As she slid her thumb under his foreskin and brushed it over the tip, he peeled his lips away and released a hot groan of pleasure.

Elizabeth didn't fight the urge to relax her arms above her head when he urged her onto her back. He slowly ran the tips of his fingers around her erect nipples and then down the hollow between her breasts. He trailed a hand between her thighs and gently caressed her, sending sweeping waves of heat through her body. Soft light from the nearby Victorian-style lamp fluttered through the room, covering her skin with a soft glow.

She dropped her gaze to his hand as he teased her, the tan of his skin a contrast to her fairness. Her legs seemed to part by their own will and she allowed them fall to open in invitation. Her vision seemed to fade as he slowly traced her with the tips of his fingers. When he stroked her apart and brushed his thumb against her nub, she was sure she was going to combust into a cloud of wanting. As he grasped a leg and hooked it over his shoulder, she had no doubt that she had died and gone to heaven. "Derek," she moaned. "Oh yes, I like that."

"God, you're lovely, Elizabeth," he groaned.

When she realized what he intended, a new flow of molten lava spread through her blood. A crying gasp erupted from within her when he bent his head and pressed a handful of kisses against her. She gripped the headboard, her cries turning into whimpers as he parted her with his fingers and slid his tongue over her flaming bud. "Derek," she cried. "Oh, yes."

She couldn't help but arch her back as a long, loud moan passed her lips. She moved fluidly against him, enjoying the silkiness of the short strands of his hair against her inner thighs and the damp swiftness of his tongue moving over her. She groaned deeply, her voice raw from her moans of gratification. The muscles of her legs tightened and her thighs began to quiver as more heat burned through her. Burning warmth ravaged her aching bud and her high, panting cries sounded deep in her ears as she drifted off into the heavens.

As she returned to earth, Derek moved away from her. He chuckled when she released a whine of protest, but then pushed his slacks down his legs and off. "Your turn, sweetheart," he prompted as he moved onto his back, his voice heavy with wanting.

Elizabeth's heart seemed to stop beating as she eyed her lover on his back with his hands resting above his head and his legs parted in invitation. She found herself dropping her attention between his thighs and eyeing his manly form with his length full in anticipation. The dark, curly hairs resting below the length of him caused her mouth to go dry and her heart to tighten deliciously.

I love you and want you so much. Before she confessed her feelings, she turned to face him. She cupped him, sliding her thumb under the foreskin and over the tip. It was already damp with his pre-release and his breathing became heavier with his desire.

He slid his fingers through the top of her hair and pressed down. "Please, Elizabeth," he groaned.

Unable to help herself, she bent her head. Her body flamed as she took the tip into her mouth and brushed her tongue over him. She tugged his length farther in, causing his breathing to become even deeper.

"Yes," he groaned. "I like what you're doing to me, babe."

Elizabeth released him and gazed at him. "Yeah?" she teased.

Derek passionately narrowed his eyes. "Don't tease me, Elizabeth," he groaned. "I cannot take this anymore. If I don't have you now, my life is over." When she grinned and lowered her head again to brush her tongue over the tip, he gave another hot groan. He widened his legs and arched his back, encouraging the sensuality of her touch.

Before she realized he had moved, he lifted her and eased her down onto his length. A loud, whimpering gasp escaped from her throat as he completely filled her. All consciousness was swept from her senses except for the movement of their bodies as he grasped her buttocks and urged her to ride him. Their combined breathing as well as their mutual cries of pleasure sounded in her ears. It were as if she had a raging fever she couldn't control and her body received the full onslaught as he made love to her. She didn't attempt to stifle the whimpering cries of pleasure that leapt from within her, their sound echoing loudly in her ears.

Derek continued to move with her, his handsome face softened as his own grunts of wanting burst from deep within him. Their lovemaking brought her to heights she hadn't even imagined and her body sang out as she reached the heavens. The joy of it swelled her heart, flooding tears of happiness into her eyes. Her cries of pleasure and love echoed his throaty grunts as he shed his warm climax into her.

She collapsed on top of him moments later, his heart pounding hard and fast in her ear equaling the powerful velocity of her own. He lifted her chin with his index finger and gazed deep into her eyes before planting an open-mouthed kiss on her lips. Their tongues briefly slid together and to her disappointment, he peeled away his mouth. He pressed a gentle kiss on her cheek and flashed her a warm grin. "Are you ready, my lady?" he asked.

Elizabeth balked, her heartbeat shooting up. There was no way she could do that again, at least without a break. "I'll be dead if we do that again without a rest," she said, her tone breathless.

Derek chuckled, the warmth of his smile fully reaching his eyes. "I meant are you ready for me to hold you," he explained, but then grinned. "Although your idea sounds great to me."

She snorted at her stupidity, although she did see the humor of what he had said. "Hello, Elizabeth," she said to herself, a small laugh in her voice. "Yes, Derek. I'm ready."

He grasped her hips, lifting her off him and urging her to his side. He slid a hand into her hair and urged it down into the crook of his neck as their legs entwined. "You are absolutely the most beautiful woman I have ever known," he said with a groan. "Inside and out."

Elizabeth allowed a languid smile to curve her lips, enjoying the heat of their bodies as they laid together. "Thank you," she said. "I like hearing that."

"Thank you kindly, madam," he returned. He sat up and held out his hands to her. "I know it is rather soon, but guess what I feel like doing?"

When he grasped her hands in his, a new wetness dampened between her thighs as her body again became sensitive with wanting. Once he had tugged her on top of him, her released her hands and held tightly onto her buttocks. Their tongues entwined a moment later, spreading a blanket of fire over her body. As she wriggled against his warmth, he wrapped a leg around one of hers and rolled her onto her back.

He peeled away his lips and chuckled as he gazed down at her. "Oooh yeah, baby," he teased. "I like it."

"Derek," she said with a teasing groan. "Stop teasing me."

Her love trailed his hand down between her thighs and slid his fingers into her hair and over the lips. He drew them out and then back in, gently stroking her.

Elizabeth couldn't help but part her legs and arch her back, offering herself as new heat flamed between them. "Derek," she groaned.

He parted the lips and lightly brushed his middle finger over the swollen bud to stroke it, tease it. "Yes?" he asked, his voice heavy with desire.

"Keep torturing me," she whimpered as he continued to caress her. "Oh yes. Please." He again slid his middle finger over her, sending another wave of fire through her body.

"Yes, Elizabeth," he whispered hotly into her ear. "Come for me again, sweetheart."

Short, high pants erupted from her throat and her mind drifted into a sea of clouds as his touch became quicker and lighter. He grasped her behind her knees and urged her legs further apart to prepare her for his entry. She slid her arms around his neck, a hard whimper bursting from her when he thrust deep inside her and filled her warmth with his length.

She moved her hips and buttocks with the rhythm of his new thrusts and wrapped her legs around his hips to urge him deeper inside her. As he moved onto his hands and passionately rode her, she floated off into a dream world. Her throaty cries echoed in her ears as she reached another sensual peak. Off in the distance, Derek released a series of male grunts as he shed another hot release inside her.

He sank onto her as he came back to earth, his heartbeat fast and heavy from their coupling. Their damp, warm bodies pressed against each other caused her along with her sense of euphoria to breathe a deep sigh of fulfillment. She let out a long, soft whistle, wanting to lose herself in him and never leave.

Derek chuckled against her. "You can say that again," he teased, his voice breathy.

They both laughed when she repeated her whistle. He raised his head and gazed deep into her eyes. She slid her hands into his hair and tugged down his head, urging him to press a lingering kiss on her lips. "Are ready to catch your breath now?" he teased as he lifted his head.

Elizabeth giggled, her heart swelling. "Go slowly, okay?" She sucked in her breath when he lifted himself off her and eased out of her.

"Maybe next time we'll actually get between the sheets."

Elizabeth's high chuckle turned into full laughter. "Works for me," she teased.

Chuckling himself, Derek moved to her side and laid his head on the curve of her shoulder as he rested an arm across her waist and grasped her hip. He slid a leg between hers, the warmth of his skin and the feel of his soft, male hairs sending a flash of warmth through her. "I like you holding me in your arms, Elizabeth," he said gently.

She grinned. "So do I," she agreed.

"I just wish the circumstances were better than in this damn place."

"I think we've made the best of it, Derek, considering the situation here. We are at least blessed to have someone care as you do. We could have been in a much worse situation. You kept us from experiencing a living hell." She had no doubt that it was true. They wouldn't have seen the improvements and the provisions he had made in the captives' favor or the kindness he had brought them. Having him here was more of a miracle than he realized.

"I never would have come here if I had had a choice. I hate what I have had to become just for having to accept this damn assignment."

Elizabeth's heart wrenched at the worry and desperation in his voice. "You said you were threatened into taking this assignment and that there were other people involved," she said. "What could they possibly have against you?"

Derek released a breath and there was a depth of emotion in the sigh. "My grandmother's companion, Miriam, is a Jew," he said. "I had identification papers falsified for her and SS Colonel Karl Heinrich found out about it, along with Miriam's true identity. He informed me that if I did not become *Kommandant* of this camp, my grandmother, Miriam and I would be incarcerated. If they were not involved, I would have taken my chances as a captive, but once my grandmother and her friend were threatened, I had no choice."

An eerie shudder rushed through Elizabeth and her eyes filled with sympathetic tears. His superiors forced him to be here under threats of arresting his family members and putting them into a KZ to allow them to die. She didn't doubt he would have refused the assignment and taken his chances here if it weren't for them. In a sense, he was as captive as most of the people here. "I'm so sorry, Derek," she said. She had believed him too caring to be the *Kommandant* of this camp, but she had misjudged him in ways she hadn't thought of until now and she regretted every bit of it. To be forced into an assignment like this by having your loved ones' lives threatened was unconscionable. She wasn't sure she wouldn't have done the same had she been in his position.

"When I walked into processing and realized everyone was being treated as if they were anything but human, I realized I had been guilty of denying what had been going on in these camps." His tone was heavy with emotion, causing her heart to flip and tears to burn in her eyes. "My friend, Hans, is involved in the resistance and has been encouraging me to join in the fight for years. I had refused, at least officially, until I realized what was going on here. I couldn't believe I had been so blind as to not know the extent of the atrocities going on in these compounds. This should have never happened to any human being and I pray to God that it never will again."

"I have to admit I am every bit as guilty of being in denial as many others," she confessed. "We have to make the best of what we can, Derek. There has to be a purpose for our being here."

"I must confess I will systematically continue to smuggle in supplies in order to make everyone's captivity even the slightest bit bearable. I refuse to sign any death warrants and I will do my damnedest to make sure everyone here now or later leaves alive and healthy. I will give up my own life in order to save theirs, if that is what it takes. They deserve no less."

Elizabeth slid from under him and turned onto her side to gaze into his eyes. Her heart constricted with love for this remarkable man and she held back a sob. She didn't ever want to be without him. "I love you, Derek," she confessed, her voice froggy from the tears she couldn't seem to shed. "I tried to deny it to myself, but now there is no doubt in my mind about how I feel about you. I am sorry for the way I screamed at you in the laundry. I was only denying my love for you."

Tears rushed into his eyes, distorting their green depths. "I love you, too, Elizabeth," he returned, his voice husky from his feelings. "I have known that since I first set eyes on you. It's been hell not being able to tell you." He gathered her into his arms and urged her head onto his chest. "Don't leave me yet, babe. Please sleep with me."

Exhausted, she exaggerated a sigh and closed her eyes. "I will," she promised. The now-steady rhythm of his heartbeat sounded in her ear and she breathed in his musky scent. It wasn't long before she slid into an oblivious sleep.

Chapter Fifteen

ELIZABETH AWOKE TO FIND THAT THEY had switched positions and Derek was lying with his head on her breasts and his right leg resting over her left thigh. His arm was wrapped around her waist, the warmth of his body bringing a smile of contentment to her lips. She found herself running her fingers through the silky strands of his military short hair, thinking how pretty it was, with prominent highlights shining in the darker chestnut brown.

"This is nice," he said gently.

Believing he had been asleep, she nearly jumped from surprise. She giggled, a bit groggy from sleep. "No kidding," she agreed. "I could get used to this. I like your hair, by the way. It's a pretty color and it's so soft."

Derek moved to his side and rested the side of his head in his hand, his eyes softening as he gazed into hers. "So could I," he agreed, but then a plea entered the depths of his eyes. "Stay with me tonight and every night, Elizabeth. I hate it that you have to go back to that goddamned barracks."

As tempting as his offer was, she couldn't stay. The guilt of sleeping in his comfortable bed while the others were lying on their pallets on those wooden so-called beds would be too much for her to bear. "I don't think we should, Derek," she said gently. Once she had explained her reasons to him, he gave a resigned sigh.

"God, Elizabeth," he relayed, anguish sounding in his deep voice. "I love you so much. Dammit to hell, why the fuck did this have to happen? I should be out there like the rest of you instead of in my cushy house or in my cushy office. I'll never be able to wipe away the guilt because of it. I'm not at all good enough for you. I don't deserve you a bit."

Agony tore through her at his words and it seemed as if someone had sliced her heart with a razor. "Derek Edwin," she snapped, unable to keep her emotional pain from her tone. Chills rushed over her skin and burning tears made their presence known in her eyes. "Don't you ever say that again! If it weren't for you, most of the people in this camp would be dead or wasting away from disease and starvation. You are giving them everything you possibly can under the circumstances and are risking your own life to do so. You're only human, Derek. You can't save the world by yourself and you know it. I love you the way you are. Don't change a thing. You are phenomenal."

Although tears blurred his eyes, a ghost of a smile curved his sensual lips. "You told me," he teased.

She couldn't help but chuckle, her heart still heavy at the fact that he would demean himself in such a way. "So watch it," she teased in return. "Now I have to get back to the barracks before the other women decide to string me up. I'm probably on their shit list as it is."

Derek slid his fingers into her hair and tugged her head down to meet his lips. He slid his tongue over and around hers, heating her body to a new level. She knew she had to leave before she changed her mind and stayed in his bed. If she did so, she would never be able to leave.

She peeled her lips away and pressed her forehead against his. "I have to go, cutie pie," she grinned. "I love you."

"I know," Derek sighed as he pulled away with a grin. "Cutie pie. I love you, too."

Elizabeth slid out of the bed and tugged on the atrocious slacks. As she pulled the top around her shoulders, she eyed the man she loved as he lay on the bed watching her. He rested on his stomach with the side of his head on an upraised hand. She ran her gaze down the curve of his back and her attention rested on the paleness of his buttocks, a nice contrast to his tan. He was so perfectly male and her hands itched to squeeze his firm cheeks in her palms. He rolled onto his back and parted his thighs in a sensual pose, leaving nothing to her imagination. Weakening, she looked back into his eyes in time to catch his leer.

"Keep looking, sweetheart," he offered with a grin.

Elizabeth's sight became slightly fuzzy as her body weakened. "No man should have the right to be so damned sexy," she found herself confessing. "I could make a mint by bottling you and selling you."

He winked as a broad smile curved his lips. "I take that to be a compliment," he said. A moment later, he slid from the bed and rose to his feet.

"We better get dressed before I attack you," she said with a teasing growl "Then neither of us will get any work done."

Derek chuckled, but he slid his legs into his black boxers and then his uniform slacks. He had just fastened the last button on his shirt when a knock sounded on the outer door.

As they left the bedroom and made their way into the office, Elizabeth caught a glimpse of her reflection in the plain, silver-framed mirror. Her cheeks were softly flushed and her lips were swollen from their passionate kisses. It was clear she was a woman who had just left her lover's bed after more than an hour of sensual lovemaking. She looked like the woman in love she was and couldn't help but smile at the thought.

"Yes, Manfred," Derek called out. "Come in."

The door cautiously opened and Manny poked his tawny head inside. His eyes briefly widened as he took in her disheveled and languid appearance, but he turned his attention back to Derek. "A courier has arrived, sir," he informed him, his voice choky. "Shall I send him in?"

"Yes, Manny," Derek returned in his normal voice. "Thank you."

Elizabeth was impressed at her lover's calmness, sure she wouldn't have been able to pull it off as he had, since she would have been stammering left and right. As soon as the thought cleared her mind, a very attractive, blonde-haired man entered the room. His coat indicated him to be a dispatch rider, but it looked more like a combination of a slicker and a jacket with the material hanging perfectly on his frame. He was a couple of inches shorter than Derek, but with a build similar to Rolf's. He looked to her as if he were in his twenties, although she suspected he was a bit older.

He took a quick glance in her direction and withheld a smile. Without saluting, he handed Derek an unmarked envelope. „*Herr Kommandant*," he said with a slight bow as he clicked his heels together.

Derek showed no emotion as he took the envelope and tossed it on the desktop. *„Danke,"* he returned.

With another quick glance and slight smirk in Elizabeth's direction, the rider again bowed toward Derek. *„Bitte,"* he replied. A moment later, he turned on his heel and walked out of the office.

Chapter Sixteen

EW BARRACKS HAD BEEN BUILT TO reduce the overcrowding associated with the camps and more were being erected as fast as the buildings could be produced. Elizabeth walked into the barracks she now shared with a much smaller number of women, who had been there before the changes, the smell of the new wood making itself known to her. She was so absorbed in thoughts of Derek that she hadn't paid much attention to her surroundings.

"Well," someone sneered as she shut the door, her tone laced with disgust. "So you are officially the new *Kommandant's* whore."

Elizabeth snapped out of her reverie to catch Naomi Rosenthal's hostile glare, as the older woman sat on the edge of the bed, her anger showing full in her brown eyes. A handful of others glowered at her as well and one looked as if she wanted to slug her, but most eyed her with curiosity more than anything. In any event, she fought to keep her alarm hidden as a shudder of dread rushed through her. She had no doubt the shit was about to hit the fan. For the first time since she had been in the camp, Elizabeth was afraid of the other captives. She had expected a bit of animosity, but not outright hostility.

"I see you are speechless, *Amerikanerin*," another snorted. "So it is true. I didn't believe it when Naomi told me, but it seems she was correct."

"So high and mighty you are," Naomi snapped. "Pretending to be one of us while you are fucking the handsome new *Kommandant*. You are a traitor and a collaborator, Elizabeth. I would advise you to watch your back from now on. You should worry more about us than those foolish young men guarding this camp."

In part, Elizabeth understood their reactions. She had been one of them, but had betrayed their trust with the man who kept them there. They had given her the benefit of the doubt the first few times she had gone to see Derek, but this time her explanations wouldn't be so readily accepted.

"I'm sorry you feel that way about me, Naomi," she said gently. "I do care what happens to you and everyone else here." When Naomi scoffed, her heart sank and tears of sadness filled her eyes. She did genuinely care about these women, but clearly none of them would believe her. Naomi's reaction proved it. This was exactly what Talia had warned her about when they first arrived.

"Leave her be, old woman," Zsuzsanna said with a yawn, as she stretched on her spot of the bed. "She is trying to survive like the rest of us. A lot of us would do the same in her position."

"I would," Dana admitted with a slight chuckle. "In spite of being our captor, he is very sexy. It's not like he asked for this damn job. Thank God we are not saddled with what other camps are."

"I say we should toss her pretty little ass outside in the cold for the next few nights," Naomi continued. "The slut has betrayed us by spreading her thighs for the bastard."

Zsuzsanna sat up and walloped the older woman with her pillow. "Give her the benefit of the doubt," she said. "Have you not already seen the changes von Vetter has made? Do we not have pallets and pillows instead of having to sleep directly on the hard wood of these beds? Are our stomachs now full of nourishment instead of empty and pained as before? Are we not alive and healthy instead of diseased and dying? He is even allowing everyone to continue with their religious practices and giving them their Sabbath days of rest as well as time for amusements. For once, we are not wallowing in filth, disease and starvation. That is unheard of for a man in his position. He has done more for all of us in the last month than the others have in the last few years. If he's the bad one, the good one must be amazing."

"It is a trick," Naomi insisted, although doubt at her own words flashed in her eyes. "He will give us comforts and then snatch them away when it is convenient. We are still being held prisoner in this godforsaken place."

"He is doing what he can," Elizabeth said, forcing herself to talk to these women when she wanted to run away and hide. Zsuzsanna was aware of her feelings for him, so she had at least one ally in the room. She would have been somewhat less worried had Talia been there, but she had been assigned to another barracks. In any case, she trusted Derek with her life and she had no doubt that he was doing what he could under the circumstances. He could help the resistance and fight back in many subtle ways. What he had already done for their benefit could get him into serious or even life-threatening danger. It was no different than what she had done for Zarah.

And he had already risked his life by hiding the identity of his grandmother's companion. He could have been killed outright for harboring a Jew, as she could have. He had been sent here, to Murrbrück, instead and had chosen to do good with what had been forced upon him. Most men in his position would have dismissed their consciences and chosen to do evil instead. Derek's love of life and humanity would not allow him to do so.

"I don't care if you believe me," she lied, but then continued with the truth. "He has been forced into commanding Murrbrück because his superiors had threatened to incarcerate his family if he did not. Having smuggled in these supplies, he is doing his part in fighting the injustices the others have no compunction in meting out. He is risking his life to do this as well. He cannot outright release us. If he did, the wrath of the SS and Gestapo would be upon our heads. God only knows what would happen."

At her own words, memories of what she had believed it would be like if she were suddenly dead entered her head. She would be alive and then it would suddenly be over. Those thoughts had always seemed to cause a surge of sheer terror to rush through her body and soul. She didn't realize the tears were streaming down her cheeks or that her heart fluttered as if she had just missed death until Zsuzsanna squatted on the floor and rested a hand on her left forearm.

"Are you in love with him, Elizabeth?" her friend asked, her tone filled with understanding. "Is he really worthy of our trust?"

She wiped her eyes and nodded. "Yes, he is," she said. "I love him and would give up my own life to save him, as I would any of you." She turned her attention to the others, meeting the remaining hostile gazes with a determined one. "Derek means everything to me, so if you all wish to make me pay for that, then do your worst. I don't give a damn any more. I've had it with this shit."

Naomi gave an exaggerated snort, but one of the younger women cut her off.

"Enough, Naomi!" Fey snapped. "Elizabeth is correct. Herr von Vetter is doing what he can and we have seen vast improvements proving this. You must admit this is true. The other *Kommandants* would have killed us outright, but he has done everything he can to make sure we stay alive and healthy. Rolf has always treated us with respect and you have no problem trusting him. Von Vetter is no different."

Naomi gave another snort, although this one had less punch. "We shall see," she said.

Zsuzsanna sat next to Elizabeth and rested her arm across her shoulders in a sisterly and friendly gesture, staring straight back at Naomi. Elizabeth rested her head on her friend's shoulder, glad she and the others were there. "He deserves the benefit of the doubt, as does our American friend. He has released that nice Therese because she was about to have a baby and she was not supposed to leave for a year or so yet. Need I remind you that Elizabeth is here because she risked her life to hide a Jew? Our new *Kommandant* is continuing to put his own life at risk by helping us. You should do well to remember that next time you plan to cause trouble."

"Do not allow those people to play us against one another," said an English girl, who had previously been silent. "That is just what has been happening here. Stop it now, because that is exactly what they want."

At Leslie's reassuring smile, Elizabeth gave her own. "Thank you," she mouthed, receiving a nod of acknowledgment in return.

To her and the others' surprise, Dana pulled a deck of cards from under her blanket. "Rolf has brought us a deck of cards, the sweetie pie," she said. "Anyone up for a game?"

Chapter Seventeen

LIZABETH STROLLED INTO THE MAIN PROCESSING room the next morning to see Rolf about shaving her head, convinced she was doing the right thing. Although relations between her and the other women were back to normal, she still had to prove that she didn't consider herself above them and that she wasn't giving herself to Derek just to cover her own ass. He had stopped the required shaving and the captives' hair was growing back, but this was her only recourse in proving herself to the others. She owed them that much.

She caught Rolf with his feet propped up on the table, his ankles crossed, while he leaned his chair back on its hind legs. He was reading an old edition of *Life* magazine, one she assumed that one of the guards had taken away from a captive. When she stopped beside his chair, he tossed back his head and stared up at her. "Hey, Elizabeth," he greeted her in guttural English.

She tossed her coat onto the bench behind the processing table. "Shear my hair," she demanded without preamble.

He raised a reddish eyebrow in amusement. "You are kidding me, right?" he asked.

"I don't believe so."

Rolf immediately yanked his feet off the table and allowed the front legs of the chair to bang to the floor. "But you're *Herr Kommandant's* m-m-mistress ..." he said, flushing as he stammered over the last word.

Elizabeth had to fight the urge to chuckle. "Yes, Rolf," she agreed. "That is true. Now, would you please shear my hair as I asked?"

"But …" he started, his eyes widening with worry. "When Übel had tried to do that to you before, Derek had threatened to, I mean *Herr Kommandant* had threatened to …"

She nearly released a boisterous laugh at Rolf's attempt to cover the use of Derek's first name, but she forced herself to withhold it. The men were close friends and Derek considered him the younger brother he never had. "I will chance his wrath," she snapped, pretending to be annoyed at his continuous hesitation. It appeared he was only going to do what she wanted if she ordered him to do it.

He reluctantly rose from his seat and tossed the magazine onto the table. "Yes, ma'am," he grumbled.

When she began releasing the buttons her top, he balked. "I'm going to take off my shirt so I don't get itchy from the hair that will fall on me," she explained. "Don't have a heart attack, okay?" Without waiting for a response, she pushed the top off her shoulders and allowed it to fall into a small puddle on the floor. She sighed and sat in the chair he had recently vacated.

When Rolf dropped his gaze to her bare breasts, he loudly cleared his throat. "I will try," he choked out. Flushing, he turned away and picked the shaver off the nearby table. It took less than five minutes for him to shave off her long hair, although he paused and groaned loudly in protest after each stroke of the shaver.

Now she was like any other prisoner who had been generally processed through the room. She raised a hand to smooth it over her head. The stubble was surprisingly soft against her palm, although it felt rather strange after all the years of long, thick hair. "Nice job, Rolf," she said in approval. "Thank you."

"I may as well go into hiding now," he complained, his voice somewhat whiny. "When Derek sees what I have done, he will shoot me on sight."

Before she could change her mind, Elizabeth grasped the waistband of her slacks and tugged them down. *God, Elizabeth. I can't believe you're about to do this. Rolf may be a sweetheart, but he is still a man.*

When they were down to her hips, Rolf turned beet red and again loudly cleared his throat. "I suppose you are telling me to shave you there as well," he surmised.

She raised an eyebrow and allowed the pants to fall to the floor.

She sat back down in his chair and set a leg on either side of it, leaving nothing to his imagination. "Yes, I want you to shave me between my legs," she said, a flush burning her cheeks at the words. "Make me as bare as a baby."

Rolf rolled his eyes, his comely face again turning fiery red. "God, I'm dead," he whined.

Later, when she had dressed and gone back outside, she headed toward her laundry assignment. *It would sure feel nice when winter was really here*, she thought as the chill of the wind flowed over her. She shivered, but this was for the best. The first person to notice her was her nemesis, Naomi, whose jaw dropped open in shock. She eyed the stubble of hair covering her head and snapped her mouth shut, although she nodded as a new respect entered her eyes. Without waiting for another reaction, Elizabeth turned and walked in the other direction.

Chapter Eighteen

"**I** APOLOGIZE FOR THE INTERRUPTION, BUT ROLF wishes to speak with you when you have a moment," Manfred said as he poked his head in the door. "He says it is important."

Derek held up his index finger, telling his secretary to wait. "Hang on a tic, Granny," he said. He had been telling her more about Elizabeth than he had been able to after his first day at the camp and she seemed to approve. He just wished he could do more for the woman he loved now.

Sabrina chuckled. "All right, sweetheart," she said. "I'm not going anywhere."

Derek cupped his hand over the mouthpiece and raised an eyebrow. "Have him wait for me," he said as he switched to German. "I will only be a few moments."

The young man nodded. "Yes, sir," he said. A moment later, he closed the door behind him.

"Do you need to go, darling?" his grandmother asked.

"Rolf needs to speak with me," he said as he returned to English. "Manny said it was important, so I'll call you back later."

"Goodbye then. Tell him and Elizabeth I said hello."

Derek grinned. "I will do that," he promised. He hung up the phone, not bothering to let Manfred know to send in Rolf. He made his way to the door and opened it to see his young friend pacing and looking very nervous. He fought back a chuckle. He couldn't possibly have done anything *that* terrible. If anything, he looked as if he were waiting on news that he was about to be a father. "You can come in now,

Rolf." Rolf grimaced, but followed him into the room. Derek closed the door behind them. "What did you need to speak with me about?"

"You may wish to sit down for this, my lord," Rolf stated with a stiff posture.

My lord? Derek smirked, but instead of sitting, he leaned back against his desk and crossed his arms over his ribs. "What's with the 'my lord' shit, Rolf?" he teased. "You don't have to be formal with me. You know that."

Rolf physically relaxed his stance and clenched his hands behind his back. "I must confess something, my lord, and I do not believe you are going to like it."

Curiosity flashed through Derek and he raised an eyebrow. "You have no reason to fear me either, Rolf," he reminded him. "I have told you that before."

Rolf looked at the wall behind the desk. "You will not feel the same after I tell you what has happened," he said, his voice shaky.

Derek couldn't help but chuckle, although he couldn't say he wasn't curious. "Will you quit stalling and tell me what the hell is going on?" he asked.

Rolf took a heavy breath and then audibly gulped. "Miss Kelley came to me today and demanded that I shave her head," he said. "I did so."

Derek wasn't sure he had heard correctly at first, but when the words registered, his heart smacked hard into his ribs and anger slammed through his body. He dropped his hands to his sides and took a threatening step forward. "You did what?" he shouted as the heat of rage rushed through him. "No wonder you keep calling me 'my lord'!"

Rolf flinched as he slid his rifle off his shoulder and held it out toward him. "Please have mercy, sir," he whined. "Shoot me and be done with it."

Derek ran his hand through the longer top of his hair and took a deep breath in an attempt to calm his racing heart. The color returned to his cheeks so hard they hurt. "So you are telling me that Elizabeth came into the processing room and insisted you shave her head," he said as if confirming that he understood. "Did you shave her ..." he started as he motioned downward, but then cut off the rest of his words. He just couldn't finish the rest of the sentence.

Rolf flushed bright red as he slid his rifle strap and rifle back onto his shoulder. „*Ja,*" he choked out.

Derek couldn't stop the stream of profanity in four languages that shot from his lips. The first thing he wanted to do was slam a chair against the wall, so hard that his body burned with it. It was clear his friend was terrified, but he didn't care. He took a deep breath in another attempt to calm his racing heart, but it did not work. He tightened his lips. "I want you to do something for me, Rolf." The ramrod hardness sounded in his voice, but the pain of what Rolf had said was in the tone as well. "I want you to bring Elizabeth to me immediately and after you drop her off, I do not want to see your face for the rest of the day. Do you understand me?"

Rolf took several deep, silent breaths. „*Ja, mein Herr,*" he said, but then momentarily hesitated.

Anger again flashed within him at Rolf's hesitation and he stepped forward. "Leave now before I change my mind!" he shouted. If he hadn't ordered his friend out, he would have hit him. If he had done that, he would never have forgiven himself.

„*Ja, mein Herr,*" Rolf said. He opened the door and left the room.

Once Rolf had gone, Derek sank into the nearest chair.

Chapter Nineteen

THE NEWS TRAVELED OVER THE COMPOUND in an amazingly short time, but Elizabeth wasn't surprised. She couldn't help but notice the numerous gapes and double takes as she made her way back to her job. She was helping Zsuzsanna plant some new winter flowers a few minutes later when Rolf interrupted.

"Miss Elizabeth," he stated, his face red from an emotion she couldn't place. He audibly gulped. "*Herr Kommandant* wishes to speak with you. How I am still alive to relay this message, I do not know."

Elizabeth forced back a boisterous laugh, but Zsuzsanna couldn't and was nearly doubled over in her amusement. "Tell Derek I'm on my way," Elizabeth said.

Rolf emphatically shook his head. "He does not wish to see my face for the rest of the day, quote unquote," he said. "I would advise that you come with me to his office. Immediately."

She hid a smile. "I will see him immediately," she assured him. She paused and rested a hand on his forearm. "Do not worry, Rolf. I'll tell him I made you do it."

He physically relaxed, although worry still filled his eyes. „*Danke*," he said.

After a conspiratory wink at the laughing Zsuzsanna, Elizabeth rose to her feet. Rolf was silent the entire way, not that she blamed him. She caught Manny's eye as he stopped typing and gazed directly at her head, gawking when he realized what had happened.

He snatched up the phone, nearly dropping the ˙receiver in the process. "She is here, my lord," he said. After a few seconds, he hung up and raised an eyebrow. "You may go in now, Miss Kelley."

"Thank you, Manny," she smiled. Without knocking, she walked into Derek's office.

When his gaze landed on her, his reaction was like his secretary's. If there had been anything in his mouth, it would have fallen out. "I swear, Elizabeth," he said a moment later, his voice strained as if he had a touch of laryngitis. "I believe you are about to see a grown man have a good cry. God, that gorgeous hair. Why in the hell would you do something like that?"

She related what had happened when she had returned to the barracks the previous night and how the only way she could think of to prove her loyalty was to have Rolf shave off her hair. "It wasn't Rolf's fault, Derek, my love," she said. "He likes you, but after he did what I pretty much demanded, he was terrified. The poor thing believes he will face a firing squad at any moment."

Derek chuckled. "It amazes me that after three years of seeing all the shit that has been happening in this damned place, he seems so naïve."

Elizabeth smirked with humor, although she knew that Rolf wasn't nearly as naïve as he portrayed himself to be. "I know." She stepped toward Derek and grasped his hand. "Enough about Rolf. I have another surprise for you. I think you'll like this one."

Curiosity flashed in his eyes and he arched an eyebrow. "Oh?" he asked in a warm tone.

She moved his hand toward her and slid it into the front of her slacks. When his fingers cupped her, a lick of fire mixed with sensitivity swept through her body. "Derek ..." she urged.

He parted the lips and slid his middle finger against her button, the action weakening her knees. "I must have you, Elizabeth," he stated hotly as a dazed look entered his eyes. "But in bed, not on the damn sofa."

"Yes," she agreed. Her heart raced when he grasped her behind her shoulders and her knees. When he lifted her into the warmth of his arms, a squeal leaped from within her. She slid her arms around his neck and rested her head in the curve of his shoulder so he wouldn't drop her. She hoped he didn't put out his back. "Derek."

He laughed. "You ain't seen nothin' yet," he teased. He carried her into his personal quarters and laid her down on the bed. He sat and leaned on his left hand, grinning at her.

She raised her hands over her head, laughing as he released the buttons on her shirt. "Something tells me you're in the mood," she teased.

He raised an eyebrow, although the laughter shined brightly in his eyes. "You think so?" he asked with a straight face.

She could only laugh harder, but when he brushed his thumb over her nipple, her laughter turned into a moan. "Derek," she groaned.

"At least I got you to stop laughing," he grinned.

When he slid his hand under her slacks and between her thighs to stroke the bud, Elizabeth groaned again as flames shot through her. She found herself raising her hips and moving against her love's slow torture, her consciousness seeming to fade.

Derek slid his finger down the canal and into her sheath, then back out again to tease the burning bud. "God, Elizabeth," he groaned. "You feel so good, babe. I want you." He released her and tugged the slacks down and off her legs. A barely-audible whimper sounded in her throat as he grasped her behind her knees and parted them.

When he bent his head to her and pressed kisses over her, her whimpers turned into cries of pleasure. She raised her buttocks at the same time that his tongue touched her. As her entire body seemed to flame, he tickled her with the tip and then allowed it to lave her. Cries sounded in the distance and it was as if someone else made them, causing her to stiffen as a climax threatened to take over her body.

"I cannot stand it any longer," Derek said as he laid against her and gazed deep into her eyes. "I must have you now, babe."

"I love you," Elizabeth said, an urgent edge in her tone.

He gave her a brief kiss. "I love you," he returned. He slid off her and quickly shed his uniform. He laid on his back and grasped her hips to urge her on top of him. Before she knew it, he tugged her down onto his length.

As she rode him, he brushed against her, teasing and tantalizing her. He raised his knees and grasped her buttocks in encouragement. "Derek," she cried at the feel of him inside her.

"Ride me, sweetheart," he begged as they moved together. "Take me."

He groaned hotly as he thrust within her, turning her body sensitive. They moved in a sensual rhythm and it wasn't long before they both reached their peaks of fulfillment.

The next day proved to be just as sensual. Elizabeth, Dominique, Katrine and the other women, who worked in the laundry were about to finish the last load of the guards' uniforms when Dominique burst out laughing.

"Maybe we should accidentally lose Übel's," she said, allowing the sarcasm to sound in her tone.

"I know what I'd like to do with it and to him," Fey supplied in the same tone. "Then do the same thing to Erich. They're both assholes."

Elizabeth and the others burst out laughing at the word, since it was one Fey normally wouldn't use. As the laughter died down, Erna strolled into the room with a knowing smirk. "I think Derek wants you, Elizabeth," she relayed.

Katrine laughed. "Imagine that," she said.

"Did somebody mention my name?" Derek asked as he followed Erna into the room. At the simultaneous, elongated yeses, his gaze landed on her and he smiled. "Can I see you for a bit, Elizabeth?" he asked, his eyes sparkling impishly.

She ignored the knowing looks that passed between the other women and smiled at him. "Sure," she agreed, not questioning him. He wanted to be alone with her and that was enough. He grasped her hand and pulled her to her feet.

"Come with me."

Before she realized it, they headed toward his office. As soon as they walked in, Manny yanked his hand from the filing cabinet and slammed the drawer shut. Elizabeth nearly burst out laughing when he stood there gaping, something he seemed to be doing a lot of lately.

"Sir?" the secretary asked.

"Lunchtime, Manny," Derek suggested. "Like now."

Manfred took a quick glance at her, his cheeks momentarily flashing bright red. "Yes, sir!" He headed toward the door and was gone a moment later.

The two burst out laughing. "I think we're wearing signs," Elizabeth teased.

Derek chuckled. "Yes," he said. "We didn't exactly keep what we wanted a secret. I may as well have said outright that we came here to fuck."

Elizabeth couldn't help but laugh harder, her cheeks burning hard with a blush. "Derek Edwin von Vetter," she said in teasing reprimand. "I can't believe that came out of your mouth."

Derek flushed. "Shame on me," he said with a grin. "I couldn't help myself." Once in his quarters, he tugged her into his arms. "God, I've missed you," he groaned. Her heart leaped and delicious heat flowed through her body as he bent his head. The touch of his tongue as it caressed hers caused her heart to pound hard between her breasts, nearly immobilizing her. She slid her hands up his shoulders and gripped them in an attempt to keep from sliding to the carpeting.

The passionate kiss seemed to go on and on, sending her mind reeling into a whirlpool of sensation. The next thing she knew, he eased the jacket's buttons out of their holes and tugged the material off her shoulders. It fell to the carpeting with a soft whomp. The "uniform" top came soon after, falling to her feet. He groaned when his gaze landed on her breasts.

"Derek," she pleaded, her body languid in anticipation of their lovemaking. The one word was all the encouragement he needed and he yanked her "uniform" bottoms down to her ankles. A shiver of wanting rushed through her as he went down on his knees. When he touched her heat with the tip of his tongue, her knees gave way from the intimacy of the touch. She dug her fingertips into his shoulders, allowing a crying groan of pleasure to pass her lips.

Derek briefly momentarily lifted his head. "Elizabeth," he groaned as he looked up at her. "Promise me you'll keep shaving yourself."

"I ... I ..." she started, but couldn't finish, since he again buried his head between her thighs. He brushed his tongue over her sensitivity and warmth gradually turned into new flames as wanting spread over her body.

He slid up her body and bent his head to hers, their tongues immediately fighting as if they were enemies in battle. He urged her down onto the bed, squirming against her as she released the buttons on his slacks. She slid her hands under the waistband and lower to grasp his firm buttocks in her hands. When she pushed his slacks down to the tops of his thighs, he rolled onto his back and tugged them off. A moment later, his boots clumped to the floor.

He pulled her onto his lap and urged her down onto his length. At his invasion, she peeled away her mouth and released a cry into the room. "Ride me, Elizabeth," he encouraged her, his tone hot. "Oh yes, babe. Ride me."

At their sensual coupling, he slid his hand between her thighs. "Derek," she whimpered as his caresses spread heat through her blood.

He released a heavy breath without slowing their pace. "I should thank Rolf for this," he said with his voice full of his desire and love for her. "You are softer than chenille. You're driving me wild, babe. Come for me now."

She drifted off into a sea of pleasure at his words and touch, riding the tide as she reached her devastating climax.

Chapter Twenty

OVER THE NEXT FEW WEEKS, CONDITIONS in the camp continued to improve, just as Derek had promised. Members of the resistance were able to get more supplies and have them gradually brought into the camp. One of the married captives discovered she was pregnant, so Derek procured new identity documents from a reliable source for her and her husband. He was able to get them out of the compound and to a new life. After that incident and as with Therese, it became easier to find ways to smuggle captives out of the compound under the guise of officiality. Since Derek's friend Hans' resistance group had many contacts, they would have places to stay until they were safe.

Thankfully, the most hostile of the guards were not aware of how much had been happening. If they had found out about the course of events and the in-camp resistance he supported, Derek would, at the very least, have become a prisoner himself.

The arbitrary abuse had stopped on the day Derek had taken command. Rolf had been stealing medications from Dr. Weidenbach's medical supply for years and giving them to captives who became ill and he continued the practice with Derek's help. Since Dr. Weidenbach was addicted to morphine and stoned for the much of the time, it did not present much of a problem. The captives were healthier and more productive than those in other camps because of it and because there was plenty of food to eat. Although Derek had stopped mandatory haircuts on the first day he was there, there was no need for them because cleanliness kept away the infestations of lice and the many diseases caused by the usual squalid conditions.

Something snapped Elizabeth awake, although she didn't know what it could have been. Maybe it was thoughts of the changes that occupied her mind. Derek laid sleeping behind her with his left arm around her waist and his left leg entwined with hers, his breathing deep and even. She forced herself to tug away from the heat of his body and face him instead of snuggling back against him. He stirred, but didn't awaken. Why was it that the more important it was to get up, the more difficult a task it was simply to get out of bed?

"Derek," she whispered as she shook his bare shoulder. "I need to go."

He snapped awake, but then relaxed and gave her a loving smile. "I told you that you could stay with me tonight," he reminded her.

Tears filled Elizabeth's eyes as her heart tightened with emotion. The last thing she wanted to do was leave, but she had no choice. "I know," she said. "But I need to get back to my barracks."

He exaggerated a pout, but then nodded. "If you're sure," he said.

She smiled. "I'm sure." She bent her head to kiss him gently. "I love you. Goodnight."

"Goodnight, my love. I love you, too." It wasn't long before he laid down his head and peacefully slept. Her heart ached to stay with him, but she did not want to get used to sleeping in his quarters. After the war was over, they could be together forever, but now that wasn't possible.

Elizabeth slid into her uniform and tugged on her jacket and shoes, trying her best not to burst into tears. The evening was a little warmer than it had been lately, but it was still very cold. The oppressive air seemed to hug her bones, although there was no wind. She made her way down the short flight of stairs only to be stopped by one of the guards. She was briefly startled, but then recognized one of the friendlier young men.

"Halt," Fritz snapped as he leveled his rifle at her. When he realized who she was, he lowered it. "Sorry, ma'am. I didn't realize it was you. I'll escort you to your barracks."

"It isn't necessary, Fritz. I'll be fine."

He narrowed his eyes. "I would rather you allowed me," he insisted. "It would be for your safety."

He was correct, since there were still plenty of guards who would enjoy harming her. "All right," she agreed. "Thank you."

Along the way, she took a quick, sweeping view of the camp. It was a very still quiet and a few guards stood at their posts. They had had a snowfall a couple of weeks ago, but it had long since dissipated, leaving blackness. The guards and the barracks seemed to stand out in spite of the night's darkness, giving the area an eerier aspect than usual. A still night was always creepy to an extent, but an impending sense of doom rushed through Elizabeth's bones. She shrugged, brushing off her nervousness. Once they arrived at her barracks, Fritz nodded. "Goodnight, ma'am," he said.

Elizabeth nodded in return. "Goodnight, Fritz," she said. She stepped inside and made her way through the darkness.

"How nice of you to join us," someone said with humor in her tone.

Elizabeth jerked, surprised that anyone was awake. She and Naomi had gotten along well in the last few weeks, although Elizabeth didn't believe the older woman really trusted her. "Sorry," she apologized.

Naomi chuckled. "Goodnight, Elizabeth," she said.

"Goodnight," she returned. She removed her shoes and jacket, and laid down in her spot at the end. She used her jacket as an extra pillow and grasped the real one in her arms. A hot tear slid down her cheek as she wished she were still with the man she loved. She hoped that the day when she would be able to stay with him would come soon. She missed him so much already. That was the last thing she remembered before she fell asleep.

Chapter Twenty-One

KARL TOSSED ANOTHER SET OF FILES into the garbage, disgusted with von Vetter. He would pay for his continued resistance and the changes he had made in the camp. Apparently, the threat to incarcerate his grandmother and her *Jüdin* companion had failed.

Übel had informed him of the goings-on at the camp, that von Vetter had been smuggling in supplies for the benefit of his prisoners and the rumors of an in-camp resistance that had von Vetter's support. Übel had also reported that his commanding officer had been giving the prisoners medical attention and an overabundance of nourishment as well as extended breaks, brief moments to relax and religious Sabbaths off. He treated them as his employees and friends, instead of threats to the Reich. It was no wonder the people in this camp were so productive. With such incentives, they were all too willing to do von Vetter's bidding. The German officer was becoming quite the humanitarian.

There was no room for such deviants in the New Order. The major had betrayed the Brotherhood for the last time. Heinrich would not have him killed outright, even if his *Führer* had ordered him to do so, since that would have been far too easy. The younger man would suffer along with the other prisoners and not live to see the end of the war, receiving a death sentence that would be meted out in a slow and merciless way. In addition to his other crimes, von Vetter was having sexual relations with one of his prisoners, an American by the name of Elizabeth Kelley, who had been placed there for hiding a Jew. Heinrich would enjoy seeing von Vetter fall apart when the woman he loved was destroyed along with him.

Karl brought his personal guards with him, since he could not trust the guards employed at the camp, with the exceptions of Übel and Erich. His first priority was to eliminate von Vetter, but he would deal with the others later. The door opened behind him and he casually turned toward the sound.

Manfred released a shocked gasp when he realized what was happening. "Sir," he forced out, momentarily paling as recognition flashed in his eyes. "I …"

"Silence!" Karl shouted, withholding a smile as the young man visibly jerked and closed his mouth with an audible snap. He stalked over to Manfred and around him, deliberately trying to instill fear in him. He allowed a cold grin to curve his lips as a sense of power rushed through him. "Where is the communiqué, Manfred?" he demanded, aware that the young man could know nothing about a fictitious document.

Manfred stood rigid and shifted his eyes to the back wall. "I do not know of what you are speaking, Colonel," he said truthfully, his eyes filled with terror.

Heinrich stepped behind the young man and whipped his pistol from his holster. He had intended to have him transferred and replace him with his own secretary, but this would simplify things. Without hesitation, he pointed the muzzle at the back of the secretary's head and pulled the trigger.

Blood, brain matter and shards of skull shot from Manfred's head and his body dropped to the floor a half a heartbeat later. "I am aware of that, Manfred," he said in a calm voice. Ignoring the splatters on the wall as well as his guards' stunned realizations, he slid the pistol back into his holster.

Heinrich chuckled at their reactions, surprised that his men were so shocked. It was not the first time they had witnessed such an action and it certainly wouldn't be the last. "Get back to work and find the communiqué," he said as he stalked over to Derek's desk. "Übel assures me it is here." There was no communiqué, but his guards did not know it. He merely wanted to add any incriminating evidence he may find.

„*Ja, mein Herr*," they choked out.

Heinrich pulled out a drawer and ran the pads of his fingertips along the underside of it, feeling the slight catch in the wood. When he passed over it again, he realized what it was. He pulled out the drawer the rest of the way and turned it over, letting the papers inside shower to the floor.

He pressed the tip of a letter opener against the seam and opened the hidden section. There were several small pieces of paper inside, but it appeared they were only personal notes. Heinrich suspected otherwise and he would try to decipher them later. Right now, he had more important things to address. "Konrad, Bernhard," he snapped. "Find that traitor and his American whore. Now."

„*Was über Manfred?*" Konrad asked, his pale eyebrows crinkling.

Heinrich eyed the secretary lying on the floor. Once his heart had stopped beating, the blood flow would begin to trickle and then coagulate. "Take him to the crematorium and burn his remains," he ordered. "If he had not happened upon us, he would not be dead."

Chapter Twenty-Two

EREK LACED HIS FINGERS THROUGH ELIZABETH'S short hair, pleased at the style. Although it was a bit boyish, it would grow out in time. His heart flipped as he looked deep into her eyes. "I've been wanting to be alone with you all morning," he confessed.

Elizabeth chuckled as she wriggled her eyebrows. "Just all morning?" she teased.

"Oh, much more than that," he groaned softly. "Care to sneak away for a tic?'

"Would I ever."

He grasped her hand and started walking toward his office. When he realized that Manny wasn't at the front desk and that his own door stood partially open, he shivered and became alert. He always locked his door when he left and his secretary wouldn't go in there without his permission. A sixth sense of dread rushed through his being when movement sounded from inside.

"Find it," someone ordered. He realized that his premonition of fear was right on the mark when he recognized the voice as belonging to the man who had put him there, Colonel Karl Heinrich. "Übel assures me it is here."

"What ..." Elizabeth started, but he put his index finger to his lips.

"Konrad, Bernhard," he heard Heinrich snap. "Find that traitor and his American whore. Now."

"What about Manfred?" one of the guards asked.

"Take him to the crematorium and burn his remains. If he had not happened upon us, he would not be dead."

Derek went numb at the words and motioned for Elizabeth to follow him. She nodded in understanding, her eyes bright with worry. He slowly walked backward on his toes, his boots making nearly no sound. He repeatedly thanked himself for finding her the leather shoes. They were cheap and worn, but they were comfortable. Best of all, they were silent on the hardwood floor. Once outside, he glanced at her.

"What's going on, Derek?" she asked.

"I can't tell you right now, sweetheart, but we have to get out of here now. I cannot protect you here any longer." He had to get her out of the compound fast. Elizabeth's safety was his priority. He would rather have allowed himself to be captured than put her through such hell. "If I don't make it, I want you to find Hans and have him help you save my granny before they get to her. I will keep trying to do what I can here." If anything happened to him, they would both be caught and there would have no way to save Miriam or Sabrina. Staying would be the most unselfish thing he could do. Elizabeth would do fine without him, especially with Hans' help. "I love you more than life itself," he reminded her as if he would never be able to tell her again. "Always remember that."

"Derek, you're scaring me." Her voice was so thick with emotion that his heart lurched. She was close to tears and stiff, as if she were forcing herself not to panic.

"Just promise me?" he asked gently.

She momentarily closed her eyes and took a deep, shaky breath. "I promise."

They made their way along the side of the building and headed toward the gatehouse without gaining attention from the other captives. Since they were receiving no new prisoners today, it was clear, with the exception of Rolf patrolling the immediate area. When he noticed them in their attempt to make a cautious exit, he briefly stopped in his tracks.

Derek slid his index finger sideways across his throat, the signal they had agreed upon if their secret was discovered. His friend barely nodded, although understanding flashed his eyes. A moment later, he turned and walked in the other direction. Derek stole a few seconds to pull a still-silent Elizabeth to him and squeeze her in a hug. "I love you, Elizabeth," he reminded her into her hair. "Just follow my lead."

She pulled back and rested her hands on the sides of his face. "I love you, Derek," she said as if it were the last time she would be able to do so.

Although a rush of panic shot through him and pushed his heartbeat to a new level, he smiled in reassurance and pressed a kiss against her thumb. "On the count of three, walk quickly toward the gate and go through," he urged gently. "I will be right behind you, I promise."

She nodded and slid her hands down, her face pale with the seriousness of the situation. It was bone-chillingly cold, but he doubted she cared any more than he did. "All right," she agreed.

"One … two … three."

Elizabeth grabbed tightly onto his hand and they walked swiftly toward the wrought iron gates. He unlocked them in record time and they went through them a heartbeat later. He took a look around as a couple of guards in the towers glanced their way and paused but then turned away as if nothing unusual were happening. Thankfully, no one else was looking their direction, since they were involved in their daily assignments. He was sure all hell would break loose of they did. A few more steps and they would be free of the compound, but as soon as the thought cleared his mind, someone yelled from behind them. He chanced a glance over his shoulder as Übel ran toward them with his rifle in his hands.

"Halt!" the sergeant shouted.

"Move, Elizabeth!" Derek yelled in English. They reached the meadow in record time and were halfway across before he could breathe. Thank God he had the guards to disable the mines since they would have been killed otherwise. The edge of the woods was a short distance away and if they made it there, they were home free.

When the crack of Übel's rifle echoed into the trees, a soft whimper of fear leapt from Elizabeth's throat and Derek's heartbeat shot off as if it were a V-1 rocket. He tugged out his pistol as he took a glance behind him and shot toward the younger man, narrowly missing his right cheekbone.

Instead of returning fire, Übel aimed his pistol at Elizabeth. Derek could not allow anything to happen to the woman he loved. As soon as he hopped behind her, a bullet sliced through his thigh and forced him down. He oomphed as the ground slammed hard against his chest and knocked the breath from his lungs.

The color drained from Elizabeth's face when she realized he had been shot. "Derek!" she screamed, her face and lips pale from terror. His heart nearly stopped beating when she ran back to him.

"Keep running!" he yelled as another bullet whizzed past her. "Don't stop!"

Tears rolled down Elizabeth's cheeks and her bottom lip quivered uncontrollably. "No!" she screamed. "I can't leave you here!"

Derek didn't bother attempting to get up, since his wound would slow them. He leveled his Walther sideways at her. "Catch," he shouted as he tossed it to her. "You'll need this." Luckily, she caught it with one hand. He watched, his heart constricting as more tears poured from her eyes. "Go before he shoots you!" he shouted back, thanking God that the guard hadn't already done so. "There's nothing you can do."

"I'll ..." she started.

Tears filled Derek's eyes and his throat muscles tightened, his thigh burning from the wound. It shattered his heart that he would have to be without her, but letting her go was the only way to save her life. "Please, my love," he tried to shout, his voice strained from emotional agony. "Go!"

"I love you, Derek," she cried. "We'll come back for you, I swear it."

Derek watched as his love turned to run the rest of the distance into the woods. A cold chill raced through his marrow at the unmistakable sound of a cocking rifle, but that chill turned into numbness when the muzzle of the rifle met the back of his head.

"Stay on your stomach, von Vetter," Übel snarled in English, with triumph sounding in his voice. "Or I will splatter your Jew-loving brains all over the ground."

Chapter Twenty-Three

ONLY WHEN ELIZABETH WAS DEEP INTO the trees did she take the time to stop. She leaned back against one of the tall trees, crying out as she slid to the ground. The air in her lungs was seemingly being squeezed out and her heart raced wildly from her exertion and emotional pain, as if someone had sliced her soul apart with a razor. She barely noticed when the pistol Derek had given her slid from her fingers and landed beside her. "Derek," she wailed to herself. She buried her head in her arms and the tears slid unhindered down her cheeks.

God, this can't be happening! She couldn't find the man who meant everything to her and then have him ripped away from her. She should have stayed there with him instead of being the selfish person she had been and left him. If he died, she would never forgive herself. As with Zarah, it would be all her fault if that were the case. The only thing that kept her from going back was seeing Derek in her mind as he tossed her his pistol and told her there was nothing she could do. She had betrayed not only her best friend, but the man she loved as well.

She cried until her insides ached and once her tears had dried, she wiped her eyes with her coat sleeve. She forced herself to rise to her feet and step away from the tree. The cold breeze whipped through her bones and numbed her, but she had more important matters to attend to than comfort. She was about to try to find her way out the other side of the woods when someone grabbed her around her arms and ribcage, pressing the muzzle of a pistol against the side of her head. She cried out as her heart seemed to come to a stop. "God, no," she said out loud.

"One wrong move and you are dead," a male voice she didn't recognize snarled in German from behind her left ear. "Nod if you understand me."

Elizabeth sharply sucked in her breath as her heart raced from fear, but she nodded.

"Good girl."

When she realized he had spoken the latter in English, it was the last straw. Rage soared through her as she began to struggle, the anger temporarily negating her emotional pain and her sense of logic. She wrapped her foot around his ankle in an attempt to trip him, but unfortunately her maneuver didn't faze him and he remained on his feet. A heartbeat later, he lifted her from the ground. Curses sprang from her lips as her legs flailed, but her actions did nothing except cause him to burst out laughing. He lowered her to a standing position, although he retained his hold on her.

"What's so damned funny, you son of a bitch?" she snapped in English, her heart pounding hard and wild from her anger.

"You must be Elizabeth," he said with a smile in his voice. "Derek said you are a fireball." The man let go of her and moved to stand in front of her. She wanted to slap him when he grinned like an idiot.

Elizabeth briefly ran her gaze over him, deciding that if he had a chance to bathe he would be a very attractive man. With his dirty, baggy brown slacks and jacket, he looked as if he had been rolling around in the dirt. An olive armband was wrapped around his left bicep, with "39/7" sewn into it. She crinkled her eyebrows, having no idea what the numbers meant. He was about the same height as she was, but with a bone structure similar to Derek's. His overlong, golden-highlighted brown hair reached to his shoulders and gave an appealing prettiness to his features. A rifle was slung over his shoulder, but she did not recognize the caliber. "And just who the hell are you, jerk weed?" she snapped.

He chuckled, the movement tightening his full lips. "I will take that answer to mean yes," he teased.

She crinkled her eyebrows, taking a deep breath to stop the annoyance that swept through her. "Like I said, who are you?"

The man clicked the heels of his boots together and bowed gracefully.

"Hans Lindberg, at your service," he said with a grin, giving a good imitation of a Texas drawl.

She raised an eyebrow at him. "Like Charles Lindbergh?" she asked.

Hans bent to snatch Derek's pistol off the ground and handed it to her, butt first. "No relation, I am sorry to say," he advised. "Besides, there is no *h* at the end of my surname."

Elizabeth took the pistol from his hand and slid it into her jacket pocket. "Oh," she said flatly.

"So where is Derek?" he asked with a smile. "He was supposed to meet me here."

Tears rushed into her eyes at the inquiry, wiping away her anger and bringing her emotions back to reality. The thought of never seeing Derek again was unbearable and her lower lip began quivering in emotional pain. The scene of their attempted escape played in her mind as if reminding her that she had chosen to leave him there. She breathed a deep sigh in an attempt to wipe away the guilt, but it didn't work. "He's not here," she said, her voice cracking. "That hateful guard, Übel, shot him. He took the bullet that was meant for me."

Hans paled. "You mean he is ..."

"No. He's not dead." Thank God for that small mercy, but who knew what would happen while he was in custody. She was too terrified even to think about it. "Although I don't know how long he'll be alive."

"When the Americans come, he will be freed."

Hope leaped in Elizabeth's heart at the bit of news, but she forced herself to remain cautious. "When are they ..." she began.

"I cannot say for sure, although I hope it will be soon. However you must know, Elizabeth, that there is a chance he may not be alive when they get there."

Elizabeth's elation turned into defeat as he confirmed her earlier thought. "That's not an option, Hans," she insisted, her heart heavy. "I will never believe he is dead until I see it with my own eyes."

Hans released a heavy sigh. "All right, Elizabeth," he reluctantly agreed. "Then will you help us with the fight until we see him again?"

She crinkled her eyebrows at the apparent offer. "You mean join your resistance?" she asked.

"Yes."

There was no question what her answer would be. She would do whatever she could to fight injustices. She had been passive far too long. "I will help you until that time arrives, but I need to learn how to shoot. I'm useless with a gun."

Hans' hazel eyes flashed with a warm sparkle as he chuckled. "I will teach you how to be a crack shot," he said with a wink. "You will learn much more than that in time."

"Thank you," Elizabeth said, intrigued.

„Bitte," he said, nodding in return. "However, we must leave here."

She shivered as a cold breeze blew over her. A soft rain had begun to fall, but it was more soothing than worrisome. Without another word between them, she followed him out of the woods and onto a dirt road that had darkened from the raindrops. She questioned the wisdom of traveling out in the open, but she assumed he knew what he was doing. They had walked only a few feet when a large, dark green tractor stopped beside them.

„Guten Tag," a cheerful-looking farmer called down in greeting. His nearly white hair and pale skin gleamed, even with the drizzly afternoon.

Elizabeth would have given anything to be as carefree as Derek's friend seemed to be. *„Guten Tag,"* she returned.

„Hallo," Hans greeted the man with a wide smile.

"My home is open to you," the farmer advised them. "I can take you to your next destination early tomorrow morning."

„Vielen Dank," Hans answered with a nod.

Elizabeth thought it was strange that the farmer had opened his home to them, since it was clear from her striped uniform that she was a prisoner from the nearby camp. If they were caught, he could be sent to the camp along with her, if he was lucky enough not to be shot on sight.

The farmer motioned with his thumb to the back of the tractor. "There is room in the back," he told them.

Elizabeth glanced at the back and suppressed a gasp of surprise. How would they ever fit back there? "You've got to be kidding me," she whispered to Hans. There didn't seem to be enough room for supplies, let alone for two adults. Since she had never been comfortable with tightly closed spaces, she took several deep breaths to force herself to hold back the panic.

Hans squeezed her arm in reassurance. "Thank you for your kindness, sir," he said with a nod and a smile.

Once they were cramped and curled together under the convenient tarp, she proposed her earlier questions to him. The rain had begun to fall more readily and the drops echoed against the tarp and the tractor. "How do we know we can trust him?" she asked.

"Do not worry, Elizabeth," he assured her, his voice gentle in her ear. "He is a contact and will forward us to our new destination. Our meeting was not an accident."

Elizabeth breathed a sigh of relief, but gritted her teeth when they went over a bump. Since she had to go to the bathroom, the bumps seemed more prominent. She brought her mind back to the farmer to keep it off the condition of her bladder. She hadn't noticed him wearing an armband similar to Hans', but then again, she hadn't looked either. "I was wondering why you would risk walking on the open road with me. My camp outfit is a dead giveaway. Not to mention that you're wearing that outfit with the obvious armband and have a rifle slung over your shoulder. You look like a recruitment poster for the Resistance."

Hans laughed. "Are you familiar with the expression 'hiding in plain sight?'" he asked.

Elizabeth rolled her eyes. "Of course I have," she snorted.

"Now the two of you have been properly introduced."

With Hans' arm snug around her waist and the length of his body pressed against her backside, she felt warm and safe. *If only Derek was here*, she thought as she breathed in Hans' manly scent. He wasn't as dirty as she had first believed and she briefly wondered if he had soiled himself to look as if he were. God, she was so worried for Derek. If there was a way to reverse what had happened to him, she would have taken that chance.

The farmer took them back to his farm and into the barn. Elizabeth stretched her aching back and legs as she stood, glad to be out of the cramped tractor. She took a quick glance around in the semidarkness and noted only a few pieces of farm equipment. The farmer led them behind a wooden door that another tractor hid and down a small flight of stairs into a cellar. Inside were various foods and blankets, but not much else. It was on the small side, but there was enough room and nourishment for Elizabeth and Hans to stay comfortably. Her nose twitched from the musty scent of dust and old wood, but she refused to complain.

"So what happens now?" Elizabeth asked as she sat down on the cobblestone floor.

When Hans sat down next to her and wrapped his arms around his knees, she noticed the gold wedding band on the ring finger of his right hand. She wondered how he could leave his wife behind and go traipsing around the German countryside, even for a good cause. "We wait," he informed her.

She had told him she would help him with his fight, but part of her was still terrified. She had no doubt they would be killed if they were caught. "Are you married, Hans?" she asked, wanting to say anything to break up the nervousness she was feeling.

"Yes. I have not seen Hannah since just after the *Kristallnacht*. Sabrina and I were able to get her out of the country and sent to England. She is staying at one of Sabrina's estates, where I have no doubt she is safe."

"Hannah is a Jew then?" she asked, assuming the answer was yes.

He sent her an angry look, his eyes flashing fire. "Do you have the same beliefs as the Nazi bastards?" he snapped, his momentary anger overpowering his common sense.

She glared back at him, insulted at the accusation. After all she had been through, he had the nerve to say that! "Come on! I have nothing against Jews," she snapped back. "I was placed in that awful camp for hiding my best friend, who is of the same faith. If I had to do it over again, I would do it the same way and hide every Jew I could. I didn't go there for this charming little uniform and I wasn't there for my health. Remember that the next time you feel like passing judgment on me. So cool it with the attitude."

To her surprise, he burst out laughing. "I do apologize, Elizabeth," he said. "I should know better. You are as feisty as my Hannah. You remind me of how much I miss her."

She was grateful when the farmer brought them a change of clothes a short while later. He handed Hans apparel that consisted of slacks, a shirt and heavy socks that he wore with his own boots.

"My daughter wears these," Jeorg Ardnt said as he handed her slacks, a heavy black cable sweater and thick socks. He shook his head, his light-blue eyes bright with affection. "I cannot understand why she enjoys dressing that way, but this is a useful way to get rid of these clothes. I will find you another coat and boots so you can stay warm while you travel. I will find you both a mat to sit or lie on. That stone floor can only be comfortable for so long."

„*Vielen Dank*," she said with a smile.

„*Bitte*," Jeorg returned, smiling. "I will return later to collect that atrocious camp uniform and burn the pieces in my furnace. I am sure you are sick of wearing it." With a nod at both Elizabeth and Hans, he made his way back up the stairs.

Elizabeth shot to her feet, placing her hands on the small of her back and stretching to relive the ache. „*Wunderbar!*" she said, not bothering to withhold her enthusiasm.

Hans chuckled, wriggling his eyebrows up and down in a teasing leer. "I am sure you will enjoy your new attire," he said.

Elizabeth good-naturedly stuck her tongue out at him and then hurriedly pulled off her camp clothing. It was sheer heaven finally to be released from the ugly material and she breathed a great sigh of relief. Although Derek had offered her some real clothes, she had refused, since she didn't need another black mark against her for accepting them. This time, modesty didn't even cross her mind, since so many strangers had seen her naked body. She inwardly laughed. *It's not as if you were that reserved to begin with, Elizabeth.*

As a young teenager, she had been cursed with a too-thin body, with barely any hips and not much in the way of breasts. She had been quite self-conscious, especially since most of the other girls already had their adult bodies. Suddenly at fifteen, she had blossomed, her hips and breasts fuller. Her shyness had vanished along with the young form.

She stepped into the slacks and then pulled the sweater over her head, only half-aware of Hans" attention on her breasts. She sat down on the cellar floor and slid her feet into the thick socks. Once they had both changed into their new clothing, Jeorg returned with the coat, boots and pallets he had promised. After thanking him again for his hospitality, Elizabeth slid her feet into the boots and breathed a comfortable sigh of relief. She had thought she would never experience wearing normal clothes again. It was sheer heaven. The farmer took away the old clothes, once again leaving them alone.

Elizabeth snuggled under the provided blanket a few minutes later and turned her gaze to her new friend. He did look better with the brown turtleneck and matching slacks. "So what happens now, Hans?" she asked.

He exaggerated a yawn before answering. "Soon we will meet our new contact," he answered. "Then we will go from there."

"What about Derek's grandmother? When are we going to get her to safety?" Since Derek had asked Elizabeth to find granny for him and take her somewhere safe, she was going to make sure she accomplished the feat. She owed him that much.

Hans crinkled his eyebrows. "Do you know who Colonel Heinrich is, Elizabeth?" he asked.

She nodded. "Yes," she said. "Derek told me that the colonel had threatened him into his position. Is there more to that?"

"Yes. He had received his post to the SS long before the *Kristallnacht.*"

Elizabeth was confused. "So what does that have to do with anything?" she found herself asking.

"Since he had threatened to incarcerate Derek's grandmother and her companion, it is probable that he would have his people watch for her. If he does happen to capture her, we will not be able to rescue her."

Elizabeth's heart sank to her toes. "We'll just have to find a way to get to her then," she said, her voice filled with determination.

Hans raised an eyebrow. "It will not be easy," he warned.

"I don't care. I promised Derek."

He ran a hand through the top of his hair, nodding. "I will have to teach you how to use the Walther soon," he said. "It would not be wise for you to be armed and not know how to protect yourself. Unfortunately, we cannot wait for you to learn before we find Sabrina. We must get to Derek's residence as soon as possible. I hope we are not already too late."

A chill of fear rushed through her and tightness lumped in her heart. "That Sabrina has been captured is not an option, Hans," she said with conviction. "I could do nothing for my best friend and I could do nothing for the man I love. I cannot allow something to happen to Derek's grandmother, too."

The corners of his lips turned in as he seemed to force back a laugh at her determination. "I am glad you are on my side," he seemed to tease. "I would be dead meat otherwise."

Elizabeth couldn't help but laugh at his use of American slang, her heart lifting a little. "You're terrible," she returned. "I like that in a person."

Hans exaggerated a proud grin, but then his expression became serious. "We must get our rest, Elizabeth," he said. "You will need it. Besides, we have a long evening ahead of us."

"Evening?" she questioned flatly. "Why? Are we going somewhere?"

"Yes, evening. And yes, we are going somewhere."

Groaning, Elizabeth moved to her side and tugged the blanket up past her shoulders. In spite of the material's warmth, she shivered from the chill in the damp cellar. A long, loud yawn snuck up on her and she snuggled into the fetal position for comfort. She swore she could sleep for a month straight if she had the chance.

"See," Hans teased. "I told you that you needed some rest."

Elizabeth exaggerated a sigh and tugged the blanket up to her ears. "Shut up, Hans," she said at his answering chuckle. As soon as she closed her eyes, her thoughts went blank. She didn't remember what happened after that.

Chapter Twenty-Four

ELIZABETH SNUGGLED DEEPER INTO HER COAT to ward off the late-afternoon chill, her heart pounding as if she had been running a marathon. She took a deep breath in an attempt to calm herself, but she was becoming increasingly more nervous as time went by. What could be taking Hans so long?

A shiver of alarm rushed over her skin as an unidentifiable noise sounded in the air. She took a glance around the ruins of the abandoned clothing store and fought back a sneeze from the dust. She dismissed the remnants of tables and various types of ragged clothing as the air's eerie stillness raised bumps on her skin and another shiver raked over her body. If it had been any later, she wouldn't have waited. As it was, there were too many shadows for comfort and she wouldn't have been surprised if she saw an apparition or two.

Squeaks sounded in the distance just before two rats scurried out from behind the counter. At the unexpected company, a loud, whimpering cry of panic leaped from within her and her heartbeat shot up. She rushed out the doorway and onto the sidewalk before some of the rodents' friends decided to join them. She moved her feet along the surprisingly intact pavement, anxious to find Hans. She would take her chances with the human kind of rats.

Elizabeth stopped at the edge of the maroon brick building and poked her head around the corner. She took a quick, sweeping look of the area, noting the empty streets and abandoned stores. The area looked like a modern ghost town. Sucking in her breath at the chance she was taking, she made her way across the road from the store where she had been. She sped up her pace, hoping to catch up to Hans. Before she realized what was happening, someone grabbed her from behind and slung his arm around her throat. The scream she was about to let out was cut off as the arm tightened.

"I thought I told you to stay where you were," the person furiously whispered.

Her wildly racing heart calmed when she recognized Hans' deep voice. As he pulled away his arm, she turned to face him and took a deep, relaxing breath. "I'm sorry, Hans," she apologized, her voice shaky. "I just couldn't stay in there any longer. I swear I would have seen ghosts if I did."

His eyes softened and he took a quick glance around the small downtown. He then tugged on her arm. "Come on," he urged. "Hiding in plain sight won't work here. Try not to make a lot of noise when we walk up the hill."

Elizabeth noticed the seemingly medieval, timber-framed buildings standing along with the modern ones, all of which appeared empty. However, just because the rest of the area looked run-down and vacant didn't mean no one else was there. As they made their way up the hill, her thighs ached from the exertion of the climb. Supposedly avoiding leaning forward helped, but it didn't seem to work. The darkening forest loomed ahead and she sighed in relief when only moments later they made their way into the trees. "What's going on?" she whispered when Hans stopped in his tracks.

"Derek's house is to the east," he told her. "It's the pale-brown Tudor with the dark roof. Two soldiers are standing guard and they watch every direction."

She took the binoculars Hans handed her and held them up to peek through the lenses. She aimed them at what she believed was an eastward direction and breathed a sigh of relief when the house Hans had described came into view. It was built in the Tudor style, as Hans had said, and set on a hectare lot. The color was more of a tawny brown with a chocolate-colored roof and she briefly thought that it should be in England instead of Germany. *Of course, silly. It is a Tudor.*

She eyed it, along with the purple flowers that made a path up the walkway to the front porch. She briefly wondered how they survived the cold, but who knew the answer. *So, this is where Derek lives.* As soon as the thought entered her mind, she frowned. *Where he used to live,* she reminded herself. A lump of emotion formed in her throat and she gulped to force it back down, allowing the numbness to return. It was easier to deal with her separation from him that way. She missed him like crazy, but had to focus on the evening ahead. It wouldn't help for her to crawl into a ball and hide within her own misery of worry for him, since it wouldn't change anything.

"Do you see it?" Hans asked. "And the guard?"

Elizabeth nodded as the young guard with pale brown hair strolling the grounds caught her visual attention. "I see him," she confirmed, noting his tall and slightly husky bone structure. But because of the distance, she couldn't tell what his eye color was or in what direction he was looking. His olive coat fell to mid-calf of his boots and his rifle was slung onto his back by a shoulder strap. Outwardly, it was similar to the ensemble Rolf wore when he patrolled the camp, but with the helmet their friend rarely wore.

"There is another guard who will be making his way around in a moment."

As if the young man had heard Hans' words, he came around the side of the house and shook his head in a bored fashion at the other guard. His hair was on the lighter side of brown and his build was somewhat larger. He shared a look of boredom with his friend and then went back around to the other side of the house. *Oh, what the neighbors must think,* Elizabeth thought with an inward chuckle. She flushed and handed the binoculars back to Hans. *Good God, Elizabeth. What's wrong with you? You really are losing it.*

Hans raised an eyebrow, a sparkle lighting depths of his eyes. "Why the grin?" he asked.

She shrugged, embarrassed at her thought. "I was just wondering what Derek's neighbors must think with the guards around his house," she explained. "It just kinda popped in my mind."

Hans surprised her with a chuckle and he slid his arm around her shoulders. "It's okay, Elizabeth," he said with a brotherly squeeze. "A sense of humor will keep you strong. Don't worry about it."

"Thank you," she sighed with relief, although she still felt idiotic. A moment later, she bit her bottom lip before asking what she didn't really want to know. "So now what do we do?"

Her body cooled when he let his arm drop from around her. Because of the situation, it hadn't registered how cold it was and a shiver rushed over her. "Care to have some fun?" he asked brightly.

Elizabeth was stunned. What could he possibly call fun? "Fun?" she asked flatly.

Hans held back a smirk. "Yes," he said. "Can you flirt with the guard so I can overpower him?"

She withheld a shudder at having to do so, but she had promised Derek that she would help rescue his grandmother. Even if she had not, the answer wouldn't have changed. "I don't have a choice," she said truthfully.

A light of respect entered Hans' eyes as he nodded. "Are you ready then, Elizabeth?" he asked.

"Yes," she gulped.

"Make your way toward the house, but don't let him see you until you are nearby."

Yeah, right, she thought, but she kept Hans' comment in mind. At least it had started drizzling. She wouldn't get too wet, but the rain would provide a little cover, so the soldier guard wouldn't notice her right away. She and Hans started making their way out of the trees when another thought popped into her mind. She grasped his forearm. "Are you going to kill him, Hans?" she had to ask. She couldn't go any farther until she knew the answer. Her heart pounded so loudly that she could barely hear her own thoughts regarding what was about to happen.

"If I knock him out, he will come to while we are still inside and then he will be able to identify us to his superiors. As you said before, we do not have a choice."

Tears rushed into her eyes and her heart tightened with dread as the heaviness of guilt already began to shroud her, but Hans was right. They had no choice. It was survival. "We'd better go before I change my mind," she admitted, her voice choky with fear.

Hans squeezed her hand and looked directly into her eyes, his flat. Ever so briefly, Elizabeth noted that it had gotten darker very quickly, but she forced herself to concentrate on her friend's words. "I will be as quick as I can," he promised. "He will never know what hit him. For what it is worth, I wish I did not have to make the choice, Elizabeth."

She sighed as her heart tightened. "I know," she said, her voice tight.

"Grab his attention and I will be right behind you."

Without a word, Elizabeth made her way out of the nest of trees. She was sure her guardian angel had been with her since she had made it down the hill without the blonde's notice. She was as far as the walkway when she caught his glance. From his view, it would have seemed as if she were merely on a stroll.

A sparkle lit his blue eyes and he ran his gaze down the length of her body. "*Guten Abend,*" he greeted her in a flirty tone.

Elizabeth allowed a phony smile to curve her lips and continued to walk toward him, although her conscience was sickened about what she had to do. Here was this man who was someone's son, someone's grandson or brother or possibly someone's husband. *Anyway, Hans is right,* she reminded herself. If they didn't do this, all would be for nothing. She snuggled into her gray woolen coat and took a deep, yet silent breath. „*Guten Abend,*" she returned. "It's a lovely evening, yes?"

The guard chuckled and cocked his head to the side. "It is," he agreed. "But you should be inside. It is not a good idea for such a beautiful lady to be out alone."

Elizabeth crinkled her eyebrows, pretending to consider his comment. "Yes, I …"

Before she could finish the sentence, Hans came up from behind the guard and slung his hand over the man's mouth. When he gave a sharp twist of his other hand at the back of the young man's neck, a muffled grunt rumbled in the blonde's throat. He was on the ground a moment later and Hans was slipping the rifle onto his own shoulder. "Come on," he urged as he stepped away from the young man. "Let's get going. We have to find the other guard before he finds this one."

She followed Hans, as if in a daze, unsure of what had just happened. She forced herself not to take a last glance at the guard, although her body burned with the opposite impulse. *Remember what happened to Lot's wife?*

They made their way to the other side of the house where the other guard stood with his left side pressed against the building. Hans stepped silently behind him and slung his arm around the young man's neck. Instead of covering his mouth, he said in English, "Gotcha."

"Shit," the man swore, his accent clearly American. He had said it so quickly that Elizabeth wondered how he hid the accent.

Hans chuckled and pulled away his arm. "I could always get you easily," he teased.

The young man turned around and exaggerated a sigh of relief. He was a bit on the cute side and had that soft look a lot of German men had, so it became clear how he blended in. "Geez, Hans," he complained. "It's about damn time you showed up." He smiled when his brown gaze landed on Elizabeth. "Hi, there."

Still numb from the killing of the other guard, Elizabeth stepped forward. "Hi," she replied, her tone soft.

Hans grinned. "Jason, this is Elizabeth," he said in introduction. "Elizabeth, this is Jason."

Confused, Elizabeth crinkled her eyebrows. "How do you guys know each other?" she asked.

The men took a glance at each other, both grinning. "I know I shouldn't tell you this, but Jason is a POW from a nearby camp," Hans explained. "He was shot while escaping and luckily one of our members found him."

"If you'll pardon the cliché, that's all she wrote," Jason added with a wink. "Now I've joined your team."

Elizabeth grinned. "It's nice to meet you," she said.

Jason bowed. "You, too, ma'am," he said. "I just wish the circumstances were better."

"Me, too."

"I hate to rush, Elizabeth," Hans interrupted. "But you need to go inside." He looked at Jason. "We need to move the guard out of sight until we can find you a new set of clothes. I will need his uniform and any weapons you find on him."

"Is he dead then?" Jason said, asking the unnecessary.

"Yes," Hans said with a nod, his eyes again flat. Elizabeth assumed his supposed indifference was to keep his emotions together. If she had been in his position, she would have been terrified of how she would have reacted once the numbness had worn off.

"Damn," Jason swore with an exaggerated sigh. "He was just getting to be a pain in the ass, too."

Elizabeth failed to stop the chuckle that bubbled in her throat, although she made no other response.

"We'll discuss in once we're all inside," Hans said.

Jason nodded. "It isn't much," he said. "But I'll tell you what I know."

As she made her way through the unlatched front door and into the entryway, Elizabeth couldn't help but notice how pretty it was, with hardwood flooring and a Victorian hall tree with a pier mirror entwined with gold flecks. She noted the salt-and-pepper marble staircase that led down to the basement and to the top floor. The combination of modern and historical gave the residence a nice touch. She had never realized how much Derek clearly appreciated history, but it was evident in his taste. She wondered whether some of the furniture was family heirlooms. Considering his ancestry, she had no doubt this was the case. They must have been in his family for at least the last handful of generations.

When she stepped through the foyer and into the main room, Elizabeth was surprised to see how tidy the house was. For some reason, she had expected it to be ransacked. The main living area was carpeted in plush dove-gray and the furniture was what she would have considered to be masculine in design, but it had that softening, feminine touch, since much of it was from the Victorian era, as in the entryway. A lump rose in her heart as she ran her hand over the modern, burgundy brocade sofa with multicolored, brocade pillows. She held back a nearly audible sob as the day's events started to overwhelm her, but then the tears began to flow.

She hadn't cried since this morning when she had left Derek back at the camp. Part of her wished she had been captured along with him, but she had a job to do. It had nearly destroyed her emotionally to leave him, but she had had no choice. Only after they had located Sabrina and Miriam could they go back and rescue him. She had to stuff her fears and worries or she would never make it through. She flinched when someone rested his hand on her shoulder.

Jason's gray eyes were filled with concern. "Are you okay?" he asked.

Elizabeth eyed him, but the words seemed to be lodged in her throat. She wiped at the tears with the back of her hand as she shook her head. She released a shaky sigh, her heart tight with emotion. She breathed a sigh of relief when Hans came into the room.

He looked at his friend. "Derek is her fiancé," he said.

Elizabeth wouldn't contradict his words, since she would marry Derek if they survived the war. She was sure about that.

Sympathy flashed in Jason's eyes. "I'm sorry," he apologized. "I didn't realize that."

"I will find something for you to change the guard into," Hans interrupted.

Glad at his subject change, Elizabeth sent a look of thanks his direction. He returned it with a slight smile and wink. As he made his way into a room northeast of the living room, she turned to Jason. "Do you know where Sabrina is, Jason?" she asked in an attempt to keep her emotions from overcoming her.

An unknown light flashed in his eyes. "I'd rather wait for Hans to come back before I say anything," he said, his tone gentle. "Then I will tell you what I know."

She nodded in understanding, although her body burned with the desire to scream at him. *Stop stalling and give me a straight answer, dammit!* She made her way over to a wood and glass china cabinet with a fold-out ledge for pictures. A small photograph of a little boy caught her attention, instantly warming her heart. It was encased in a pewter frame, but that did not distract from the picture. As soon as she noticed that the boy was Derek, she picked up the frame.

He sat in a batch of wildflowers with his lips curved into a smile and he held a wooden toy train. The bottom of his pale-blonde hair was cut close to his scalp, but the top was a little bit longer. Her heart melted as she eyed his little boyish overalls and short-sleeved shirt. The white socks with little boots in combination with his ensemble made him look as if he were a small angel. Just by looking at the photo, she could tell that he had been a warm, happy and loving child. The man he was today proved this. A lump of emotion rose in her throat as new tears rushed into her eyes. She lifted her hand to wipe them away, but jerked when someone touched her shoulder.

"Derek was about five then," Hans told her.

Elizabeth sniffed. "He was adorable," she said with a smile, her tone filled with emotion. Her heart tightened and her body seemed to burn, not from desire, but because she wanted nothing more than to be with him now. *I miss you so much, Derek.*

"We need to be going, Elizabeth. We do not have much time."

She nodded, but held onto the photo as if it were her lifeline to sanity. She just didn't have the heart to set it back down. Sabrina and Miriam must have been in a hurry for Sabrina to have left it behind.

Hans handed the black slacks and sweater to Jason. "You can explain everything after you change him," he said.

Jason nodded. "I'll do that," he agreed. A moment later, he left the room.

Elizabeth couldn't help but smile as she took a second glance at the photo in her hand. *He was as adorable then as he is now.* She took a glance at Hans as he stepped toward her. "Is it okay if I keep it?" she found herself asking.

"It directly relates you to him," he said, his words sinking her heart. "I would advise against it, Elizabeth."

Although Hans was correct, tears welled in her eyes. "I miss him so much already," she said. Another picture of Derek pleading with her to save his grandmother popped into her mind and she took a deep breath to stifle the tears. "I just keep seeing him in my mind. I tried to wipe the image away to keep from losing it, but it didn't work."

Hans slid his arm around her shoulder and pulled her against his body, urging her head onto the curve of his neck. "I know," he said in a soothing tone.

"I just keep seeing him on the ground when he's holding his gun out to me and pleading for me to go on without him. I hate this shit, Hans! *I hate it!*" Her tone had begun soft, but had turned harder and louder at each word, ending as she nearly shouted into his shoulder.

"Go ahead and cry," he said, his tone again soothing. "It does help, I promise."

For some odd reason, a chuckle bubbled in her throat. She pulled away and raised an eyebrow. She still wanted to cry, but Hans had helped. "And how would you know?" she teased.

Hans sheepishly rolled his eyes and shrugged. "Believe it or not, you're talking to the biggest crybaby in the world."

"Uh-huh," she teased. "The next thing I know, you'll be telling me that you blush." She couldn't picture him blushing for any reason.

Hans chuckled. "Never," he agreed.

"Here's the uniform, Hans," Jason said, the interruption startling Elizabeth.

Hans took the folded uniform and long coat from his friend's hands and stuffed both into his satchel. "Okay, Jason," he said with a sigh. "No more stalling. Tell us what's going on and where Sabrina and Miriam are."

"Sabrina and Miriam are with Miriam's family and they're safe." Elizabeth breathed a sigh of relief. Unfortunately, that relief turned to more disappointment. "One of our members discovered that Heinrich had found out about what had happened and they were able to relocate Sabrina before the colonel was able to send someone to arrest her. We don't know the whereabouts of Miriam's family." An apology shined in his eyes. "I'm sorry I can't give you any more information."

Hans swore. "Thanks anyway, Jason," he said. "When you find out something, have someone get in contact with me."

"I'll do that."

"Thank you," Elizabeth added, although he hadn't told them much. *We had to wait for that?* "I have to say, I'm impressed that you received this information so quickly."

"You'd be surprised at how many of our people are around here, although they can't always find the answer to everything."

Hans gave a brief nod. "Have someone keep in touch, Jason," he urged.

Chapter Twenty-Five

EREK'S MEMORIES OF BEING BROUGHT BACK into the compound after his capture continued to replay in his mind. Most of the guards had had no compunction in revealing their pleasure in the situation, as they stood with their rifles pointed at the captives they had brought into the main yard. There had been no mistaking the gleams of satisfaction in the depths of their eyes as they stared back at him. He was fully aware that he had been on their "shit list", as Elizabeth had described it, since day one and that they would make his life a living hell.

The tie wraps dug into his wrists while his hands were behind his back and the back of his thigh burned from his wound, but he was too emotionally numb to care. The despair and terror shined in the captives' eyes, but there was nothing he could do to stop it. He prayed that Elizabeth would meet up with Hans and save his grandmother. He missed her so much already.

Übel had not bothered hiding his pleasure as he pushed Derek along with the muzzle of his rifle. "I have been waiting months for this day, milord *Kommandant*," he had sneered. "I will personally see to it that you and living hell become acquainted in many different ways. Your titles will not save you this time."

Derek had refused to acknowledge the threatening comments even with a look. He had stared straight ahead without expression, catching a glimpse of Rolf standing directly behind a teary-eyed Katrine. His friend had had a rigid, angry air about him as he eyed the other guards. His rifle had been aimed more at the ground than at a particular person, but no one had seemed to notice, with everything that had been happening. The men had exchanged a long look, but had hidden their feelings.

"This will be the last time you see this *Kommandant* in uniform!" Übel had announced. "Take a good look. He is about to become one of you!"

Someone roughly shoved Derek back in the chair and the wooden rungs dug into his back and arms, forcing his mind back to the present. He gritted his teeth when the tightness of the rope burned into his already raw wrists and his biceps ached from the exertion.

"These rope burns are the least of what you deserve for betraying the brotherhood, Herr von Vetter," Heinrich said, his voice cold.

"Fuck you," Derek said in English with a facetious snort.

Heinrich hauled off and slapped him with the back of his hand. Derek's bottom lip split as Heinrich's ring slammed against his mouth. The warmth of his blood gathered on his already-numbing lip and his mind swam, but he assumed the latter was more from his thigh wound than the physical abuse.

"Just as you did to your *Amerikanerin* whore," Heinrich sneered, trying to incite a reaction Derek refused to give. "When we capture her, maybe we can share her with Übel, yes? Elizabeth is a passionate woman, is she not? I imagine she would enjoy my rod inside her as she had yours." His former superior officer grinned "You remember Lina Weimar, do you not? You were her first lover and I take it she was yours."

A jolt rushed through Derek's system at his former lover's name, although this commentary wasn't unexpected. He realized he had reacted to Heinrich's confession because another rare smile curved his lips. "Now about Miriam, the *Jüdin* who is the Lady Sabrina's companion," Heinrich continued taunting, his voice filled with pleasure. "I believe you refer to her as Maria. Do you fuck her as well?" When Derek refused to give him a response, the colonel sighed as if bored with the conversation. "When this hour is finished, you will speak again." He turned his attention to the door. "Übel. Come in here now!"

As Übel strolled into the room, Derek did not miss the bright light of satisfaction in the guard's eyes. „*Ja, mein Herr*," the guard smirked.

"Take this filthy prisoner out of here and clean him up. Give him something to keep the infection from his leg. I do not wish his time to end too quickly. When you are finished, bring him back to me."

"Yes, sir."

Once they were in the main processing room, Übel turned to Derek and cut the ties from his wrists with his knife. "Remove every stitch of that uniform from your body, von Vetter," he ordered. "You are no longer entitled to wear it. Then sit down in that chair and do not even *think* of moving."

As if he were in a dream, Derek removed the uniform jacket and shirt and tossed both onto one of the chairs. It was the processing room where he had first witnessed the humiliation that the captives suffered, but this time he would find out how it felt to be the victim and he at least deserved, firsthand, to understand it. For now, his emotions were so numb that it was as if this weren't really happening, but logic told him that it was. When he started to remove his *Erkennungsmarke*, known by Americans as "dog tags", Übel stopped him.

"Keep them. I will enjoy the irony."

As the sergeant watched with a telltale gleam in his eyes, Derek slowly took off the rest of his uniform and sat down in the chair as "requested". His mind briefly swam, but he forced himself to remain conscious. The loud buzzing of the shaver sounded in his ears as if taunting him. The strokes were swift and sure, but he was barely conscious of them. Derek was reminded of when he had first had his hair shorn, but then the purpose wasn't to dehumanize and humiliate him. Even at such a young age, it was not nearly as traumatic. He refused to allow himself to be made to feel any less than a man.

"Spread your legs, von Vetter," Übel chuckled.

When Derek sat still, passively refusing to comply with the order, Übel shoved his foot against the inside of his knees and forced apart his legs. He then lowered the shaver to between his legs and Derek felt the vibrations rush through him. When his phallus leaped to attention as if of its own free will, his face burned with embarrassment.

"This is your lucky day, von Vetter," Übel sneered after he had finished. He tossed the shaver onto the tabletop and it made a clatter as it hit the hard wood. "No new prisoners today but you. Otherwise the men would be jealous of the thickness of that stiff *Schwanz*."

Revulsion burned in Derek's gut as Übel grasped him between his legs and cupped the base. "You had better let go of that before you are slapped with a pink chevron," he sneered in return. Expecting the other man to become angry at his comment, he was surprised when Übel chuckled and released him.

"You are well known for your sense of humor, von Vetter. Let us see if you still have it in a few days."

Derek pretended a boredom he didn't feel, although his first thought was to see how far he could piss off Übel. "As charming as this little subject is, I am bored with it," he said with a sigh. "When did you become such a lousy shot, Übel? I had believed you were an expert marksman. Maybe I was mistaken in my assumption."

Übel burst out into maniacal laughter. When it died down, he curled his upper lip into a sneer and shoved the muzzle of his pistol hard against Derek's jaw. "If I had wanted you dead, you would be so," he snarled.

Derek's heart and breath tightened, but he refused to give the slug a reaction. "So go ahead and kill me," he taunted. "I'm sure you can't wait to do so anyway."

Übel pulled the gun away and placed it back into his holster. "*Nein*, von Vetter. That would be much too easy for me." He shrugged. "Besides, Herr Karl has other plans for you. I will be around to enjoy every moment of your suffering."

Less than an hour later, Derek had been given his barracks assignment and taken to the doctor. Weidenbach said that the wounds were merely grazes and he expected them to heal in time. He wrapped Derek's thigh and gave him some mild painkillers along with something to fight infection, since Derek had flat-out refused morphine. He wanted to be alert, not in a drug-induced state. His body still ached, but he ignored the pain as he focused on the scene before him. He noted the glazed blankness in the doctor's eyes, so it was obvious Weidenbach had been abusing the drugs in his office. His condition, however, didn't keep him from doing his job.

Only a short while later, the colonel and a handful of guards had their rifles casually pointed at the prisoners as they dragged the pallets and thick blankets out of the barracks. Numbness reached to the core of Derek's soul as he was forced to stand back and watch everything he had worked for in the captives' favor being destroyed. The air was so deafeningly quiet that he was sure everyone could hear his heart pound.

One of the men had the misfortune of stumbling over the corner of a blanket and was rewarded with a powerful jab at the back of his head from the butt of a rifle. He whoomphed to the ground and was given another hit in the same spot, causing him to whimper in pain.

With rage burning all the way to the core of his being, Derek stepped forward and swore. "You son of a bitch ..." he spat at the guard. A heartbeat later, the muzzles of the guards' rifles were pointed at a handful of other captives.

Derek's ears rang as he became light-headed and expected to pass out from his sudden panic. The guards would have no compunction about killing them on the spot if Heinrich ordered it and he knew it. He also had to mask any fear he had because the guards were already aware that the others' safety was his weak spot. He did not wish to give them anything else.

Heinrich stepped toward him and pressed the muzzle of his Luger against his forehead. "Shut your fucking mouth, von Vetter," he snarled in English, his pale eyes gleaming with anger. "If you open it again, what happened to this Jew will be nothing compared to what will happen to the others here."

Before Derek could think, Karl hauled off and slammed his pistol back down, whipping him across his temple with the butt. It was all he could do to remain on his feet as his mind reeled and he found himself crying out. He fought to hold on to his consciousness as the warmth of his blood began to stream down his cheek. *Maybe I should have taken the morphine after all.* A hysterical laugh threatened to bubble in his throat, but he was able to stifle it.

The cleaning of the barracks lasted into the late hours of the evening and it was after midnight when the captives fell into a nearly unconscious slumber in the cramped, overcrowded beds. Having been *Kommandant* of this camp, Derek expected to be a target for the other prisoners, even though he had improved their living conditions and made this place less of a hellhole. Although he had treated them with as much respect as he could, he had still been their captor. That alone was unforgivable. Those guilty of Crimes Against Humanity would be sent to trial and no doubt executed. Even with the changes he had made, he had his own guilt in these crimes. Justice would expect that he, too, be sent to trial for these crimes, regardless of his improvements here and his participation in the Resistance.

In spite of being physically and emotionally drained, Derek found he couldn't sleep. Breathing a deep sigh, he made his way through the horde of men and found an empty spot on the bare floor. His head still throbbed from Heinrich's pistol whipping and lying on hard wood wouldn't help. He sat down and took a glance around the semi dark room. The large, wooden sleeping area was made to hold forty people, but there seemed to be two times that. After being forced to the camp, he had read smuggled-in accounts of these barracks in the larger camps that held more than ten times that number. The beds were not very long and a tall person was cramped even more than the shorter people were. Even if the area had been larger, there wouldn't have been enough space.

Some camps held either men or women, but Murrbrück held both. Some of these men had spouses in other barracks and Derek had allowed them a separate one so they could have at least some semblance of a marriage. Now that Heinrich had taken over, they were separated again and everyone was crammed together. The buildings were relatively clean and the people healthy, but he did not know how long that would last. He couldn't help but notice that the captives' food portions were less than what he had given them. He had no doubt that they would be reduced even more. It wouldn't be a drastic reduction, but a slow and nearly unnoticeable one.

Once when Derek had first arrived at the camp, a young man had had a cold that he had tried to hide, but it had turned into Strep throat before anyone had realized how sick he was. Derek had ordered Weidenbach to administer the newfound penicillin to keep the infection from turning into pneumonia. Aaron had recovered, but the next time something like that happened, the person wouldn't be so lucky.

He tried to ignore the deep shivers that rushed through his bones, but he drew his knees up to his chest in an attempt to warm himself. He placed his arms across them and rested his chin on the backs of his hands. He rocked forward and his bare toes and the balls of his feet came off the floor as he rocked back. His body ached to hold Elizabeth and he would have given anything to feel her in his arms again. He missed everything about her. He missed the thickness of her silky, red hair and the light that entered her beautiful green eyes when she smiled. He missed her cries of pleasure as he made love to her and the softness of her skin when he touched her.

Derek prayed that she had been able to meet up with Hans. He had no doubt that his friend would protect her and help her rescue Miriam and his grandmother, but it didn't stop him from worrying about all of them. A fluttering tickle rushed down his cheek, but he ignored the irritation. His cheeks itched for him to wipe the invading tears from his face, but he fought the temptation. Some of the wetness ran into the corner of his mouth and he could taste the saltiness on his tongue. His bottom lip threatened to quiver and he bit it to keep a sob in his throat. What had happened in the last few days seemed to be unbearable, but things would only get worse. Hell would be a mild term to describe what he suspected lay ahead. A movement out of the corner of his eye caught his attention and when he turned toward the interruption, a slender, thirtyish man he knew to be an American rabbi walked up to him.

Samuel Benjamin sat down to his left and linked his arms around his upraised knees. Sympathy filled his dark-brown eyes as he gazed at him. "If you would like to talk with someone, I am here for you," he offered.

Dumbfounded, Derek returned the man's gaze. It wasn't Benjamin's casual use of his first name that surprised him, but the understanding and the concern he seemed to exude. "Are you sure you wish to associate with me, sir?" he asked. "After all, I am one of *them*, in spite of my current status."

Samuel crinkled his dark eyebrows, seemingly confused. "Why would you believe that, Derek?" he asked gently.

Guilt and disbelief swept through Derek and he took a deep breath. "I was *Kommandant* of this camp, even for a short while," he said. "That makes me just as guilty as they are."

"How so?"

Derek shook his head, not understanding why the man would take this type of approach. All the questions were nonjudgmental and they seemed to tug an answer from him. In any event, he had the urge to bare his soul to Samuel and didn't bother fighting it. "The position speaks for itself," he explained.

"Have you forgotten what you have done for the people here?" Sam asked. "If it weren't for you, many would be dead or dying." He paused for a moment as if deciding whether to say something else. "Elizabeth told us you were threatened into your position. Is this not correct?"

New tears burned Derek's eyes and the rabbi's image was briefly distorted. He blinked quickly to force away the tears. "That is correct, Rabbi," he said. "But that changes nothing."

Benjamin nodded in understanding. "My first name is Samuel." He shrugged. "I go by Sam. You may call me that. Anyway, you did the best you could under the circumstances, Derek. God will reward you for that."

"Why would He do that for me when He has turned his back on those who are suffering here?"

"Do not blame God for what has happened," Sam said gently. "It is the evil some men have *chosen* that has brought us here. They are the ones who have turned their backs on God."

The rabbi's words were true, but that didn't make Derek any less guilty. "You are correct, but that still doesn't release me from my responsibility."

"You have done everything humanly possible to make everyone's incarceration here bearable. There is a reason God has put you here. Have faith, Derek, and remember that."

"But what can I *do*?" Derek asked, his emotional pain full in his voice. "I feel so damned helpless." There was a movement beside him and he turned toward the intrusion.

"I could not help but overhear your conversation," Aaron Dahlberg commented as he sat down, his tawny eyes inquisitive. He was tall and slender, but for some reason beside the physical he reminded Derek of Rolf. "If you were anyone else, I wouldn't be saying this, but Sam is correct. Most of us were ready to condemn you when you first arrived, but the changes you made and the kindness you brought us made this hellhole bearable. We were as low as any human being can be, but you gave our humanity back to us. We will never, ever forget that."

More hot tears burned behind Derek's eyes and his heart tightened as if a vice gripped it. "I appreciate that more than I can ever say," he said, and the men acknowledged him. A thought came to mind and he decided to present it. "Has anyone been documenting what has been happening here?" He knew full well that they were, but he didn't know the extent of it.

Sam and Aaron exchanged grins. "Funny you should ask," Aaron said cheerfully as he rose to his feet.

"Watch," Sam advised.

Aaron made his way to the bunk and bent down to one of the floorboards. To Derek's surprise, he pressed down on the edge and the other side opened a loose piece of wood. He pulled out some items and made his way back over to Derek and Sam. He held out a hand.

In his palm rested a boxy item that looked remarkably like a small camera. "Is that what I believe it to be?" Derek asked.

"Rolf gave us supplies in order to make this," Aaron explained with a grin. He showed Derek everything and told him that he had also been documenting Derek's treatment of them as well as the previous *Kommandant's*.

"As you can see, we document everything we can," Sam remarked. "Someday the world will see the real truth about what has happened here. If we don't, nothing here will be remembered. We cannot allow that to happen."

Aaron nodded in agreement and flashed another grin. "You would be surprised at what photos we have taken and developed." At these words, he selected a photograph from near the bottom and handed it to him. "This one nobody would have believed if we had not taken the shot."

Derek took the photo, along with the written documentation, from his friend's hands and with the full moon there was enough light to see. It showed him in an embrace with Elizabeth, his arms wrapped around her and his chin resting on top of her head. It took him a mere heartbeat to realize that this was the day after she had had Rolf shave off her hair. Her arms were around his waist and her head rested against his shoulder. With him in his full uniform and her in that atrocious, striped prison clothing, it was a loving embrace that no person on earth would believe had happened had it not been photographed. A knot of emotion caught in his throat. It was absolutely stunning. Is *this* what the people had seen? "My God," he said in a hard whisper. He turned his attention back to Aaron.

The young man's expression was serious. "If any of the guards, with the exception of Rolf, find out about what we have been doing, we are dead," he warned.

Derek's heart tightened with a small sense of dread, but it was a risk he was willing to take. "Then so be it," he vowed.

The men briefly clasped hands in a gesture of support. "We will continue with our own documentation," Sam said. "And do everything we can to help you with yours."

"Ditto," Aaron agreed. At Derek and Sam's raised eyebrows, he shrugged with a grin. "I have heard that Americans sometimes use that expression."

Derek couldn't help but chuckle, as did Sam. Elizabeth had said that a handful of times.

He and Sam exchanged a glance of amusement and then Sam rose to his feet. "We need to get some sleep," he said.

Aaron exaggerated a yawn, but nodded in agreement.

"I cannot sleep, in any event," Derek said. "So I will start now." As the others went back to the cramped bunk, he began to write.

Chapter Twenty-Six

ERICH KURTZ CHUCKLED AT THE HATE flashing from Katrine Lipinski's dark eyes as he eased her shirt off her shoulders. Her breasts beckoned him, surprisingly full and large for such a small-boned girl. That, along with the fact that she was Rolf's girlfriend, made this all the more exciting. He had to remind himself to thank his friend and cohort Übel for bringing her to him.

Übel had previously informed him as to why she had been sent to the camp. She and her older sister had organized a protest against his people and were arrested soon after it had begun. The sister had been sent to Auschwitz and was no doubt dead at this point. You would be more likely dead than alive if you were ever sent to the death camp. The majority were gassed soon after arrival, if they were lucky enough to live that long.

Erich mentally thanked Heinrich for taking over the camp when he had incarcerated von Vetter. He had been given more power and control than he had had anywhere he had served. Now his friend had allowed him use of the *Kommandant's* personal quarters in order to show Katrine the pleasures of the flesh. The Nazi ideology considered her to be subhuman simply for being Polish, but she was too tempting to ignore. Erich found it ironic that he was allowed to bed her in the same rooms where von Vetter had bedded his American lover.

He took a glance back down at the sensual young woman, allowing a smile to curve his lips. He had enjoyed watching as she had been brought into the compound. Her large breasts and the gentle curve of her hips had enticed him to the point of physical obsession. He had wanted to take her on the spot in front of the others, but unfortunately von Vetter had interrupted. As long as she continued to please him in bed, she would have all the food and comforts she wanted. If not, she would meet her fate with the others.

"I hate you," she spat at him.

He tugged her slacks down her legs and off her, leaving her bare. "That is too bad, Katrine," he chuckled as he eyed her down the length of her body. "Because you will be my lover. If you choose not to enjoy my lovemaking, that will be your decision."

She dared to snort at his explanation, but it was not important. His desire to take her far overwhelmed the desire to strike her. He wanted a more of a fiery response than a docile one. "You call it lovemaking," she sneered, "while it is nothing but rape."

Erich grasped hold of her wrists and raised them over her head to press them against the sofa's armrest. He eyed her lush breasts with the light, chocolate-brown nipples and his swollen length urged him to ram into her on the spot, but he had promised Übel he would share his prize with him. "You will enjoy it once you are used to the feel of my hard cock thrusting inside you," he couldn't help but remark. He released her wrists and trailed his hands down the soft skin of her arms, over her stomach and to the insides of her thighs. He parted them to cup her shaved mound and gently pry her lips apart with his fingers.

"Never," she spat.

He slid a finger between her lips to caress the bud between them. "Never?" he asked. He chuckled when she gritted her teeth and stiffened to keep her anger in check. When he was finished with her, she wouldn't be protesting any longer, no matter how silently she did so now. For now, he would wait for Übel to arrive. How he would enjoy sharing his prize with his friend. "We will be having a guest in a moment. While he is here, you will continue to do as I tell you."

"And if I refuse?" she had the nerve to ask.

Erich grinned. "Are you willing to risk the consequences, my dear?" he asked. "If so, I can find any number of *Frauen* who would enjoy a pretty young thing like you. Besides, I should think you would not want Rolf to become a prisoner along with you. If you reject me, that is exactly what will happen."

Katrine's lovely brown eyes grew wet with tears of horror, yet she managed to spout hate from them at the same time. Erich chuckled as a knock sounded from the door. After a brief pause, Übel entered the quarters. Erich noticed that he was dressed as casually as he was, with blue jeans and a gray shirt that matched the steel gray of his eyes. He eyed the young woman on the sofa and raised a blonde eyebrow in amusement. "Hello, lovely *frau*," he said with a smile in his voice. Contrary to non-German opinion, the word '*frau*' merely meant an adult female, married or unmarried. He didn't feel it was *that* difficult to understand.

Katrine's cheeks reddened with a flush. She pulled down her arms and turned on her side away from him to face the back of the sofa.

Erich enjoyed her modesty, but once they showed her how to take pleasure from their lovemaking, she would no longer hide herself from them. He exchanged a grin with his friend and then turned back to her. "Do not turn away and close your thighs to me, Katrine," he said. "You will protest no longer." He grasped her shoulder and rolled her onto her back, inwardly grinning at the hostile glares she continued to send his way. He urged her hands over her head again and widened her thighs, tightening his grip when she deliberately stiffened her legs.

Übel chuckled as he sat in the adjacent chair and slowly ran his gaze over her body. "She is as feisty a one as Derek's whore," he said. "How well does she respond?"

Erich trailed his hand between her thighs and slid her lips apart with his middle finger. As he raised an eyebrow at his friend, Katrine gritted her teeth and turned her head to face the back of the sofa. "Not unfavorable for a virgin, although there is still room for improvement," he said. She might pretend his touch disgusted her, but his finger had become damp with her moisture as he continued to stroke her. He leapt in anticipation of sliding into the warm tightness of her virgin sheath.

Übel crossed an ankle over a knee and placed his elbows on the chair arms, resting his chin on the tips of his upraised fingers. "Speaking of Derek," he continued. "Karl is wearing him down. He is impressed that von Vetter has lasted this long." He laughed. "We should all be physically blessed with a male organ such as his. I admit I am envious."

Erich chuckled in agreement. He took a glance at the young woman on the sofa and grinned at the flush that entered her cheeks. "I have enough to satisfy you, Katrine," he said. "However, I shall enjoy sharing you with my friend Übel." Just the thought of the scene made him want to go ahead and take her, but he wanted to take his time with her and show her how it was to be pleasured by two men.

New tears rushed into Katrine's eyes. "No," she pleaded, the fear full in her shaky voice. "Do not do this. I beg you."

Erich slid his fingers slowly from her nubile femininity and rose to his feet. He watched the dread resurface in her eyes as he removed his civilian clothing. Once bare, he positioned himself between her open thighs, his rod shouting to be eased into her heat. He took a glance at Übel just as he finished removing his jeans. When his gaze dropped to his friend's erection, he was unable to stop a grin from curving his lips. "Are you ready to partake of this tasty morsel, *mein Freund*?" he asked unnecessarily, his voice husky in anticipation of their conquest.

„*Ja*," Übel agreed, his breathing heavy and uneven. He moved to the sofa next to Katrine and grasped her hands, holding them above her head with one hand. With the other, he grasped her chin and bent his head to openly slide his tongue into her mouth. A small wail bubbled from her throat while she tried to pull her mouth away from his, but his grip on her was too strong.

Erich grasped her quaking knees and rammed through her maiden barrier. He released a loud groan at the action, his pleasure at the take covering up her anguished cries.

Chapter Twenty-Seven

VERY ASSIGNMENT DEREK HAD BEEN GIVEN within the last month had conveniently had Übel as the NCO guard in charge. The younger man had no compunction in singling him out as a target for ridicule.

Today, he was assigned to the notorious gravel pit and his only job was to shovel gravel continuously into a wagon. The act itself seemed pointless, but it was used to wear out the person assigned to the job. Derek's back ached as if he had been sleeping on bare concrete for the last week and his biceps screamed in protest at each movement of his arms. With the blistering on his palms, he didn't want to let go of the shovel because the rawness of the skin seemed to sting through the layers at a greater intensity than if he continued to hold on to it. Sweat gathered on his skin in spite of the coldness of the winter air and it had seemed to pour down his back. Without thinking, he paused to take a deep breath.

Übel slammed a handful of gravel at him. "Keep moving you filthy, stinking pig!" he snarled into his face. "If you cannot handle this, maybe I will make you carry the concrete bricks. Move it, asshole!"

Stifling the urge to whack Übel with his shovel, Derek quietly resumed his duties. Several minutes later, he watched from the corner of an eye as Übel slung his rifle over his back and began strolling around the pit. The guard slowly eyed the others as they continued to work and when he returned to Derek, he stopped behind him.

Derek was about to toss another shovel full of gravel onto the wagon when Übel rammed his jackbooted foot between his shoulder blades and shoved him forward, slamming him to the ground with a loud whoomph. The impact knocked the breath from his lungs and it was as if someone had slugged him in the chest with a sledgehammer.

At the same time, the gravel fell onto his head and body as if it were a heavy rain shower. The shovel fell back to earth, nearly landing on another captive. Derek wanted to snatch the rifle from Übel's hands and unload the bullets into him when he and the other guards burst out laughing. Not only would it not do him any good, but it would make it worse for everyone else. They would be the ones to suffer most for his transgressions and he refused to allow that.

A couple of the other captives paused to gawk at the reactions, but most continued their jobs as if nothing unusual were happening. Derek forced himself back to his feet and brushed the dust off his body.

Übel laughed, his gray eyes lit with his enjoyment of the situation. "The show is finished!" he bellowed as if he had become angry. "Get off your fucking lazy asses and get back to shoveling the shit that's too good for you!"

As the men continued to work, Übel strolled back to his watching spot and sat down. Derek watched from the corner of his eye as the guard propped up his foot on a large boulder and swatted the dust off the toe of his boot. He casually lit a cigarette and took slow drags, blowing the smoke out in perpetual rings. After several minutes of silence and amusements with the cigarette smoke, he laughed as if something humorous had just popped into his mind. "Our ex-*Kommandant* here is a limey marquess among other things," he sneered loudly. "You are not so noble now, are you, pretty boy lordship!"

Since Karl had taken complete control of the camp, Derek assumed it was the way it had been with the old *Kommandant* in charge. He watched the changes, for which he had worked so hard being cast aside. These guards were behaving like childhood bullies who had never grown out of their power kicks.

Used to the previously allowed rests, another captive briefly stopped his work to take a breath and wiped the sweat from his forehead with his sleeve. Erich rammed his booted foot into the man's back, knocking him from his feet. Abraham oomphed as he sprawled down onto the ground on his chest. Although Derek continued to shovel the gravel into the pit, he tightened his lips in remembrance and watched the anger that burned in the young man's dark eyes. This seemed to be Erich's choice of copycat bullying for the day as well.

"You do not stop until I tell you to!" he shouted, his cerulean eyes flashing with amusement. "Now quit humping the ground and get back up on your feet, asshole."

They all ignored him as he continued slamming the others with various slurs on their character. The guard had no compunction about shoving the butt of his rifle into someone who gave him even the slightest bit of attention, but in many ways this was worse. The physical pains would soon disappear, but the emotional ones would take much longer to heal. The guards' taunts would remain with him for as long as he was alive.

Erich walked around the other men with a smirk of satisfaction curving his lips. "What are you looking at, you whore-fucking, Jew-loving pretty boy?" Erich snapped. "Going soft by letting everyone have their way. Eh, traitor?"

Derek ignored the guard, but his insides quickly numbed again. "Eat shit, fucker," he muttered under his breath, resisting the temptation to flash him the finger. Like Übel, Erich wouldn't hesitate to punish the others. Derek remembered that in school the bullies always had a little buddy who hung around them and Erich reminded him of this little buddy. The toady was usually harmless, but this wasn't true in Erich's case.

The guard stepped directly in front of him, stopping his work. "I'm talking to you, traitor," he sneered in his face, though his amusement was full in his eyes. "Traitor" seemed to be the newest "pet name" the guards had decided to call him to ridicule him, but he didn't much give a damn. When Derek stood, but continued to ignore him, Erich snatched the shovel from his hand and tossed it onto the ground. "Pick it up, your lordship."

It was all Derek could do not to ram the shovel down the younger man's throat, but he forced himself to squelch the temptation. Since his arms and legs burned from his rage and his heartbeat seemed nearly out of control, he no longer noticed the biting cold of the mid-February air. Without verbally acknowledging Erich, he bent to pick up the shovel.

"Your hair is getting too long, traitor," Lorenz Bauer, another guard, piped in. "Get it shaved off. Maybe you will look like a man again."

Without a word, Derek tossed the shovel onto the ground, refusing to satisfy them with a verbal response. As the other guards burst out laughing for a second time, he made his way toward the processing room. He ignored them as they then shouted more slurs at his back. It hadn't bothered him so much at first, but now it cut deep within him. There was no way around it, no matter how much he tried.

Allowing his thoughts to take over, he ignored his surroundings and the others who dared to watch him as he made his way to processing. Even an extra breath was met with either a degrading comment or a slam with a fist or the end of a weapon. Yesterday, one of the guards had shoved a woman to the ground and beat her nearly to death with the butt of his rifle because she wasn't planting a flower fast enough. Sometimes nothing was the cause and they abused the prisoners for the sheer joy of it.

Derek had watched Rolf walk Katrine toward the infirmary and it was obvious she had been raped, just by her demeanor. She had been shaking so hard that if Rolf hadn't been holding onto her, she wouldn't have been able to stay on her feet. Her face was flushed and the tears of pain and humiliation showed clearly in her eyes. Rolf was deeply in love with Katrine, as he was with Elizabeth, and he looked to do murder. What surprised Derek the most was that none of the other guards had stopped him from helping her.

He thanked God that Elizabeth was free of the camp. If she had still been there, who knew how they would have treated her, considering that she was the woman he loved. That alone would have made her a target. He hadn't yet received word whether or not she and Hans had rescued his grandmother. Rolf had said that Hans hadn't contacted him as of yet, but he would let Derek know when he did.

Derek brought his mind to Heinrich, whose words and actions he wrote down each night. The colonel had informed everyone that even passive resistance would not be tolerated and if anyone dared to cross him or even send a glance his way, there would be hell to pay. Arbitrary abuse was again commonplace and medications that had been given to those who needed them when Derek had been in charge were no longer being used. No one had become seriously ill, though it was only a matter of time before someone did.

Just outside the processing room, Derek breathed a deep sigh, his emotional pain evident. The young guard coming through the door stopped him.

"What can I do for you, sir?" Wolfgang asked. The question was calm and the sympathy was clear in the young man's eyes.

A little prick sent me here. "I was told to come for a haircut," he said instead.

"Rolf's in there. None of the assholes. We're not busy today."

Derek smirked. "Thanks," he said.

Wolfgang flushed when he realized what he had said. He swore. "I mean ..."

Derek couldn't help but chuckle. He knew the young man was referring to the other guards, not the captives. "Don't worry about it," he assured him. "I know what you meant."

Wolfgang flushed again. "Go on in, sir," he said.

Derek made his way inside as Rolf was talking with Jeorg. When he approached, his friend turned to the other guard. "Out," Rolf snapped. "And keep your mouth shut if you ever want to raise a family."

Jeorg smirked, but left without a word.

"Thanks, my friend," Derek said. "That little shit, Lorenz, sent me for a haircut."

Rolf nodded. "It will give us a chance to speak," he said. He motioned to the nearest chair. "Have a seat."

Derek sat down and breathed a deep sigh of relief. He didn't realize how much his legs ached until he did so, but it was good to take a rest. He nearly whimpered in relief.

Rolf snatched up a nearby shaver and turned it on. "How are you holding up?" he asked as he began trimming Derek's hair.

Tears burned behind Derek's eyes and he blinked to hold them back, his heart so tight that it physically ached. "Like shit," he snorted. "I'm glad Elizabeth isn't here to go through this. God only knows what they would do to her." He paused as a thought came to mind. "Shave it off. I don't give a flying fuck about it at this point." There was no doubt that this would cause more comments, but he didn't much care.

His friend paused. "Are you sure that's what you want?" he asked.

"Yes."

There was another brief pause before Rolf released a shaky breath. "When Katrine told me what Übel and Erich did to her, I wanted to kill them on the spot," he said, confirming Derek's earlier thoughts. "If she hadn't begged me not to because she was terrified of what would happen to me, I would have. Without a doubt."

Derek gave a humorless chuckle. "I have been tempted to do exactly that numerous times," he confessed. "But part of me gets satisfaction knowing I'm documenting everything they're doing. One day they will pay for it."

"Let me know if you need any more supplies."

Derek's heart lurched, but he appreciated the offer more than he could say. "You'll be in deep shit if they find out about this," he reminded Rolf.

Rolf finished shaving Derek's head before he answered. "I'll risk it," he said.

If it weren't for having faith that he would one day be reunited with Elizabeth, Derek wouldn't have been able to handle this. In spite of everything, if given the chance, he wouldn't have done anything differently than he had. "I just wish ..." He stopped as his throat muscles clenched with emotion.

Rolf sat backward in the adjacent chair to face him, resting his arms on the back in a reassuring gesture. "I swear I will do everything I can for you, Derek," he promised. "Including getting you out of here as you have done so many times yourself for others."

Although it was tempting, Derek wanted to prove to the others that he could and would survive, in spite of their wanting otherwise. "I cannot say the idea isn't tempting, but I have to stay here. I have to help gather proof of the shit that's going on here. I can't let these fucking psychos get away with it."

"As you wish, but I want you to keep the offer in mind."

"Thanks," Derek said, his voice tight. "Could I have a few moments alone?"

Rolf rose to his feet and reached out to squeeze his hands in a supportive gesture. "No problem," he said. "I'll wait outside. It's about time for your meal anyway."

"Thanks."

Once his friend had gone, the tears he had been withholding spilled down his cheeks. He rested his forehead against his upraised palms and bit his bottom lip to withhold the heavy sob. God, he missed Elizabeth so much and would have given his right arm to get out of this atrocious place. She had been free of the compound for over a month, but it seemed as if she had been gone for an eternity. If he lived through this purgatory, he would marry her. He had no doubt about that. He just wished he had done so anyway. There were a few priests held captive, so it would have been possible.

The sob he had been withholding bubbled in his throat, shifting his attention from his thoughts of Elizabeth to the present. "Oh, God, help us," he prayed, his tone filled with anguish and desperation. It only took a heartbeat to realize he had pleaded out loud and that his body burned along with his soul. "Why the fuck did this have to happen? Why? Why? *Why?*"

Before he realized he had moved, he shot to his feet as a hard rage sliced through him. A heartbeat later, he slammed the chair Rolf had been sitting in against the wall, wishing it were a sledgehammer against Heinrich's skull. As he eyed it in pieces, he couldn't help but burst out laughing. His emotions were at the breaking point, his heart was racing wildly and his breathing was quick and deep, but it felt so good to release his rage.

Rolf shot into the room. "Good God!" he swore as he eyed the chair. "What the hell happened here? Are you okay?"

Derek stopped laughing and grinned at his friend. "It must have slipped out of my hands," he lied, not bothering to hide his sarcasm. "Whoops! How 'bout that."

There was a brief moment of dead silence, but then they both burst out laughing.

Chapter Twenty-Eight

LIZABETH SAT AGAINST THE GRAYING, CONCRETE wall of the semi-dark cellar room in another contact's house. The musty smell tickled the inside of her nose, but she ignored it. Although she and Hans had been playing a game of Gin, she couldn't concentrate on her hand. She had admitted to herself that she had fallen in love with Derek the day she had broken down in the laundry area, though she had kept denying it until she could no longer. She had told herself that the swiftness of her feelings was reason to disavow them, but she knew deep within her soul that her feelings were genuine. Not a day had gone by when she didn't think about him, but she hated to think about what he was surely going through. She realized that most of the guards despised him for treating the captives as the human beings they were and that they would target him for their abuse. She couldn't help but wish he had been the one to have escaped instead of her. She didn't care what happened to herself as long as Derek could be spared.

When Japan had attacked Pearl Harbor on December 7, 1941, her father had begged her to leave Germany and go back to the States with him. Although his assignment was over, she had refused to leave, since Germany was also her home. But after learning the extent of the atrocities that had been happening, she had decided she was going back to Texas after the war was over. She had hoped to convince Derek to go back with her, but now she prayed only that he would survive. God, she loved him so much. She remembered the love shining in his eyes as he looked at her and his smile, which never failed to brighten her day.

The gentleness of his lovemaking and the memory of his arms around her made her ache to be held within them again.

Before she realized it, a lump rose in her throat and tears slid from her eyes. She wiped them away with her fingers and a moment later, Hans pulled her into his arms as if she were a child he was trying to console. The touch of his hands as he stroked her hair soothed her and halted the trail of tears just as her father's had done when she was a child. She didn't know what she would have done without him these last few weeks. Besides Derek, he was the best friend she had ever had and that made her appreciate him all the more.

They had followed lead after lead, but had come to nothing except dead ends. As far as they knew, Sabrina was relatively safe. For how long that would be, she did not know. No matter what they did, she still worried for Derek. What they might be doing to him terrified her more than anything and she found she could do nothing to stop her worries.

"I felt this way when I was first separated from Hannah," Hans explained. "I went through a grief process similar to what people go through when a loved one dies. It will hurt like hell for a while and then the ache will start to fade."

Elizabeth smiled. "I'm sorry for going all weepy on you," she apologized.

He chuckled affectionately. "Don't worry about it, Elizabeth. You are entitled." He shrugged, looking sheepish. "I told you I was the biggest crybaby around."

She found herself running her gaze over his strong jaw and the lush lips any woman would envy. He had the most beautiful eyes she had ever seen, next to Derek's, blue like the depths of the ocean with small flecks of green running through the irises.

Before she realized the gravity of what was she was doing, she slid her arms around his neck and tugged his head down to hers. Guilt and shame made a shroud over her, but her blood warmed when he nudged her lips apart. When she opened her mouth, he eased his tongue into her mouth to gently brush against hers. Their tongues entwined, wrestling and hotness made a path through her bones. Her body burned at the exchange of their tongues as they brushed them against each other's. *I love you, Derek, with all my heart, but I need Hans. I need him to ease the pain. Please forgive me.*

Hans pulled his tongue away from hers and let a groan escape from his throat. "Elizabeth," he said against her lips, the desire clear in his voice.

"Yes," she whispered in return. When he slid his hand under the hem of the sweater to close over her breast, she forced back a gasp of pleasure as fire swept over her body. When he touched her nipple and traced the tip with his thumb, it leapt to attention.

Hans moved down his hand and slid it inside her slacks. She widened her thighs, inviting him to ease his fingers through the feminine hairs and urge her wetness. He gently moved his hand over her, sliding a finger between the lips to stroke against the sensitive nub.

Elizabeth groaned as she humped against him in encouragement. *I miss you so much, Derek. God, I wish this was you.* She ran her hand down Hans' hard length, covered by his slacks, and gently cupped him, urging him to groan out his own pleasure. She needed the touch of his hands, the taste of his lips on hers and his tongue brushing against hers. She needed him to ease the pain of separation from the man she loved.

Hans lowered his head again and their tongues immediately entwined, the action bringing another flash of heat through her body. He peeled his lips from hers and pulled back to take a deep breath. "I cannot believe what we are doing," he groaned.

She moved back toward him to slide her hands up his chest and around the back of his neck. "Please?" she pleaded as she gazed deep into his eyes, her tone husky with yearning.

He cupped her cheek in his hand and gazed deep into her eyes, wanting shining in his. "Are you aware of what you are saying?" he asked, his tone matching his look. "If we do not stop now, there is no turning back."

Elizabeth took a deep breath. "Yes," she said. "I know what we're about to do."

He tugged her head back and bent his, allowing a groan to pass his lips. When their tongues met in another passionate frenzy, flames spread over her skin and she released a whimper into his mouth. He peeled his lips away and gazed back into her eyes. "I have to have you, Elizabeth," he groaned. "I cannot wait any longer."

He rose to his feet and pulled his sweater over his head. When he tossed away his slacks a few moments later, she raked her gaze over his body. Broad shoulders led to a flat stomach, trim waist and slim hips. Golden-blonde hair covered the length of his long legs, defined by his extensive walking during the last several years. She brought her attention back to his features as a sensual smile curved his lips and a rush of wanting charged through her.

Rising to her feet, Elizabeth pulled the sweater over her head and tossed it to the ground. As she eased down the slacks, Hans eyed her down the length of her body. He stepped toward her and grasped her hands to rest them on top of her head, his actions causing her body to flame hotter at each movement. He moved behind her and cupped her breasts while pressing his aroused length against her buttocks. She arched her back when he began brushing his palms against her swollen nipples. He pulled his hands back and let his fingers tease the tips, the actions causing her to suck in her breath.

"Hans," Elizabeth found herself begging hotly, her body on fire for him. "Please." Before she had realized it, he was again standing in front of her.

Grasping her hands, he moved them behind her to the small of her back and bent his head to her breasts. Elizabeth arched her back, encouraging his assault on her as he trailed his tongue over her swollen nipples. When he released her hands and slid his over her hips to grasp them, she laced her fingers through his overlong hair and tugged his head closer to her body in encouragement. His suckling caused her femininity to tighten and it was all she could do not to release the cry she had been holding.

He slowly moved his tongue away and pressed wet kisses up along the curve of her neck. Just as she was sure her knees were about to give way, he urged her down onto the cellar floor and onto her back. He pressed on the insides of her knees and widened her thighs. He slid his fingers into the hair and then drew them back out before sliding them back in again.

When he bent his head and slid his tongue between them to stroke the tip over the sensitive button, she couldn't help but release a loud cry of wanting. She found herself squirming against the torture, her pants of pleasure sounding deep in her ears. As her body soared, he moved slightly away and grasped her hands. He raised them above her head and stared deep into her eyes. "I am going take you, Elizabeth," he told her, his tone husky from passion.

"I know," she answered in the same tone.

He moved between her thighs and grasped her hips with his hands. When he thrust his fullness inside her, she sucked in her breath. Their fingers entwined and she found herself squeezing them as if they were a lifeline. She grasped the cheeks of his buttocks with the backs of her knees and urged him deeper inside her.

Their passion brushed all worries and thoughts from her mind, causing only her body to be aware of how he was pleasuring her. As he continued the movement of his hips and his length, he cupped her breasts and her nipples become sensitive in response. She failed to stop the sensual groan from sounding in her throat as he ran the tips of his fingers over them and it was as if twinges of pleasure shot through them. She nearly groaned in protest when he pulled himself from her. With a sensual male groan, he urged her onto her hands and knees and pressed his chest against her back and thrust hard into her from behind. He eased his hands between her thighs and along the feminine lips, parting them to bare the swollen bud between them.

"Hans," she whispered, as her mind swam away in tides.

"Come for me, Elizabeth," he begged in the back of her mind. "Reach it for me."

She had a death grip on the blanket beneath her and bucked back against him in their continued rhythm. When he teased her enflamed sensitivity, she cried out and floated off into a sea of stars. Hans shouted out at the same time, shedding his heated climax inside her.

He swore loudly a few moments later and pulled himself out of her. He collapsed onto his back and slid his fingers through the top of his silky hair. "What the *hell* am I doing!" he snapped a few heartbeats later.

As Elizabeth sat back on her hands, her body burned from the passion they had shared. She was so aroused at the sensual encounter with him that she had ignored her conscience about what she had done. When she realized this, shock at what she had just done sliced through her. She had used her involuntary parting from Derek as a reason for falling into the arms of his best friend. She had tried to convince herself that the stress and uncertainty of worrying about him was a good excuse for her behavior, but her conscience knew better. Her guilt was like a physical blanket of consciousness that had wrapped itself around her, hounding her about her treachery.

Good God, Elizabeth! What have you done? When you screw up, you do it with a vengeance. "We will just have to make sure that it doesn't happen again," she said, tight-lipped. Her tone indicated she was angry at him, but she was angry with herself more than anything. "It doesn't mean anything, right? It was nothing more than physical release and we're both still in love with other people."

"Yes, Elizabeth," he agreed, his tone and eyes flat. "That is true."

She turned and laid down on her side, facing away from him, pulling the blanket over her naked form. "Goodnight, Hans," she said quietly.

"Goodnight, Elizabeth."

As the new silence in the room became oppressive, she squeezed her eyes closed to keep the tears from falling.

Chapter Twenty-Nine

HE NEXT AFTERNOON, ELIZABETH HAD HER first lesson on how to shoot a pistol. She found it hard to concentrate, since she was haunted by the memory of the nightmare she had had about Derek the night before. She had dreamed that he had met another woman and he had exaggerated his intentions toward the blonde as if taunting her in repayment for her own mistakes. He had merely laughed when she had released tears of despair as she confronted him and let him know that his behavior hurt her. The pain was as much physical as it was emotional, so much so that the nightmare seemed painfully real. She had shot awake to tears streaming down her face and her heart wildly racing.

"Are you ready, Elizabeth?" Hans asked, his words pulling her from her reverie.

Elizabeth shuddered with a smirk and shrugged a shoulder. "I guess," she replied. "I'm just a little nervous about learning how to shoot." She was also nervous about being around him after her behavior of the previous night. He hadn't brought up the subject so far and she refused to. They would just have to pretend that nothing had happened. *But something did and you know it. No wonder you had that dream last night. You deserve every bit of the guilt you've placed upon yourself.*

"It is easy," he said. "I have faith in you." He bent to snatch Derek's Walther P38 off the ground and then handed it to her.

When she took it from him, her hands shook somewhat from touching it. She didn't have this reaction when she had taken it from

160

Derek, but she put it down to the intensity of that particular situation. "Thanks, I think," she said cautiously.

"You are welcome," Hans grinned. "Now, are you right or left-handed?"

"Right-handed."

"You should be familiar with this, since your policemen are skilled in this method. It is similar to how I was trained in that same profession before they gave me the boot. Hold it in your right hand, but do not put your finger on the trigger until I tell you to. Then wrap your left hand over the fingers of your right and move your feet apart to steady yourself. Do not shoot one-handed as I have seen many do. It will keep you from shooting too many wayward bullets and hitting something or someone you do not wish to. You don't have to pull the trigger back, since the first bullet is loaded automatically. You will not have to pull the trigger as far after you have discharged the first bullet. Since you can get off more rounds in a shorter time, this pistol is mucho easier to shoot than many."

Elizabeth nearly giggled at the word *mucho*, since it was so unexpected. She moved into position and then lifted the P-38 and pointed it at the target, which was a burlap potato sack filled with hay from their last hideout. She gripped her shooting hand with her left hand as Hans had directed and took a deep breath. "Now what?" she asked, but then chuckled. "Besides shoot."

She only half-listened as Hans gave her the directions. She was nervous because of the situation, but she got the gist of what he was telling her. Ignoring her racing heart, she pulled the trigger back as far as it would go with ease, then stopped. She forced the trigger the rest of the way back and seemingly a long moment later, the bullet hit the target just outside the necessary circle. She shot at the crude target, but she became less nervous each time. At the sixth round, she was much more relaxed and actually beginning to have fun learning how to shoot.

"How about another magazine," he suggested once she had finished. "You are doing much better since you relaxed."

Elizabeth grinned, feeling a sense of accomplishment. "Thank you," she said. She had always been leery of guns, but today her anxieties were waning.

"After that you can step further away from the target."

"All right."

The nerves that had been calm earlier now tingled with awareness of Hans beside her as he watched her progress. Her heart pounded and a nervous flutter moved in the pit of her stomach. She wasn't sure whether it was desire she was feeling or just her guilty conscience working overtime. Someone chuckled in the back of her mind and she again brought herself out of a reverie by turning to Hans. "What?" she snapped in a high tone, angry with herself for letting her mind drift for the second time.

He raised an eyebrow and smirked. "You killed that poor ant," he told her.

"Pardon?" she asked cautiously as she lowered her arms. She briefly wondered if he could have read her thoughts, but quickly dismissed the idea.

He slid an arm across her shoulders and flashed her a smile. "I am just teasing you," he explained. "Are you okay?"

"I'm fine," she said with an attempt at a small smile, but the slight nervousness sounded in her voice.

Hans dropped his gaze to her lips and her body warmed at the near physical touch. His eyes briefly darkened and her cheeks burned with a flush as their time together popped into her mind. She nearly jumped when he slid his arm from her shoulders.

"Let us finish out that mag," Hans suggested. "Then we will take a short rest."

Elizabeth gave him an uneasy smile. "Okay," she agreed.

As the days went slowly by, her heels became blistered from the kilometers of walking. She and Hans had stopped at several places along the way and continued to change their clothes in front of each other. She was fully aware that they still held a degree of desire for each other, but they had to keep it in check and not repeat their sensual encounter. It would be so easy to give into their desires and to lose themselves in each other's bodies so they wouldn't have to deal with the pain of their separation from the people they loved.

Her mind was drawn back to reality when she caught a sheen of water rushing over multicolored rocks below. As soon as she realized that it was a waterfall, a squeal of excitement leaped from her throat. It was small, but big enough that it invited a nice bath. It was a bright, sunny day and the air was chilly, but nothing could take away the joy of the situation. *The water's probably chillier than the air,* she thought.

"Hans!" she cried. "A waterfall!" *And people think there are no waterfalls in Germany. Hah!* If she had had a camera, she would have taken a picture. It was absolutely beautiful. She couldn't help but jump up and down, leaping at her friend to hug him.

Hans stumbled, but was able to stay on his feet and retain his hold on her. "I am glad that you are excited and all," he said with a slight chuckle. "But try to contain it some. You never know who may be lurking."

She failed to stop the grin from curving her lips although she pulled away from him. "Of course," she said brightly. "So who gets a bath first, you or I?"

"Ladies first," he said with a graceful bow. "I will be back in a few minutes. Enjoy yourself." With a wink and a grin, he trailed off.

While he was gone, Elizabeth stripped off her clothes and set them down on a large boulder. The cool wind shivered over her, but she was beyond caring, since the warm sun more than made up for it. She made her way down the embankment and into the falls below. The tension seemed to fall off her body as the cold water rushed over her skin. She let it soak into her hair and continue to run down her body. Even without soap, the bath was wonderful. A groan burst from deep within her diaphragm as the soft pounding of the fall eased her tired, overworked muscles.

A shiver rushed over her body a few minutes later as she realized she was being watched. It had to be Hans coming back from wherever he had gone and she looked back over her shoulder just as he stopped short. Without thinking about what she was doing, she took a slight step back and turned around to face him. She leaned her head back and raised her arms to squeeze the water from her hair.

When he ran his gaze over her body, her nipples tightened and the warm wetness between her thighs had nothing to do with the waterfall. She flashed him a slow, encouraging smile as he looked straight back into her eyes. She tried to justify to herself that if Derek were in this situation, she would expect him to take a lover. There wasn't really anything wrong with it, she convinced herself. It was physical release, nothing more.

Hans raised a knowing eyebrow and tightened his lips. "Finish up," he snapped. "I need a bath, too."

Chapter Thirty

HANS STEPPED UNDER THE COLD WATER of the fall and moaned in relief as it eased the sore muscles of his shoulders, chest and back. When he had stumbled onto the sight of Elizabeth still taking her shower, he had become instantly hard at the sight of her bare body. It was all he could do not to take up the girl on her offer. He still wanted to kick himself for giving into her before.

He groaned to himself at the word 'girl.' It just didn't fit. Elizabeth was all woman. It didn't matter that she was young enough to be his daughter. He physically ached to have her sensual warmth around him again. The chill of the water had no effect on his arousal, which had a mind of its own. The more he kept thinking about the firm roundness of her luscious breasts and the gentle curve of her hips, the more he had trouble keeping his hands and body to himself. When he had walked up, it was clear that she had deliberately turned to face him. It was all he could do not to shove her against the nearest tree and take her on the spot. She was the most passionate woman he had ever encountered and he was becoming physically obsessed with wanting to take her again.

The sunlight shone on his wedding band and he lifted his right hand to kiss it. It was not wise to wear such an identifier, but he didn't have the heart to rid himself of the gold band. He remembered his promise to Hannah that he would not be disloyal to her by making love with another woman. Guilt slammed through him at that thought. He had kept that vow for two years, but the chances of his being faithful had grown slimmer as time had passed.

Adrienne Martin had been as tempting as Elizabeth, but he had

---

given in to her in one wild moment and had been disgusted with himself ever since. Now he had betrayed his closest friend, which was inexcusable. Although they had agreed never to have sexual relations again, his body burned every time their sensual encounter popped into his mind. He didn't know how long he could keep from ravishing her again unless he immediately put a stop to her attentions. It was difficult, since she didn't have a shy bone in her body. *Oh, what a body,* he groaned to himself. She had no compunction about undressing in front of him or offering her body to him as she did today.

"Come on to me again, Elizabeth, and you may get more than you bargained for," he swore. He then wondered if the warning was for Elizabeth's benefit or for his own.

Chapter Thirty-One

EREK LAY ON TOP OF THE hardwood table, his back aching after being in the same position for over an hour. Heinrich had taken away his clothing and restrained him naked, in an attempt to degrade him, but he wouldn't give the older man any satisfaction. Heinrich had said little in the time they had been in the room, but had paced as he had stared, endeavoring to incite a reaction from his captive.

God only knew what the sack of shit had planned for him. When he had first been restrained, a sense of panic had lit though him as if it were a shock of electricity. His heartbeat had sped up to a ballistic rhythm and perspiration had made a sheen over his skin. It had taken every bit of willpower he possessed not to beg his superior officer to release him. Heinrich would have had no compunction about conveying his pleasure at this.

Derek dragged his thoughts back to the present just as Heinrich stopped his pacing and rested his hands on the left side of the table. He forced back a shudder of disgust when the colonel dropped his gaze between his thighs.

"Übel is correct," he said in satisfaction. "You are truly blessed to have such a large cock. I must say I am quite envious."

"I will not be a toy to humor you, Heinrich," Derek sneered.

Heinrich linked his hands behind his back and resumed his pacing. "Remember our conversation before I gave you the command of this camp?" he asked without looking at him or acknowledging his statement. "You will obey your orders without question and divided loyalties or suffer the consequences. I would say that working for the Resistance is dividing your loyalties, von Vetter."

Even then, Derek had had no intention of following those orders. "I lied," he said, not bothering to keep the sarcasm from the tone. "Besides, it does not matter. We have been losing the war for a while now and you are as aware of it as the rest of us." He chuckled without humor. "That is why you put me here, not because I was harboring Miriam. I am merely a convenient substitute, a fall guy for your Crimes Against Humanity."

Heinrich had the nerve to laugh and he again rested his hands on the table next to Derek's hips. "Of course that is merely one of the reasons, von Vetter," he agreed with a rare smile. "Surely you do not think I would have chosen you to command this dreadful place unless you were expendable. When the Americans arrive, you will be eliminated instead of me. Think of it as a matter of self-preservation on my part." His usually pale-blue eyes were bright with humor as he gave a maniacal chuckle. "Until that happens, I will personally see to your suffering and I will enjoy every moment of it."

Derek forced away all other emotions but his anger. "Fuck you," he snapped.

Heinrich let a cold grin curve his lips and he cupped Derek's phallus. "I do not think so," he said. He nonchalantly slid his thumb under the foreskin and brushed it against the tip.

Disgust rammed Derek in the gut, but unfortunately he couldn't keep himself from swelling.

Heinrich continued to touch him, sliding his fingers over his length. "I have told you before, Derek, that I would hate for you to lose what you are blessed with," he reminded him in a low voice. "Such a lusty young man you are."

"You cannot seem to be able to keep your hands to yourself, Colonel," Derek couldn't help but taunt. Heinrich continued to touch him and if he didn't know him so well, he would have thought that doing so was arousing him. "As well as your faithful lapdog, Übel. Are there other instances that others are not aware of where he comes panting to you? He may become jealous if he finds out you have been touching me so familiarly."

As Derek finished his comments, Heinrich gave his penis a sharp twist and agony sliced through his testes. The colonel's face became distorted as fuzz penetrated his thoughts. Derek took several deep breaths in an attempt to force away the pain, but the intensity remained. "Dare you question my sexuality, von Vetter," Heinrich shouted, as if from a distance, "when you are the one rising in my hand?"

Derek gritted his teeth in hopes of keeping from begging Heinrich to release him. A mewl of pain sounded in his throat and Heinrich took away his hand in the next moment. The intense pain gradually faded to a throb as Derek floated back to reality. "You fucking bastard," he forced out.

Heinrich burst out laughing, the reaction doing nothing for his fading looks. When the laughter died down, he raised a white eyebrow. "Übel has told me what you had threatened to do when he was about to shear your whore's red locks," he relayed. "Would you rather I removed your testes from you in his stead?"

Derek paled at the threat and he gritted his teeth to keep from releasing a cry of anguish. The thought of never seeing a baby with Elizabeth's red hair and lovely green eyes was almost unbearable. He would rather die than not father the children she deserved.

Heinrich grasped him again and a new slice of pain rushed through him. "Answer me, von Vetter!" he shouted. "Shall I castrate you with my bare hands or shall I call on one of the dogs?"

„*Nein*," Derek whimpered through his teeth at the horrific threat. The pain was more intense than before and his abdominal muscles constricted as he fought to keep from attempting to draw up his knees.

"I cannot hear you, von Vetter!" Heinrich shouted into his face. "What is that you say, Major?"

"No!" he returned in English, his throat muscles straining as he tried to shout out the word. Heinrich released him and Derek began hyperventilating as he tried to catch his breath, his heart and lungs tight from a seeming lack of air.

As the colonel rested a hand on either side of his waist, Derek forced himself not to spit in his face. That was the least of what the bastard deserved.

"See how much better things will go for you when you cooperate?" Heinrich said in guttural English, satisfaction curving his lips and brightening his eyes. He patted Derek's right cheek in a patronizing gesture. "You will learn that as time goes on. Do you understand me, von Vetter?"

„*Ja*," he lied, having no intention of cooperating. Doing so would be giving up and he refused to. Tell those like Heinrich anything they wanted to hear and they believed everything you told them. The reaction here proved that.

"That is good," Heinrich said, once again speaking in German. He straightened and linked his hands behind his back. "I was beginning to wonder if you had forgotten your mother tongue. I am glad to see you have not done so."

"Oh, life's little victories," Derek scoffed breathlessly in German. The throb between his thighs was turning into a dull ache, which was something of a relief.

Heinrich laughed again, stunning him. "I see you have not lost your sense of humor, von Vetter. Keep it up, so to speak. Let me show you."

He shouted out a command and the door opened a moment later. Übel shoved a young woman about Elizabeth's age into the room and slammed the door behind them. Her shoulder-length hair was a tawny brown and her gray eyes were bright with tears. The prisoner's uniform hung on her slender frame, but it did not distract from her earthy beauty. Her wrists were tied in front of her and she was pleading in French for them release her.

Derek's gut and heart tightened with rage, but since he was restrained, he could only move a short distance. He cursed Heinrich and the guard, not bothering to hide his rage at them and the situation.

"A small gift," Heinrich explained. As he cupped the woman's cheek, she yanked her face away from him. When she verbally spouted her hatred for him, he brought his hand back in an arc and then slammed it back down and across her face. She cried out as his palm connected and her head moved to the side, but she gave no other reaction.

"Silence!" the colonel shouted, causing her to cower against the wall. He turned his attention to his smiling guard and raised an eyebrow.

In response to the nonverbal command, Übel released the buttons on her top. She gritted her teeth as more tears rushed into her eyes.

Knowing he was unable to help the young woman, Derek watched as the guard cupped her chin and turned her face toward his. Übel grinned at him and then bent his head and covered her mouth with his. The woman could not keep the disgust from her lovely face as the guard openly slid his tongue into her mouth. When he roughly squeezed her breast, a small cry of pain sounded from within her. He released her breast a moment later and trailed his hand under the waistband of her slacks and between her thighs. Not bothering to hide his actions, he rammed his finger inside her.

The woman yanked her mouth from his and released a terrified cry of anguish into the room. Übel hauled off and slapped her with the back of his hand, leaving a red mark on her soft skin. A tiny whimper sounded in her throat and she sank to her knees to bury her head in her hands.

With rage burning through his being like a physical pang, Derek fought the ropes that confined him, but he could do nothing except thrash around.

"When we are through, my lovely *mademoiselle*," Übel snarled, "you will give us what we are seeking."

Heinrich stood back and watched everyone's reactions, as casually as if this were a Sunday picnic. If he weren't strapped to the table, Derek could have killed him with his bare hands. "I hope you understand, Derek, that we must do whatever possible to gain the absolute loyalty we are seeking," he warned with a smirk. "If you do not, I promise you that I will break you, von Vetter. You will be begging me to destroy you."

A cold premonition of horror rushed over Derek's skin, but he refused to allow the other man to see how deeply his treatment had cut him. "I would watch my back if I were you, Heinrich," he snarled, his entire being burning with hatred for this man. "If it comes down to you and me, you will be the one to suffer."

Heinrich's pale eyes burned with an emotion Derek couldn't place, but he was beyond giving a damn. "It is a shame your American lover is not here to share this experience with you, so I am leaving you with a temporary surrogate." He yanked the woman to her feet and shoved her sprawling onto the floor beside the table.

She cried out as she went down and the table leg creaked in protest as her head struck it. She grasped her head and rocked back and forth in a fetal position, the action causing a nauseous leap within the pit of his stomach.

Übel stalked toward the cowering female. "On your feet!" he shouted. "Do you think that because you are a woman that we will give you preferential treatment?" When she refused to answer or move, he grabbed hold of the lapels of her top and yanked her to her feet.

She refused to look at him as her tears made a path down her cheeks, but she kept silent, her eyes flat as she seemed to withdraw into herself.

"Your silence will change nothing, my dear. Need I remind you that if you do not give us what we want, you will wish you had never been brought into this world? Do you understand?"

The girl continued to remain silent, refusing to give the guard a response. Übel grabbed her by the back of her shirt and slammed her down on the table on top of Derek. Both captives oomphed as their bodies roughly connected.

"Perhaps you will change your mind after being held in this room for a while," Übel said with a smile in his voice. "Or perhaps you may even enjoy your time with our ex-*Kommandant*. He seems to have a predilection for fucking his female prisoners."

There were plenty of rumors about captives being shut away with each other just too see what would happen and Derek wondered whether this was a ploy in order to do so. He wouldn't put it past either man to achieve some voyeuristic pleasure from watching them copulate. Unfortunately, with the young woman draped over his abdomen and her breasts pressed against his chest, he began to harden.

It seemed years since he had held Elizabeth's body against his and the memory of her passionate responses rushed through him as if it were wildfire. He attempted to force his feelings of arousal from his mind, refusing to consider the actions the other two men seemed to expect. Too bad his body betrayed him by having its own ideas. He found himself staring into the woman's eyes, stunned when amusement flickered in them. He barely kept his eyebrows from crinkling in confusion at her reaction. It was as if she were enjoying this scenario. Who was this woman?

"She is quite arousing, is she not?" Heinrich sneered, causing Übel to laugh in agreement. "You may not have another chance to take such a luscious morsel. Enjoy her while you can, von Vetter. Think of her as my parting gift to you." At that, he and Übel left the room.

After both men were gone, the woman gave him a nearly undetectable smile, startling him. "My name is Adrienne Martin," she said in a soft tone, her accent Midwestern American. "And I have a message for you."

Derek's heartbeat shot up, not from the closeness of her body, but from her comment. It was all he could do not to allow his jaw to drop. "From?" he asked, his voice equally quiet. He had an inkling of suspicion about her, but gave her the benefit of the doubt. For now.

"I will untie you and then we can discuss it." As she slid off him, his gaze dropped to the curves of her breasts exposed by the open top. "We must keep our voice levels to a minimum unless it's relevant to our act. They may have bugged the room."

"Bugged?" he asked, as if unfamiliar with the term.

Adrienne moved to the head of the table and began releasing the rope that surrounded his wrists. "Planted listening devices," she explained. "Also, do your best to hide your reactions. They will be watching."

Derek brought his arm down as she pulled the rope away and the bicep ached in protest. She walked to the other side of the table and repeated the process. When she finished with his wrists, she held her hands out to him in a silent request that he untie her. He released the leather strap and tugged it away, tossing it onto the floor. "Thank you," he returned gently.

"Shall I help you with your ankles?" she asked with a bright light in her eyes.

Derek held back a smile. "I believe I can manage," he said. Taking a deep breath of anticipation, he forced himself into a sitting position. His head briefly swam as his muscles cried out in protest, but he scooted to the end of the table. He swiftly released his bindings and knocked them onto the floor in disgust.

"Play along with me, Derek," Adrienne requested. She stepped toward him and slid her arms around his neck. He held back a groan of anticipation as she tugged his head down to hers. Before he realized what was happening, their tongues were entwining. After being so long without Elizabeth's touch, heat swept over his body as his phallus leapt to attention. With their mouths still attached, he slid off the table and rose to his feet.

He found himself wrapping his arms around her waist and pulling her against him, deliberately allowing her to feel his hardness. How tempting she was, with her breasts and her body pressed against his bare form. He had no doubt he was using her, but he needed to find out if he could sustain an erection after Heinrich's assault on him. At that thought, he peeled his lips and tongue away from hers. "What were you saying about a message?" he asked.

Adrienne stood, her eyes glassy as if she were in a daze. A moment later, she shook her head. "I ... I have a message from Kurt," she explained.

"Kurt?" he asked, prompting her for another identifier.

She softly cleared her throat. "Your supplies contact." She slid her arms around his neck and pressed kisses along the line of his jaw, making a path to his lobe. "Remember to play along," she urged into his ear. "Our sexual play is a ruse."

Derek released a husky chuckle. Her statement might be true, but he couldn't help but be physically aroused by her. He bent his head close to her ear and nuzzled her lobe, sending a responding shiver through her. "I will remind you of that the next time a shiver runs over your body," he teased.

A nearly undetectable smile curved her lips. "You're quite the charmer, aren't you?" she teased.

"About that message."

Adrienne gulped. "You're quickly making me lose my head and I'm getting sidetracked." She sighed. "I am to inform you that your grandmother is hiding with Miriam's family and she is relatively safe."

It was all Derek could do not to give a whoop of joy at the news. He briefly brushed his lips against hers, remembering to continue with the act. "And Elizabeth?" he asked, wishing with all he was worth that this was Elizabeth in his arms.

Another ghost of a smile curved Adrienne's lips. "I am to meet with her and Hans within the next few days," she told him. He held back a sigh of relief. "Kurt is the only one who knows this and he says they are both well. He will be contacting them before we meet. That is all I have for now."

"Shall we continue with this sensual pretense, Adrienne?" Derek asked as he hardened even more at their petting. *Forgive me for my physical reaction to this woman, Elizabeth,* he thought. *I am only doing what is necessary.* Even though that was the case, guilt slammed into him.

"Just for a short while longer. I will let you know when to stop." She grasped his wrist and urged his hand over her breast.

He brushed his thumb over the hardening nipple as he rose to full attention. He forced himself to hold back a groan of lust as she pressed her breast into his palm. "I would advise you to do so quite soon. I do not wish to provide a peepshow for my captors. I am providing enough of one as it is." If she did not, he wouldn't be able to stop himself from taking it all the way. She had become far too tempting.

"Now," she informed him with gritted teeth. She unclenched her jaw and sent him a hard glare. "Do not take this personally, Derek, but I'm going to slap you."

She yanked herself away and brought her arm up in an arc. He could barely take a breath before her palm connected hard with his cheek. His skin burned with the sting of her slap as she spat curses at him, although the light of laughter filled her eyes. She rushed up to him and slammed her fists against his shoulders as Elizabeth had done when she had become enraged with him. "How dare you speak to me in such a way!" she shouted, but then continued with a soft, "I need to go."

"How will you escape from here?" he asked, cringing somewhat from her strength. Even with her slender build, she was surprisingly strong.

She again slammed her fists against his chest as if angered by his behavior. "You deserve what you get for treating me like this, you bastard!" she shouted. "I will not be a plaything for you people!" She grasped hold of his shoulders and sank against him as if genuinely enraged by his imaginary responses.

"Bitch," Derek snarled, although it took every ounce of willpower not to laugh. "If I were in charge, you would not have a choice."

Adrienne moved away and flashed him a fiery glare. "You are not in charge now, so I do not give a damn. I will risk death before I give myself to a filthy traitor." She stepped forward again. "Heinrich believes me to be Gestapo and that I am here under the pretence of being a prisoner in order to gain information from you, but he is no fool. I must be very careful with him."

"Godspeed, Adrienne."

"Thank you, Derek."

His throat muscles tightened. "When you see Elizabeth, tell her I love her and miss her. Can you do that for me?"

A ghost of a smile curved her lips. "I will do that, Derek," she promised.

She shot away from him and toward the wall to sink down against it, onto the floor. Sudden tears filled her eyes and she let out a phony wail. It was all Derek could do not to burst out laughing. Adrienne was some actress.

A fuming Übel came back only moments after he and Heinrich forced her from the room and tossed Derek his camp uniform. "Get the fuck dressed," Übel snapped, his eyes flashing with rage. "Karl has other plans for you."

Derek withheld a boisterous laugh at the guard's anger. *What's the matter, asshole? You look a little pissed off there. Didn't get what you wanted?* He fought for all he was worth not to taunt the younger man with his thoughts. He put back on the uniform and allowed the guard to shove him from the room, barely able to contain his satisfaction.

Chapter Thirty-Two

ELIZABETH WANTED TO SMACK HERSELF FOR eating so much bratwurst at the last contact's house. She had been so happy to eat satisfying food for the first time in ages that she had practically inhaled it. She had been queasy for the last couple of hours and she had had to stop along the way for a few rests, but had thought little of it until a few minutes ago. At least the sun was shining, instead of the dreariness of the last week and the temperature seemed warmer. Food poisoning was the last thing she needed. She and Hans had passed through an area with a few trees when the worst nausea of the afternoon clenched her stomach muscles. She crossed her arms over her stomach in an attempt to hold it down.

"Are you all right?" Hans asked.

She attempted to smile but couldn't muster the energy to finish it. She wanted to do nothing but curl up in a protective ball until the nausea disappeared. "I don't feel so well, Hans," she whispered.

He gave her a gentle smile. "We can stop to rest again," he offered.

She shook her head, knowing that if she sat down, she wouldn't get back up again. "No, I'm ..." she started. As the bile started rising to her throat, she took off into the trees, but had barely made it when she began emptying the contents of her stomach. She retched so hard, she expected to toss up her insides. She hated being sick like this anyway, but it seemed to be compounded today. *This is so disgusting*, she couldn't help but think as she retched for a second time. When she had finished, her body was bathed in sweat and ravaged with shakes. *When was the last time you had your period, stupid?* She sharply brought her head up at the thought, having no understanding of what had triggered it. It was as if someone had flipped on a switch in her head.

Hans squatted down beside her and rested a hand on her shoulder. "Are you all right now?" he asked gently.

Elizabeth sat on her bottom with her knees up and rested her chin on her hands. "Maybe the bratwurst didn't agree with me," she said with a small scoff, hoping it was a convincing explanation. She had no doubt that nausea was a sign of pregnancy, but she shoved the thought from her mind.

"It has not bothered me," he said as he raised an eyebrow. "Maybe it could be something else."

She forced herself to hold her suspicions inside and let a grin cross her face. "No," she contradicted him.

Hans gave a nearly girlish-sounding giggle. "Maybe you're pregnant," he quipped.

Elizabeth shot to her feet and glared down at him, her eyes flaming. *How could he possibly know that?* "Hans Markus Lindberg," she snapped. "That is not funny!" A bubble rose up in her throat and to her horror, tears began spilling down her cheeks. The crying jag took all the emotions she had been holding inside and released them so hard that she shook and plopped to the ground before she fell.

Hans tightened his lips into a grimace and he stood up to pull her into his arms. "I'm sorry, Elizabeth," he apologized. "I didn't mean to upset you."

"Don't be," she found herself saying into his shoulder. "I hear pregnant women are supposed to be emotional." When she realized what she had just confessed, a shock of emotional electricity rushed through her. She shot away from him and swore.

Hans coughed and loudly cleared his throat at the same time. "Lucky guess?" he seemed to tease.

There was no point in denying it now. She couldn't take back the admission. "No," she admitted, trying to ignore his attempt to cheer her up. "It's true."

He rested a hand on her shoulder and gave it a gentle squeeze. "Derek is the father of your baby, Elizabeth," he said with conviction. "There is no doubt."

Elizabeth balked and moved away to face him. "But it could be yours, Hans," she told him, but then blushed. "We didn't use protection and you came inside me." *Did that just pop out of my mouth?*

He released an affectionate chuckle, apparently not bothered by her graphic description. "It cannot be," he corrected her. "If the baby were mine, we would not be having this discussion. It has only been three weeks since we were together."

Elizabeth flushed at his reminder, but breathed a sigh of relief. She realized that his statement was true. There was no way he could be the father of the baby. It had to be Derek's. Her heart warmed at that and she prayed that one day the baby could see his or her father.

Hans excused himself and went farther into the trees. Not wanting to sit down lest she not want to get back up, She unconsciously rested her hands on her abdomen as she wondered what Derek's child would look like. Would it be a boy or a girl? Would the child look like her or like him? Would she be a good mother? She didn't know, but she didn't doubt for a moment that Derek was the father type. He was too loving and gentle not to be.

She was several feet away when a man her height wearing a black uniform caught her attention. As soon as she noticed the ominous *Leibstandarte SS Adolf Hitler* uniform with the red and white armband and the telltale black swastika in the middle, a lightning rod of fear shot through her. *Move it, you idiot!* Unfortunately, her body refused to obey her mind.

The officer leaned back against a tree and lit a match before encircling the tip of the cigarette with the flame. After taking a deep drag, he glanced up. His jade gaze landed directly on her.

Her heartbeat shot up in terror and the color drained from her face.

"What are you afraid of, woman? he snapped, his voice cracking as if it were a whip slicing through the air.

Her lips moved, but she could not force out any words. Her feet seemed to be cemented to the ground and her knees shook as her entire body weakened. *Don't pass out, Elizabeth. There has to be a way out of this.* She fought to keep from moving back as he stalked toward her in slow, deliberate steps.

"Is there something wrong with your tongue?" he asked, his tone louder and harder this time.

A twig cracked as Hans approached, but it was too late to warn him.

"Hallo, Kurt," Hans surprised her by greeting the man warmly. "What has taken you so damn long to meet us?"

With a wide grin, the "SS officer" walked over to his friend and enthusiastically shook his hand. "Hans, my friend," he greeted just as warmly. "It is good to see you." He glanced at Elizabeth and smiled. "You must be Elizabeth." He clicked his heels and briefly bowed his head. "I am Kurt Dietrich. It is a pleasure."

Elizabeth dragged herself out of her frozen reverie and turned on Hans. "You two know each other?" she asked loudly, her question sounding more like a accusation than an inquiry. "You son of a bitch! He scared the shit out of me! I expected to be shot on sight and you know him?"

Hans burst out laughing and Kurt whistled long and soft as he held back his own. "I ..." Hans tried to say, but he was laughing too hard. Elizabeth thought he was about to clutch his stomach and fall to the ground. She continued to glare at him, but he sobered a few heartbeats later. "It was worth seeing you speechless for once."

She was about to tell them both off when the proverbial light bulb went off in her head. She had first seen Kurt when he had come to the camp as a dispatch rider, but now he wore the stark black uniform of an officer of the elite bodyguards of *Leibstandarte SS Adolf Hitler*. Although they had generally branched into a paramilitary unit, there were still members of the original unit remaining. *He is a little young and was by himself, dear, but then again, who's going to notice when they're scared shitless.* "First a courier and now a member of the original *Leibstandarte*?" she demanded, as she ignored her thought. "Some master of disguises you are. Who will you be next? *Der Führer?*"

Kurt chuckled, his eyes bright with the laugh. He turned to his friend and raised an eyebrow. "Derek was not joking," he said.

"*Nein,*" Hans laughed in agreement. "*Spitfire* seems to be such a lame term. I would rather meet up with a real SS man any day of the week. It would be safer."

Exasperated, Elizabeth tossed her hands in the air. "I give up," she said loudly. "You men are hopeless."

Hans slid his arm around her shoulder and gave her a brief hug. "I am glad you are on our side," he said, amusement still in his voice.

Kurt chuckled. "I am, too," he agreed.

That evening, at a resistance sympathizer's home, Kurt pulled a change of clothes from his black rucksack and handed them to her. The room was in the basement, as usual, but was comfortable in spite of the bare gray, tile flooring and the gray steel sink oxidizing to a flat appearance. At least there were a couple of pretty throw rugs to brighten up the place and a couple of cots where they could sleep. The musty scent she could deal with, since she had slept in far worse places.

Elizabeth squealed in excitement as she snatched the black top and the long, olive skirt from his hands. She turned her back to the men and stripped off her sweater. She yanked her slacks down and stepped out of them. She kicked them aside, not bothering to hide herself from their view. She and Hans had previously made a compromise because a couple of times they had not had a choice about changing in front of each other. Either it was that or wear the same clothes day in and day out without being washed, which wasn't an option.

Once she was naked, Kurt loudly cleared his throat behind her. "Does she always take off her clothes in front of you?" he asked with a catch in his voice.

"*Ja*, she does," Hans said, his tone laced with humor. "At least now she is turning her back. Derek has his hands full, yes?"

She deliberately faced them and placed her hands on her hips. "I'm still in the room, guys," she snapped. She caught Kurt as he ran his gaze down her body and deliberately turned an icy glare his way before she turned her back again.

As Kurt swore, he slapped Hans on the back. "I am impressed that you are still breathing, my friend," he said, his voice choky.

"So am I."

Ignoring the two men, Elizabeth slid her arms into the sleeves of the surprisingly soft woolen top and buttoned the front.

"Remember what she did to poor Rolf?" Hans asked.

"Yes, I do," Kurt laughed. "The poor kid nearly died on the spot. 'Make me as bare as a baby,'" he mimicked.

Twenty-two is a kid? Elizabeth thought. *Rolf is older than I am.* She quickly tugged on the skirt and turned back to the men. "Stop talking about me like I'm not here," she snapped. When realization seemed to smack her in the brain at what Kurt had said, she abruptly stopped. "Hey, wait a minute! How do you know Rolf?"

Hans and Kurt grinned. "You didn't know," Kurt realized.

"That he is part of your resistance? No, I didn't."

"Now you do," Hans said with a nod.

Not caring whether she was acting like a proper young woman or not, she sat down beside her friends with her ankles crossed and sighed loudly in relief. "Thank God." No normal person could see what Rolf had seen and not be affected by it. Things weren't what they seemed. "Why didn't Derek tell me?" she found herself asking.

"If you were caught in the escape also, God only knows what Heinrich would have done to you," Hans said, his tone solemn. "It was for your protection, Elizabeth, and for Rolf's. While I am thinking of it, if I had not known Derek before all this started, you would not know my true last name. Or Kurt's. We know far too much about each other as it is."

A sick shudder rushed through her marrow at his words. They all aware of what happened to resistance members who were captured. They were beaten and tortured until they either gave out the names of other members or gave in to their own deaths, although by some miracle some of them survived. She wasn't a member at the time she was in the camp, but Heinrich wouldn't have cared. He would have harmed her for nothing more than being the woman Derek loved.

"Speaking of innocent," Kurt said. "Why were you at the camp, Elizabeth?"

Her heart constricted at the memory of Wil and the SS coming to arrest her along with Zarah. She had seen the panic surface in her friend and a terror she had never known had flushed through her; not to mention the guilt of having told Wil where Zarah was located. It was something she would have to live with for the rest of her life, no matter how long that would be. The only positive thing was that she had met and fallen in love with Derek. Maybe one day, she would be able to find her friend as well. She just prayed that Zarah was alive and would survive her captivity.

"I was hiding my friend, Zarah," she explained. "I made the mistake of telling her boyfriend, Wilhelm, that I was doing so, not knowing he was Gestapo." She took a deep breath. "We were taken away early the next morning."

Kurt crinkled his eyebrows, his green eyes flashing with unknown emotions. "Zarah?" he asked in surprise.

"Yes," Elizabeth said, confused by his reaction. "Why do you ask?"

A hard mask crossed his face. "What last name did she give you?" he asked.

"Her last name is Levy." When realization dawned about what Kurt had actually said, her heart took a heavy nosedive. "What do you mean by what last name did she *give* me?"

Kurt and Hans took a glance at each other and both released a long whistle. Something was going on and Hans hadn't said a word to her. Apparently, this information was no surprise to him.

Kurt swore as Hans cringed. "I'm so sorry, Elizabeth," Hans apologized. "I just didn't make the connection."

"Okay, guys," Elizabeth drawled at their exchange. "What's the scoop?"

"Your arrest was a setup, Elizabeth," a solemn Kurt explained. "The woman you knew as Zarah is Gestapo and Wilhelm is one of her many lovers."

Shock raced through the core of her system, her heart seeming to have stopped beating. She couldn't have been more stunned to find out that her time with Derek had been a mere dream. "No!" She traded another glance with the two stolid men and swallowed hard to keep from bursting into tears. "How do you know this woman you're talking about is the same Zarah?" she asked hopefully. *They have to be mistaken. Zarah isn't that uncommon a name.* "That first name isn't that uncommon. What did I say to you to make you ask me what her last name was?"

Kurt pulled his satchel onto his lap and opened the clasp. "Something clicked in my mind when you told me your friend's name was Zarah," he said. "Here's why." He extracted a manila envelope from it and handed it to her.

Numb, she opened the envelope and pulled out several sheets of paper. Each communiqué came with a summary and a photograph in the top left hand corner. The first was of her friend Zarah Levy, although the name showed Louisa Zelig instead.

The photograph showed her above the waist, wearing a dark-colored outfit, but Elizabeth couldn't tell from the picture what the color of her eyes or her hair was. The information given indicated that her hair was dark-blonde, her eyes a dark blue and that she had a fair complexion. There were two official seals, one near the top and the other on the bottom. The physical statistics were correct, but the information before proved Zarah's, or she should say Louisa's, treachery. Tears rushed into her eyes when she realized without a doubt that this was the same woman she believed she knew. She had been surprised that Zarah didn't practice her religious beliefs, but she had disregarded that fact.

"But she's a Jew," she exclaimed in quiet disbelief, her voice strained as if she had a touch of laryngitis. How was that possible? Her friend had offered memories of her childhood and her beliefs. She glanced over at Hans, who so far hadn't said a word. Tears burned in her eyes at the sympathy that lit his. She looked back at Kurt. "But how?"

"She may have portrayed herself as a Jew with a few carefully placed memories and beliefs," Kurt explained. "But she isn't. She is the typical Aryan with Aryan attitudes. A cold, calculated, first-degree bitch. She is very good at what she does. She will do anything to accomplish her goal, including using someone on a personal level to gain information and to see if a person is loyal to the Reich."

"Why me?" Elizabeth asked herself out loud, her voice still choky. "What did I ever do to her?" The harsh, cold reality of the situation lit into her and it was as if someone were stabbing her heart. She had been betrayed in the worst way possible and she would never forget the anguish she was feeling at that moment. All guilt about what had happened fled from her. If Zarah/Louisa had been there, she had no doubt that she would have taken her life. She turned her teary-eyed gaze to Hans, her bottom lip quivering as the tears began streaming down her cheeks. "Hold me, Hans," she said quietly. "Please?" A wail bubbled in her throat and she gulped to hold it back.

Without hesitation, he pulled her into his arms and she slid hers around his shoulders to squeeze him to her. He laced his fingers through her hair, urging her to rest her head on his shoulder. When her quiet tears became audible sobs, he rested his chin on the top of her head and began to gently rub her back with his free hand. "Go ahead and cry, my friend," he urged. At his words, he began to rock her as if she were a child he was urging to sleep.

"I wish Derek were here," she cried softly, her heart and body heavy with emotional anguish. "I miss him so much." Her body ached to have his arms around her again and if he died because of her selfishness or any other reason, she would never forgive herself. Her mind went back to when he had told her of how he came to be *assigned* to the camp and that he didn't believe he deserved her. *If anything, Derek, I don't deserve you.*

"I know," Hans said into her hair.

"What would I do without you, Hans?" she asked as she wiped the tears from her cheeks. "You've been a real friend." She hardened her heart against the woman she had believed was her friend. Now she understood why it had been so easy for Zarah to keep from being arrested. Elizabeth had assumed that she had just slipped through the cracks, but everything she believed she knew about the woman was a lie. Louisa Zelig had known exactly what she was doing. All the signs were there, but Elizabeth had never caught on. There was no doubt about it now. "How could I have been so blind, Hans?" she asked as the weight of guilt shrouded her once again.

"Don't torment yourself, Elizabeth," he said gently. "You believed in her and thought you were doing the best thing for her. No one can blame you for that."

It wasn't until Kurt came into the room that Elizabeth realized he had been gone. "The contact is here, Hans," he said. "He will only speak to you."

When Hans slid away from her, her body instantly cooled. "*Einer Moment,* Elizabeth," he said. A moment later, he was gone.

Elizabeth wiped the tears from her cheeks and gave Kurt a shaky smile. She forced her mind away from the betrayal that was crushing her heart. "How are you able to keep anyone from looking through your satchel?" she asked lightly.

Kurt raised a blonde eyebrow and chuckled. "Would you question an SS officer and demand to look through his satchel?" he asked, the tone teasing.

"Hell, no," she replied, the idea of questioning such a person unimaginable. "I may as well walk up to one and hand him a gun, saying, 'Go ahead. Shoot me now.'"

He chuckled again, winking. "I thought you would see it my way," he teased.

Elizabeth couldn't help but chuckle as she teasingly popped him on his shoulder with her fist. "All right," she prompted, feeling more cheerful since she had made a new friend in the process of this trauma. "Since I'm supposed to be involved in this, show me the other summaries."

Kurt slid Zarah's summary under the others and handed the stack to Elizabeth. She took a glance at the first, immediately recognizing the blonde Wilhelm. He had started out in the Jügend-Korps and had eventually become an agent of the Gestapo. Another showed a woman named Dagmar Lambrecht, naturally a blonde, who looked to be a cold-hearted bitch. Elizabeth thought the woman would be striking if she weren't so mean–looking, with such a hard expression in her eyes. The summary also showed that Louisa was one of Dagmar's lovers, along with another named Adrienne Martin, who was supposedly an agent for the Americans.

"Typical Aryan, you said?" Elizabeth smirked at the hypocrisy. Not only Louisa, but Dagmar as well.

Kurt chuckled, shrugging. "The women's only vice," he said as if explaining. "Neither makes a habit of female lovers and since they are so active in the cause, it is possible their relationship is overlooked. In any event, such a thing is not uncommon to gain information from another. They will resort to any measure, as you can see."

Elizabeth shuddered. "I didn't realize women actually did that kind of thing with each other," she found herself saying. "I mean, it's rather risky, considering the regime they belong to."

Kurt withheld a smile. "It does happen," he said. "In Louisa and Dagmar's cases, they are willing to do anything and everything to get the information they want, including taking another woman to bed. They are calculated and systematic beyond obsession. They are not to be trusted and will stab you in the back without a thought, as you have found out the hard way."

Another shudder rushed over Elizabeth's skin as her eyes burned with anger. She would never be so stupid as to fall back into that type of trap again. "God, I hope I never see the bitch again," she swore.

"There's always the chance, Elizabeth," he said solemnly. "I wish I could tell you otherwise."

She breathed a shaky sigh. "I know," she said softly.

Kurt breathed a sigh as well. "Now, with that finished, I have a little present for you," he said.

"Oh, goody," she said drily. *Geez, what now?*

"It's not bad," Kurt said with a chuckle. He snatched a thick envelope from the satchel and handed it to her.

Inside were various identification papers, with her fictitious identification being Elisabeth Killes, which made it easy to remember. The German derivative of her first name was one she liked, plus it was so close to her real pronunciation. Along with that was a dark-olive armband with the numbers 39/7 sewn into it, the same armband Hans and other resistants in the group wore.

Hans had only recently told her the full story. He had been ordered to leave his job because of his wife's religious beliefs and had he refused to do so, he would have been charged with race defiling. *How difficult it must be for them to be separated from each other.* She didn't know whether she could handle it if she were separated from Derek for such a long time. It was bad enough being separated for just a little more than a month. "So what happens now?" she asked.

Kurt sighed. "Hans and I will continue to train you," he said. "Then we will go from there."

A nervous shudder rushed through her, but she smiled. "So, I'm in?" she asked.

"Congratulations," he said happily. "You are now an official member of our friendly little resistance."

Chapter Thirty-Three

ELIZABETH'S TRAINING HAD BEEN GOING WELL and her shooting had greatly improved, but she nearly panicked when Kurt came upon them again in his uniform. Ever since she had found out that Zarah/Louisa was Gestapo, she had been continually on edge, as if an invisible monster were stalking her. Maybe it had been a mistake to tell her.

"Elizabeth, we need to desensitize you from jumping like you are a scared rabbit every time you see someone in any type of SS or even non-SS German uniform," Hans told her.

Elizabeth snorted. "It was only a couple of times," she pointed out. "Besides, with all that noise you made the first time, I'm surprised he didn't see you. How was I to know that you already knew Kurt?"

"Kurt isn't SS, Elizabeth," he reminded her with a smirk. "If he was, he certainly wouldn't have been alone when he came upon you."

She childishly stomped her foot and glared at him. "But I didn't know that!" she insisted.

Hans raised a brown eyebrow. "Do you believe I would be so absentminded as to step on a stick when I was trying to keep from being heard while a so-called *Leibstandarte SS* officer was standing right there?" he challenged her. "And didn't you think he was rather young for that type?"

His words brought Elizabeth up short. "Hey …" she protested as the incident popped into her mind. She had been standing, stunned, while she had seen their friend in that damned uniform. She had heard Hans as he had come up behind them. He wouldn't make a mistake like that. Sometimes his silence was ghostly. She quickly turned to face him. "I knew it!"

Hans burst out laughing and backed away from her, his hands up and out in a gesture of surrender. "You should have seen the look on your face, Elizabeth," he said with the laughter heavy in his voice.

Elizabeth gnashed her teeth. "Damn you!" she growled.

Hans chuckled harder at her reaction and when his laughter finally died down, he slid an arm around her shoulders. "Let us go catch up with Kurt," he said. "He is waiting on us."

Elizabeth breathed a heavy sigh to force herself to relax. She really had to stop letting her friend tease her into a rage. He wasn't being cruel. He was just being a friend, or at the very worst, an *ornery* big brother. "All right," she agreed.

They walked out of the barn and were about to round the corner when someone dressed in a black uniform nearly ran into them. As soon as Elizabeth noticed the armband with the swastika, a screaming squeal leapt from her diaphragm. When she realized the visitor was Kurt, she realized they had gotten her again.

As the men burst into uncontrollable laughter, Elizabeth's stunned heart shot off into cannon fire and she couldn't hold the tears of humiliation in her eyes. "This is not funny, damn you guys!" she found herself snapping. She was more infuriated at herself than at them for tricking her again, imagining that this would be like having *two* brothers who continually pestered her. The men sobered and exaggerated a pout at each other. It was Kurt's turn to slide his arm around her shoulders. "Do you see why we have to practice this, Elizabeth?" he asked, his tone sober.

"If we do by any chance run into a real SS man or anyone in uniform, and we will, you have to be prepared," Hans warned. "Do you understand how important this is?"

Elizabeth sighed, admitting to herself that they were right. "Yes," she begrudgingly admitted aloud, although it was the last thing she wanted to do.

"I know it's partly my fault," Hans shrugged. "I should have helped you over this sooner."

She found herself smiling. He did not have to take part the blame, but she was glad he did. "Thank you, Hans," she said. "You're a good friend."

Her friend winked. "Don't mention it," he said.

After that, she made a conscious effort to be alert. She didn't know when or where Kurt would put on the uniform and it took several attempts before she kept from being stunned. She was still cautious, but she didn't allow her feelings to show. She hated the fact that she had to watch her back at all times, but it was their key to survival.

Chapter Thirty-Four

EREK'S NERVES BURNED WITH AWARENESS AS Heinrich's guards continued to watch him eat one of the three meals a day the colonel made sure he was given. Heinrich wanted him healthy enough to prolong the abuse administered and force him to do his bidding, which usually came in some form of menial or degrading labor. He had long since been separated from the others during mealtimes, so he wasn't aware of how much or what they were given. He unintentionally took a quick glance at Übel as the guard raised an eyebrow and turned the corners of his lips into a derisive smirk.

"Has something gotten your attention, traitor?" the guard snorted.

Derek ignored him and continued to eat his roll. He usually ate quickly because he was given a time limit on his meals. If he weren't finished within the regulated amount of time, a guard would snatch away the plate.

"You think that because you are ignoring me, I will ignore you?" Übel continued.

"I think not, traitor," Erich answered for him with a chuckle in his voice.

Derek continued to ignore both of them, but when both men burst out laughing at his silence, he wanted to do nothing but pound the pricks into the floor.

"I would say he does not ignore his American whore too often," Übel continued. "What would you say, Erich?"

Erich chuckled. "I would say that," he answered cheerfully.

Derek took a gulp of his water and then set the tin cup back down onto the decrepit wooden table.

"No answer again, your lordship," Übel snorted. "See? Even Erich agrees. That hot little wench is no doubt the sensual piece of ass. That is true, yes?"

Derek paused, forcing down the rage that burned through him. He reminded himself that their taunts only had one purpose, which was to provoke an angry response. He wanted to refuse to satisfy them, but the chance was becoming slimmer each minute.

"I have heard you took her in a guard tower a couple of months ago. Such a passionate slut she is. Enjoyed the ride you gave her, yes?"

His eyes burned with anger at Übel's description and he clenched his free hand into a momentary fist. The rumor had no truth to it, but it didn't matter at this point. The clunk of the guard's jackboots sounded on the wooden floor as he stepped toward Derek.

"No answer?" Übel snorted.

Derek ignored him and resumed his assault on his cold potatoes. They tasted like he assumed soft, wet chalk would and he forced himself from to keep from spitting them into the younger man's face. His body burned with the urge to do so.

"Such luscious tits she has. Eh, von Vetter? That was clear when she was first brought here. The rest of her body seemed just as fuckable. Did you enjoy fucking her, my lord?"

He sat back in his chair, unable to mask the hostility that soared through every nerve in his body. He caught the rare smirk on Heinrich's face as he stood back and watched. It was obvious that he enjoyed this little scene as much as Übel enjoyed taunting him. He watched to see what kind of reaction Derek would give, but he wouldn't give the colonel any more satisfaction. He had already showed too much of a reaction.

"I would say she no doubt howls in pleasure each time you thrust that stiff *Shwanz* deep inside that tight pussy of hers," Erich taunted. "Is she tight, my lord? I would bet much to say she is."

Derek gritted his teeth and resumed his meal. The unmistakable sound of someone walking around him, the soles of his boots clunking against the hard floor, was the only thing he heard. The other guards stood by and watched, so silent one wouldn't have realized that they were there. Assuming his mealtime was about over, he started inhaling the rest of his food before one of them took away the plate. He had stopped tasting it a while ago.

Before he could finish, Übel slammed his arm over the table and knocked the plate with the remaining food onto the floor. "Clean up the mess you made, you fucking slug!" he bellowed. "Lap it up like you are tonguing your whore's cunt!"

Rage soared through Derek's being as he shot to his feet, slamming the chair to the floor in the process. *"Clean it up your fucking self!"* he shouted in English. He could no longer allow them to degrade Elizabeth in this way. Before he could stop himself, he leaped onto the guard. The force of the contact hurled both men onto the hard floor. He slammed his fist into the sergeant's jaw, but the other guards yanked him off before he could get in another hit.

Someone slammed him onto his back, knocking the breath from his lungs. The guards piled onto him as if they were a pack of dogs going in for the kill and then someone rammed his fist into his abdomen. He attempted to curl up when another guard slammed a fist between his legs, forcing out a groan of pain. Fire burned through him at that last connection, but before he could attempt another breath, someone's foot connected near his right kidney. He arched his back in an attempt to lessen the pain, but it wasn't meant to be and a hard cry leaped from within him. Someone got the last slam into his face and his nose immediately seemed to swell to double its size. When the guards moved away from him, he prayed that that was the last of it.

Unfortunately, everyone seemed to hit him at once, but this time they used the sides of their jackboots instead of their fists. One solid kick after another seemed to rail into his body until he was sure every bone had been broken. The physical afflictions were far worse than any of the aches that had pained him during his previous hard labor. It seemed as if several hands squeezed his insides into a tight bundle and how he managed to hold down the food he had eaten was beyond his comprehension. All of a sudden, everyone stopped and moved away from him.

Laughter came from a distance, as if he were living a dream. "Now do what I fucking tell you to do next time, you fucking traitor!" Übel shouted. At the words, someone lifted him from the floor.

The cold blew inside the room when someone opened a door. The next thing Derek knew, he slammed down onto the pavement. The impact knocked the breath from his lungs and his muscles screamed in protest. He wanted to force himself to his feet, but his body refused to cooperate. As the chilling rain poured down onto his battered body, his mind slipped into oblivion.

Chapter Thirty-Five

HE RAIN CAME DOWN UPON ROLF's slickered shoulders as he strolled over the grounds. It was so damned cold that his fingers seemed frozen to the barrel of his rifle. If it hadn't been for the strap slung over his shoulder, he wouldn't have been able to hold on to it.

Up ahead, someone lay facedown on the pavement and he made his way over to him. Two guards deep in conversation strolled up to the person and stepped over him without looking at him. It wrenched his insides that any human being could treat others as if they had no more importance than a stray mutt. Even the dogs on the compound were treated better than the captives.

As the figure began to look familiar, Rolf quickly forgot the cold and sped up his pace. When he discovered that this victim was Derek, fury soared through him and chilled him to the marrow of his bones. He released a blasphemous curse as he knelt down beside the man he considered his best friend.

Derek was the only commanding officer he had had who had treated him as an equal instead of an insignificant subordinate. If he had had a choice in whether or not he had an older brother, he would have hoped that he would be like Derek.

"Derek," he said gently, although inside the rage of his emotions even scared himself. "Who did this to you?" *My guess is Übel and Erich.* If someone had asked him to describe what he was feeling, he wouldn't have been able to give the person an explanation.

His friend's right eye was swollen shut and blood was caught where his bottom lip was split. Since he seemed to have no inclination to move,

Rolf hated to think about how severe his other injuries were. It went without saying that he would do everything possible to aid his friend back to health.

Derek's lips had a slight blue cast, but Rolf doubted his friend even had the energy to shiver from the wet and cold. "U … Übel … Erich," Derek forced out, slowly forming the words. "And Heinrich's guards.

Rolf bent down and slid an arm behind his friend's back. He knew he should check for injuries before moving him, but his first priority was to get him out of the harsh elements. "I will help you, Derek," he said in attempt to reassure him, although he inwardly prayed that he didn't hurt him more. "I am sorry in advance if I pain you."

Derek attempted a smile, but it came out as a smirk. „*Danke*," he whispered.

With a nod of acknowledgment, Rolf helped him to his feet and placed Derek's arm around his shoulders. "Hold on to me," he urged. "I will take you to your barracks and warm you."

Brutal shivers wracked Derek's body and he released a low moan. "Shit, I hurt," he said unnecessarily. "This sucks. I don't like it." He attempted to laugh, but it came out sounding as sluggish as his speech.

Unsure about how to answer, Rolf slowly started to walk. Supporting Derek was like carrying dead weight and his back ached as they took their steps. Not only did his friend have very little energy, but he was the larger of the two men, both in weight and bone structure. Thankfully, the distance to the barracks wasn't much farther.

Once there, Rolf led him up the short flight of stairs and opened the door to urge him inside. He breathed a sigh of relief when he realized that the barracks was empty of other people. He had to help his friend before the others came back from their day's work. As he laid him at the end of the bunk and stretched out his legs, Derek released a slow groan of protest.

Rolf knew the bed wasn't at all comfortable, since he had lain down with Katrine after Übel and Erich raped her. After he had seen the nearly hysterical condition she was in and understood the reason why, he had wanted to gun down both guards. Only her pleas for his safety had kept him from continuing. She wouldn't have been able to handle it if he had been killed.

He slid his rifle off his shoulder and laid it down on the floor. A moment later, he pulled his helmet and slicker over his head and laid them next to his rifle. He slid off his overcoat and laid it on top of his friend to warm him.

An unexpected grin curved Derek's lips, although his body continued to rack with shivers. "I am so fucking cold. I hurt so bad I don't know if I'll be able to move tomorrow," he said, his voice still a sluggish whisper. "I know this will sound crazy, but when I get out of here I'm going to America and taking Elizabeth with me. Then we're going to have too many kids."

That made Rolf smile, although his heart went out to his friend. "That sounds good, Derek," he agreed. "I may do so also and take Katrine. I believe she will like that."

Derek raised an eyebrow. "Are you in love with her?" he asked.

Rolf flushed, seeing no point in hiding his feelings. *Yeah, like we aren't obvious anyway,* he thought with an inward grin. "Yes," he admitted. "I am in love with her."

"Good for you."

Rolf knew Übel and Erich enough to suspect that their missing Derek's vital organs was intentional. If they had wanted to permanently damage him, they would have. "If you feel any worse, let me know," he said. "I will try to sneak you in for an X-ray. For now, I will get something for your eye."

At his second comment, Derek crinkled his eyebrows as if he were confused by it. "I do not remember anyone hitting me in my eye," he said as if telling himself.

"At first glance, I had thought it was swollen shut, but it is somewhat puffy. You may have only gotten something in it."

"Besides Übel's fist?" came the sarcastic reply.

Rolf's jaw dropped at the quip, but a heartbeat later he couldn't help but laugh. "That may be," he said. It was good to see such a positive reaction. Übel and the others may have attempted to break Derek's body, but they hadn't broken his spirit or his sense of humor. He rose to his feet. "I will get some water for your eye to take down the swelling."

He moved to the toilets and luckily, they were temporarily clean, along with the water. Who knew how long that would last? He tugged the hem of his shirt from his slacks and ripped the material so he could have something clean to press against Derek's eye. After wetting the cloth, he walked back to his friend. "Here is some wet material," he explained. He didn't miss the brief grimace that passed over Derek's face. "I promise it is clean. This time."

"I'll take your word for it."

Rolf laid the material over his friend's eye and helped him place his hand over it. "Tell me what happened," he urged.

"They beat the shit out of me."

"How did it start?"

"They keep feeding me, Rolf," he stated in response, his voice flat. "I have only a certain amount of time to eat it and if I don't finish within that time frame, they snatch away the plate."

Rolf had seen similar abuse as this before. The guards would give food, but sometimes they would deliberately toss it onto the floor. The captives were so starved, they would scramble for it. The dehumanizing scenes stayed in his mind, causing him to have ongoing nightmares. He assumed he would always have them. "Is that what happened?" he asked.

"No," Derek continued, his voice cracking with emotion. "They were taunting me about Elizabeth and degrading her in ways I could not fathom. Übel knocked my plate off the table onto the floor and then demanded I clean it up. After he made a very crude analogy, which I won't go into, I lost it. I leaped at him and started slugging him. The next thing I knew, the others were dog piling me. After slamming me simultaneously with their fists, they moved away. I thought they were finished, but unfortunately they started kicking me. I finally curled up in a ball, but only after they had tossed me outside into the cold and rain."

Rolf shook his head, his eyes burning as his anger returned. Übel had no doubt wanted a fight to begin with and Derek had given him one. He probably would have fought back himself in spite of that. "I don't blame you for fighting back," he commented.

Emotional pain passed over Derek's face and he took away his hand. "I am sure Übel wanted me to. It gave him the excuse he has been looking for since Heinrich took charge. At least there was no one else he could make suffer along with me."

"Yes, that's true." Rolf rose to his feet. He had to return to his duties or else the others would realize he was helping his friend. If they found out what he was doing, there would be no one to save Derek. "Roll call has been canceled for tonight," he lied. "That will give you time to recover some strength. I must return to my duties before they realize what has been happening."

Derek handed him back his coat and snatched a thin blanket off the floor, cringing at his slow movements. "Thank you for helping me, Rolf, even though you do not have to."

Guilt sliced through him once again, but he had no doubt he would give his life to help his friend if it came to that.

"I do have to," Rolf responded, standing up to slide his arms into the sleeves of the overcoat. "I must." After pulling the slicker back over his head and sliding on his helmet, he bent to snatch the rifle off the floor and sling the strap back over his shoulder.

"Thanks again, Rolf," came the worn-out reply.

Rolf nodded in response. "I will check on you later," he promised. Before he got to the door, the deep and even keel of Derek's breathing indicated that he had fallen asleep.

Rolf left the barracks, his emotions numb from what Derek had told him. There was no doubt in his mind that the colonel wanted Derek to suffer, not to kill him outright. His friend's explanation and condition showed this to be true. He had to stuff his fear inside or else he would never confront Heinrich. He was so enraged at this point that he felt nothing. Even though what he planned would accomplish about as much, he stalked across the compound and toward the acting *Kommandant's* office to confront him.

The first person he ran into when he slammed into the outer office was Corporal Anton Schönberg, the colonel's personal assistant. Beneath crinkled reddish-brown eyebrows, his dark-blue eyes flashed with annoyance at the intrusion. Even the hazel uniform was severe, just as rigid as the person who wore it. "May I help you?" he asked, his voice equally whiny and snobbish.

Snobby little worm. „Nein," Rolf sneered. "I am just going to have a chat with *Herr Kommandant.* Do not concern yourself."

The younger man stepped in his way and raised a hand at him.

„*Nein*," he said, though an unsure light entered his eyes. "You cannot go in."

"Get the fuck out of my way," Rolf snapped. He knocked away the secretary's hand and whizzed past him through the door.

„*Nein*," Anton repeated as he came through the door after him.

Heinrich glanced up from the paper he was signing and raised an eyebrow, smirking. The guards stood by and watched, no expression on their faces or in their eyes. The colonel briefly turned his attention to his assistant and raised an eyebrow.

"I could not stop him, sir," Anton said.

"Dismissed," Heinrich ordered. As the secretary left the room, the colonel turned his gaze to him and curved his lips into a sneer. "Is there a problem, corporal?"

Rolf's eyes burned with rage and he saw nothing but the colonel and what the monster had done to Derek. "*Psycho bastard!*" he shouted in English. Before he could stop himself, he leaped across the desktop. He seized two handfuls of Heinrich's uniform, ready to slam him to the ground and put his fist into his jaw. Paperwork slid from the desk along with the half-filled cup of black coffee. Someone yanked Rolf off Heinrich and slammed him back against the wall. The next thing he knew, the muzzles of two rifles were pointed at his heart. He caught the cold glares Heinrich's personal guards Konrad and Bernard sent him, but the rage was still too great in him to be intimidated.

The colonel shot to his feet and leaned on his fists on the desktop. "If you do not wish what happened to von Vetter to happen to you, you will shut your *fucking* mouth and return to your duties!" he shouted in English, an unknown light flashing in his pale-blue eyes as he glared back at Rolf. "*Now!*"

Without acknowledging his superior officer's order, Rolf turned and slammed out of the office.

Once he had gone, Heinrich turned to his guards and the three men simultaneously burst out laughing. When the laughter died down, Karl raised an eyebrow at the others. "It seems our unflappable guard has quite the temper," he said, more amused at Rolf's outburst than angry. "Watch him."

Chapter Thirty-Six

A FEW DAYS AFTER THE BEATING THE changes began. Derek's muscles still protested when he moved, but he suspected that that would be over soon. Most surprising was the fact that he hadn't come down with any form of sickness after being out in the cold and rain. He assumed that was because he was still relatively healthy. He had a meal every day and seemed to get enough sleep, even with the tedious, nightly roll calls.

Unfortunately, his food portions were becoming smaller with each passing day. The change was gradual, but it was noticeable enough to where he had become suspicious. Of course the guards, especially Übel, insisted he was losing his mind and that even if he weren't, he did not deserve the portions he had been given. They did not taunt him about Elizabeth, but they were far from silent. Their comments had no purpose except to degrade and humiliate him, but he would not give them the satisfaction of allowing them to bring him down again.

They continually reminded him that deviance such as his in society would not be tolerated and that those who did not conform to the new ways would pay for their mindlessness. He was also informed that his humane treatment of the Jews as well as the other captives was unacceptable at the least. He never understood why those of the Jewish faith were persecuted as they have been since the beginning of time. They were no different from anyone else who just wanted to live and be happy.

All that had been happening in this part of the world was due to one man who was power-hungry, evil and so full of hate that he could never find his way out of it. It also amazed Derek that so many others had disregarded their consciences and their souls to follow him. How could those who called themselves human beings ever be so blind? People were put into concentration camps for any excuse that the Nazis could find and many times they did not need a reason.

Anyone who spoke out was treated as a criminal and many who had resisted had lost their lives as a result. The Nazis controlled with fear and viciousness, forcing anyone who might dissent into submission and to live under the control of a dictatorship; all for a madman who made himself a self-proclaimed "god" whose goal was apparently to control the world and wipe out anyone who did not fit into his twisted ideology.

These were the reasons he had to continue with his documentation. The world had to know what had been going on here and he would see to it if it were the last thing he did on this earth. He had been silent long enough.

Chapter Thirty-Seven

HEN ELIZABETH HAD BEEN TO ROTHENBURG before, it had been so beautiful with the many buildings cutting into the small hills. The city was built within a medieval wall that dated back to the end of the twelfth century. Now many of the buildings had been reduced to rubble as a result of the shelling, but amazingly most of them remained intact. Her nose twitched at the dust remnants that floated through the air and she did not know how long it would be before the dust dissipated.

German soldiers had been stationed there, but they had surrendered after the bombings and the city was now in Allied hands. That gave her hope that they would be able to rescue Derek, Sabrina and Miriam.

They were to meet with their next contact at St. Wolfgangs Church, which dated from the late 1400s, with its high, Gothic ceilings and vaulted chambers. When Elizabeth first walked into the sanctuary, the sight took her breath away. It had been years since she had been in a church and tears filled her eyes at the peace that flowed through her.

There was only one other person there besides her and Hans, a woman with short, tawny hair, who was kneeling in the right, front pew, directly in front of the St. Wendelin's altar. Her black shirt and slacks fit well on her slender frame, cupping her gentle hips and small breasts. When she turned her attention over her shoulder and to them, her soft, gray eyes sparkled in recognition as her gaze went directly to Hans.

Elizabeth raised an eyebrow in understanding as the woman and Hans exchanged intimate glances. Obviously, this was Adrienne Martin. When Hans realized she had caught their looks, he flashed her an obnoxious grin and wink. She again raised an eyebrow and gave him a soft smile. *Maybe you two shouldn't be sharing such lusty looks in a nearly five-hundred-year-old church.* Although it was clear something had gone on between them in the past, it certainly wasn't her business.

Hans cleared his throat. "Adrienne, this is Elizabeth. Elizabeth, Adrienne," he said in a half-hearted introduction. "I promised Kurt I would catch up with him when you two met. We will meet you at the *rathaus* once you have had a chance to talk."

Elizabeth smiled at him. "Thanks," she said.

With a friendly wink, he turned and made his way back down the aisle.

Adrienne rose to her feet and made her way out of the pew. She held out her hand. "I'm glad to finally meet you, Elizabeth," she said warmly.

Elizabeth shook her hand in return. "Hi, Adrienne," she said, almost unsure of how to react.

A look of confusion came over her face as if she weren't sure what to tell her before it softened. "I was at the camp a few weeks ago," she said, her voice solemn.

Elizabeth's heart constricted in anticipation and it was all she could do not to burst into tears. "Please, Adrienne," she asked softly. "I must know if Derek is alive."

The other woman gave her a gentle smile. "He's alive and he seems healthy," she said. "He misses you. I promised him I would tell you that."

Elizabeth released her tears, but this time they were tears of happiness. God, she couldn't believe she had at last heard about him and that he was well, in spite of being held as a captive. "Thank God," she said with a deep sigh of relief. Her heart was leaping with joy, but unfortunately it was short-lived.

"Even though he's okay right now, you must know that that could change at any time."

Elizabeth's heart sank to her toes at Adrienne's words, although part of her had already assumed this. "I hate to give you the worst-case scenario, but you must be aware of what could happen."

Elizabeth nodded. "Did you tell him you were going to meet with us?" she asked hopefully.

Adrienne gave her a broken-down version of what had happened, relating what Derek had told her. "You have a wonderful man there, Elizabeth," she said with a small grin.

Elizabeth couldn't help but chuckle in agreement, not realizing that the other woman had withheld information of their sensual play-acting. "He is," she agreed. She sobered as tears sprang to her eyes. "I just pray to God that he'll still be alive when we get there. If there is any mercy left in this world at all, he will be." Before she had realized it, they were exchanging a friendly hug.

Adrienne pulled away and gave her an empathic smile. "Praying is all we can do, Elizabeth," she said, reminding her of similar words Talia had spoken.

Elizabeth released a sigh, her heart heavy. "Now …" she said with another sigh. "Let's go find the men before they think we've been captured." She laughed. "And before I become a basket case."

After catching up with Hans and Kurt at the *rathaus,* the four made their way out of the old town and to the smaller town nearby in order for Adrienne to meet with one of her people. When she returned nearly an hour later, she had disappointing news. "I have found that Sabrina and her companion are no longer here, since the bombings forced them out of their hideaway," she said. "They had to leave for their safety."

Tears burned behind Elizabeth's eyes "Do you know where they have gone?" she found herself asking.

Adrienne shook her head. "No," she said. "I'm sorry. As you probably know, the word is out that you are looking for them. But unfortunately, our contact is not always able to meet us for various reasons. I promise you that we will do our best to find them, Elizabeth. When that happens, I promise we will let you know."

Chapter Thirty-Eight

THE COOLNESS OF MARCH HAD CHANGED into a warmer April and the number of daylight hours was increasing. Derek's food had been cut down to one meager meal a day, if he was lucky, and his camp clothing was becoming looser. He was fully aware that he was losing weight, but he had no idea of the extent of it, since all the captives were becoming thinner.

He did not notice the gaunt cheeks or the darkening, hollowed eyes of the others. He did not notice when others became ill with sickness and depression, since everyone was in their own private hell. He no longer noticed the chill in the air or the rain as it fell on him and his friends. Even the gravel pit seemed a distant memory and he often wondered if he had imagined it all.

He wondered how Sabrina and Miriam were and whether they were free from the worry of capture. He was certain that Hans and Elizabeth would have rescued them by now. His beloved Elizabeth with the glorious red hair that fell to her waist in flowing waves. He remembered her coming to him after she had had Rolf shave off her tresses. He imagined her belly swollen, as if his child were growing inside her. He still intended to make her his wife if he lived through this purgatory, but he would give up if anything caused her to lose her life. As it was, he merely existed. If Heinrich and his cronies had their way, he would be dead as well. He believed they only let him live now because they took sadistic pleasure in watching him suffer.

As he heard had happened at Dachau, he was now being forced along with several others to build a new crematorium, since so many people had already been put to death. It seemed impossible that everything had happened in so little time, but it had. A wail of anguish sounded in the distance and it was several moments before he realized that it was coming from deep within him. His body burned with the desire to curl up into a ball and let his misery take over his mind. The haunting smell of human ash had emblazoned itself on his soul. He was sure it would linger for years to come.

"Don't do it, Derek," someone said in the back of his mind. "Don't let them do this to you."

He turned to the voice and recognized Sam Benjamin. His friend had lost as much weight as he had, but there was a bright flicker of determination in his eyes. "I'm so goddamned sick of this shit, Sam," he said, his voice filled with the emotions of rage and despair. Tears burned down his cheeks and distorted his image, but he was beyond caring. "Who the fuck do those bastards think they are? What did any of these people do to them? They have done nothing, absolutely nothing."

Sam crinkled his eyebrows, although he nodded in agreement. "I know, Derek, but you have to fight this," he insisted. "This is what they want you to do. If they see you break, they will have succeeded in what they have been trying to accomplish and then they will kill you."

"I know that," Derek admitted, although his insides constricted with horror at the words. "But knowing cannot stop my feelings."

"I know," Sam agreed with a humorless smile. "But you need to control your emotions instead of letting them control you. You are a survivor, Derek. You have managed this far and will do so long past the end. I'm not going to lie to you."

Derek's friend said it with such conviction that a smile tugged at the corners of his lips. "You are one tough son of a bitch, Sam," he teased.

His friend burst out laughing. "That's it," he said with the laughter heavy in his voice. "That sense of humor will do wonders. Now get back to work before Übel starts throwing around his weight. I'm surprised he hasn't heard us as it is."

Derek did not bother holding back his laughter a few moments later when Sam chuckled out a repeat of his words, "You are one tough son of a bitch."

Throughout the day, the other men continued to give Derek their support. He knew they had to do so covertly, since they weren't allowed to speak or even acknowledge one another's presence unless it directly pertained to their task. When the others traded a piece of equipment, they took an extra second to grasp his hand in a gesture of support.

Derek had long ago been accepted, but it was reassuring to be reminded of that fact. He had treated them to the best of his ability under the circumstances and they realized that by his doing so, he was forced into giving up the position of *Kommandant* and becoming one of them. He had no doubt that if he were given the chance to do everything over again, he would have done exactly the same thing. He owed his people that much.

Among the captives in the small camp, there was no longer any race, religion, nationality or other difference. They shared a bond that no one else in the world could ever understand. If they survived this living hell, they could survive anything.

Chapter Thirty-Nine

ELIZABETH AWOKE FROM HER NIGHT'S SLEEP as the baby give a quick kick against the walls of her uterus. She let a smile of contentment curve her lips and gently rubbed a hand over her distended abdomen. Lord, she wished Derek were here to touch it. *I wish he were here. Period.*

In spite of the extensive traveling she and Hans had done, she seemed to be physically invigorated. Two weeks after she had realized she was pregnant, she had cried at the most insignificant of details. That, along with the worry of capture, kept threatening to turn her into a basket case. She could live with the sore feet, the blisters, the continual weather changes and having to relieve herself in places she thought she never would. But the pregnancy wreaked havoc with her hormones, on top of everything else, and it was almost more than she could take. But thankfully her crying jags had slowed for the time being. At least she felt human again.

God, she was sick to death of sleeping outside and in basements, cellars and abandoned pillboxes! But at least it was April and the trees provided cover from the elements. The night wasn't so cold either. Thankfully, Adrienne had helped supply them with bedrolls and blankets, so they were able to keep warm enough. And Hans had shown her the trick of piling up rocks around them to keep out most of the cold air, which usually helped. Just as the thoughts left her mind, a chilly breeze ruffled her hair and she buried herself deeper into the bedroll.

They were to meet again with Kurt a few kilometers away in hopes of new information about locating Sabrina von Vetter, but they wanted to get a decent night's sleep for once. Since they had been unable to locate Sabrina and Miriam in Rothenburg, they had to continue with the task of finding them. They had no definite leads so far, but they were still searching. When the baby kicked again, Elizabeth couldn't help but giggle.

"What is so funny?" Hans asked.

Elizabeth glanced over at him, seeing him with his arm across his eyes. He always seemed to be able to sleep like that, which never ceased to amaze her. If she had done that, her arm would have been numb. "I swear, Hans, this baby will come out walking. He's kicking me like crazy."

Hans removed his arm and moved to his side to raise an eyebrow at her. "How does it feel?" he asked.

Elizabeth rose on her left forearm and allowed a grin to curve her lips. "It feels like someone is kicking me from the inside," she said, half-joking

"No shit," he said with a chuckle in his voice. "I meant besides the obvious."

Elizabeth laughed. "Would you like to feel it?" she offered.

A sparkle brightened his eyes and he nodded with enthusiasm. „*Ja*," he said with another nod. He scooted over toward her and rested his warm hand on her abdomen through the layer of material. As hard as her baby kicked, he wouldn't have a problem feeling it do so. It wasn't long before the baby gave her another quick kick. As if in a trance, Hans drew away his hand. "Cool," he drawled.

Elizabeth laughed. "I'll have you talkin' Texan yet," she teased. "You have gone from High German to a southern drawl."

"I suppose this is what happens when I spend most of my time with an American Southern girl."

"Even after living half my life in Germany, I still can't rid myself of that drawl."

"You speak *Deutsche* like a native most of the time, but when you're pissed off, I can catch the accent."

She smiled, though new tears welled in her eyes. She laid on her back and breathed a deep sigh to stop them. "Derek used to tell me that," she said. "I wish he could be here. He should be able to feel what it's like to have his baby kick against his hand."

She tried to keep her mind occupied to keep from being depressed about Derek's absence, but nearly everything seemed to remind her of him. Rolf had given them no indication of his condition, which made it all the more difficult. He probably didn't want to worry her more than he had to, but part of her wondered whether his condition were so horrible that Rolf hadn't wanted to tell her. She might give up if she discovered the truth.

She didn't know what she would have done without Hans these past months. His friendship gave her the strength to endure her separation from the man she loved. "We may never know why this had to happen, Elizabeth," he said gently. "But Germany's involvement in this war is coming to end. It is closer than you may believe."

"But what if we can't find Sabrina?" she asked, her voice filled with her tears. "What if he's dead when we get back to the camp?"

"I have no doubt that Derek is still alive. He is strong and he will survive."

Elizabeth's heart constricted and more tears rushed into her eyes. "But what if he doesn't?" she asked, her voice froggy.

"That is not an option, Elizabeth," Hans answered, the determination clear in his voice. They were words she had once spoken herself, but now she wasn't so sure.

The next morning, Kurt was able to catch up with them, so they would be able to go into the next town together instead of worrying whether anything had happened to him. Elizabeth sat on her folded-up bedroll and watched as he began to shear off the length of Hans' hair. She withheld a hard groan. The locks were so silky that most women would be envious of them and now they were lying on the ground. She now understood why Derek had reacted so strongly when he had seen her shaved head. She wanted to burst into tears. "My God," she said, releasing a groan with the words.

"Now you know how Derek felt," Hans said without looking at her, his tone teasing.

"Oh, shut up," she teased in return. His answer was one of his deliberately girlish-sounding giggles. When he turned around to face her, her jaw dropped. The longer hair had given a slight prettiness to his features, but now he was every bit as handsome as Derek.

"What is it you Americans say?" Kurt teased with one eyebrow raised. "Put your tongue back in your mouth?"

Elizabeth rolled her eyes. "You guys," she said, her voice slightly whiny.

"I must look the part," Hans supplied. "An officer would not have hair that long. Sloppiness would not be tolerated. There are allowances at the front, of course, but that is beside the point."

"I wasn't questioning that, Hans. I was just …" She flushed. "Damn, you look good."

When Hans and Kurt burst out laughing, she couldn't help but glare at them as anger soared through her. *Here go the hormones again,* the sarcastic side of her thought. She rose to her feet. "And I've just about had it with you two laughing at me," she snapped.

Kurt exaggerated a pout and Hans made the few steps to rest his hands on her shoulders. "Take it easy," Hans said, his tone gentle.

She childishly crossed her arms and shook his hands off her shoulders. "Oh, go away," she grumbled.

He chuckled. "It was a compliment, I assure you," he said.

She shot her arms down and narrowed her eyes at him. "Then say thank you instead of laughing at me," she snapped. "It pisses me off to no end." As the words came from her mouth, she didn't miss the expressions that crossed their faces. They exchanged a raised-eyebrow look and a long, silent whistle.

"Thank you then," Hans said, although the confusion was clear in his eyes.

"You are going to have to hold back your temper when we are near these people," Kurt reminded her. "Many of them have killed for far less."

Elizabeth shuddered as she released a sigh, knowing he was right. So much for the over emotionalism being over with. "If I can hold back my temper with Übel around, I can do it with anyone," she grumbled.

Hans winked. "I know I can count on you," he half-teased. "Just don't let those mom-to-be hormones get you."

"All right, children," Kurt interrupted. "Time to go into town. We have a long afternoon ahead of us."

Kurt was to meet them at the *gasthaus* after Elizabeth and Hans had met with their latest contact. Both men wore their stolen uniforms and the field gray of the material, along with Hans' hair made him appear darker than usual. She had to admit he was spectacular looking.

Kurt's thin, fake mustache and his slicked-back blonde hair were the perfect contrast to the material. Elizabeth was to masquerade as Hans' wife and she had on a real dress for the first time in months. She wasn't sure when her pregnancy had started showing, but it was clear in the outfit she wore. The dress was an olive that went surprisingly well with her flame hair and it molded to the outline of her tummy. The length fell to mid-calf and the material swirled softly about her legs, which were encased in knee-high boots. Despite the color being similar to her friends' uniforms, she hadn't felt or looked so feminine in ages. If only Derek could see her dressed this way.

Elizabeth and Hans had planned to meet separately in front of the three-story brick *gasthaus*. As she made her way down the street, she didn't miss the admiring looks from the various uniformed military men and officers. One even released a soft wolf-whistle, but she ignored him as she walked by. She found Hans waiting in front of the *gasthaus*. When he noticed her, he gave her a warm smile as if he were actually her husband. „*Guten Abend*," she greeted him warmly.

Hans pressed a kiss on her cheek and she shivered. „*Hallo, mein Liebling*." They were about to walk toward the door when a dark-haired young man in black slacks and brown jacket started to walk by. Hans held his hand out with his palm facing the man. „*Papiere, bitte*," he ordered in a calm tone.

The man stopped, his black eyes showing no reaction to the request. „*Ja, mein Herr*," he said. He pulled his papers out from inside his jacket and handed them over to Hans.

After briefly running a gaze over the documents, Hans calmly handed the them back to the man. „*Danke*," he said.

The young man nodded. „*Bitte*," he returned. With a nod at Elizabeth, he made his way into the crowd.

"Ready, my lovely wife?" Hans asked in pretence.

As they made their way inside the entrance of the restaurant, a brown-eyed, blonde hostess wearing a blue smock greeted them. The matching skirt and white blouse underneath the soft jacket were a lovely complement to her hair and brown eyes. "Lunch for two?" she inquired warmly.

„*Ja,*" Hans replied with a nod. "Could you find a quiet corner for my wife and me?"

The hostess smiled. "Of course, sir," she said.

As she showed them to their table, Elizabeth took a quick, sweeping glance around the room. It was decorated mostly in brown and gold, and there seemed to be as many military men inside as outside on the sidewalks. She was decidedly uncomfortable, but forced herself not to react. There would have been hell to pay if the others had realized there were at least three resistants in their midst. Having Hans here was a greater relief than he realized.

They were shown to a table/booth near the back where there were only a handful of nearby guests, nearly all of the men being military personnel. Hans allowed her into the booth seat on the far side and slid in beside her. The hostess laid the menus on the table in front of them. "Enjoy your lunch," she said.

"Thank you very much," Hans returned.

"Did you enjoy your shopping, Elisabeth?" Hans asked, using the subject they had agreed upon to make them sound legitimate.

It was a good thing she spoke and understood German so well or else this would have been nearly impossible. As it was, she was jumpy, as if they both wore a sign identifying them as resistants. It was as if everyone knew their secrets.

„*Ja,*" she said with a nod. "Although I did not find anything I liked."

Hans chuckled, the laugh flickering in his eyes. "It does not matter, no?" he teased.

The field-gray-uniformed lieutenant across the aisle chuckled. "It does not matter with my wife," he said with a knowing sparkle in his gray eyes. "Even with the inconveniences of the last few years, she enjoys spending my money."

Elizabeth chuckled, although inside she was anything but amused. The war was more than just an "inconvenience" although of course she couldn't say so. To be so free with money while people were starving and deprived of their livelihood seemed to her disgraceful in the least. She understood the phrase 'go on with life' and enjoyed shopping as much as most women, but this was ridiculous.

"I understand quite well," Hans said in agreement.

Elizabeth couldn't help but send a fiery glare his way.

The lieutenant chuckled as he caught her look. "She gives me that look rather often," he said.

Hans grinned. "Good day to you," he said.

"You as well."

Hans slid his arm around Elizabeth's shoulders and bent his head to her ear. "You did well, Elizabeth," he whispered. "Now laugh as if I have said something funny."

That last comment was so unexpected, she couldn't help but do as he requested. She leaned closer to him. "That was easier than I thought," she admitted.

He grinned and pressed a lingering kiss on her lips, the latter action sending a brief flash of warmth through her body. Although they were both playing a part, she couldn't stop herself from being affected by him. But what had happened between them was over and would never be repeated.

When their waitress arrived, a pretty blonde with blue eyes, she knew right away that this was Kristal and that she had to make it seem as if they were friends. Before Elizabeth realized it, Kristal handed her what appeared to be a tube of lipstick.

"Hallo, Elisabeth," she greeted her, her voice femininely husky. "You left this last time you were here. I would hate to see you lose such a lovely shade."

Elizabeth took the tube from her hand and smiled. "Thank you, Kristal," she said with heavy relief in her voice. "Autumn Sunset has always been my favorite. I'm glad you found it."

Kristal laughed. "I like it, too," she said as if in agreement. "It goes with everything." She cocked her head. "Can I get you two anything?"

They ordered their food and it wasn't long before it was on the table in front of them. It had been so long since she had had satisfying food and the schnitzel seemed to melt in her mouth. She had cleaned her plate before she had realized it.

They continued with their pretense after Kristal took away their plates. Hans bent his head to her again. "We were successful at our last meeting," he stated.

Elizabeth leaned into him, sliding her arm around him and resting her hand on his left shoulder. "How so?" she asked.

He smiled and gave her another brief kiss. "Smile, Elizabeth," he urged. When she did, he continued. "We will have to get a room. I will explain then."

She couldn't stop the flush from entering her cheeks at his suggestion, although it pertained to their scenario. If anyone noticed her reaction, they would believe that they were exchanging love words. "I see," she smirked.

"Kurt is here and he will meet us there."

Elizabeth forced herself not to take a glance around the crowded room. "Where is he?" she asked.

"He is at the left end of the bar."

She let her eyes wander that direction without moving her head. Kurt nursed a drink and took a glance around at the other patrons. He blended so well that she wouldn't have known he was there if Hans hadn't told her so. She turned her attention back to him. "I see him," she said.

Hans slid his index finger under her chin and lifted her head. "Kiss me, Elisabeth," he said loud enough for the officers near them to hear. He bent his head to kiss her and eased his tongue into her mouth.

Elizabeth's body flooded with heat as she kissed him back. She let her hand find its way into the hair at the back of his head and the short strands were silky against her fingertips. When he pulled away, her swirling mind returned to normal.

"Are you ready, my wife?" he said, his voice husky.

"Yes."

Hans laid the small additional tip on the table and then they stood up to leave. They went up to the front of the restaurant to pay the bill and the hostess greeted them. "Did you enjoy your lunch, sir?" she asked. "Ma'am?"

"It was quite enjoyable," Hans returned. He had moved to set the payment on the counter when the hostess shook her head.

"*Nein*," she smiled. "It's all right."

"*Vielen Dank*," he said with his own warm smile. "Can you show my wife and me to a room? I will insist on paying for that."

The hostess smiled knowingly. "I can do that, sir," she said.

A few minutes later, Hans opened the door and let them into the room. Elizabeth took a quick glance around, noting that the color of the decor was similar to that of the restaurant. The bed was against the middle of the left wall as you looked from the doorway. Its brown headboard and gold-colored bedspread covered the mattress, each a lovely complement to the other. By the right wall sat a small table and chair made from the same oak as the bed. An armoire sat at the far wall, also made from oak. The small bathroom was to the immediate right as you walked into the room, in which a bright, multicolored rug rested on the floor.

Elizabeth plopped down onto the mattress and released a deep sigh. She relaxed fully into its thick softness and closed her eyes to get the most of out the feeling, nearly groaning at how comfortable it was. "Whoa-ho!" she said happily, her bones seeming to soften as she continued to lie there. "A real bed. I had almost forgotten what one feels like."

When Hans chuckled, she opened her eyes. He sat in one of the chairs with his booted feet propped up on the tabletop. "You may not be able to get up if you lie there," he warned. "That is why I chose to sit here."

She good-naturedly stuck her tongue out at him. "You're just jealous 'cause I beat you to it," she teased.

He stuck his tongue out at her in return. "Am not," he teased.

Elizabeth exaggerated a groan. "Don't get me started," she warned.

"Are you afraid I would win?"

"No," she said, although she attempted to withhold the laugh that bubbled in her throat.

"Are too."

"Hans!" she growled. Before she could say anything else, a hard knock on the door made her heart and body jump.

Hans slid his pistol from the holster and made his way over to the wall next to the door, waving her toward the bathroom. She slid silently off the bed and stepped inside. As he had taught her, she removed Derek's P38 from her purse and held it down to her side. Her heart raced, but she forced herself to remain calm.

Hans pointed the weapon toward the entrance and slowly opened the door. „*Ja?*" he asked, his voice hard.

Relief spread through Elizabeth's body when Kurt poked his head in the door and gave Hans a silly, wide-toothed grin. She put the Walther back into her purse and made her way back into the main part of the room.

Hans returned to his previous seat as Kurt closed the door. "Did anyone follow you, Kurt?" Hans asked.

"No one," Kurt said with a shake of his head. "A couple of SS men watched you leave, but they were not suspicious. You two looked like you were supposed to, a married officer and his wife having a lunchtime rendezvous." He wriggled his eyebrows and sat down in the chair opposite Hans. "Was it hot?"

Hans wriggled his eyebrows as well. "Oh, yeah," he teased.

Elizabeth rolled her eyes, her cheeks burning with a flush. "You two are terrible," she said. *And Derek,* she added silently. It was no wonder the three got along so well. *Make that four,* silly goose. *You get along with them terrifically yourself.*

"It seems you are the bad one, Elizabeth," Kurt teased. "I had begun to believe the kiss you and Hans shared was about to catch the room on fire. I was tempted to pour my drink over your heads."

Elizabeth pretended a sigh of annoyance as both men laughed, but it was wonderful to be able to smile through such a tragic time.

"So what can you tell us, my friend?" Kurt asked a moment later.

Hans turned his attention to her, letting her know to give him the message. She tugged the lipstick tube from her purse and tossed it at him. He pulled the message out, took a quick glance at it and set the paper on fire before she realized what he was doing. She found herself silently sucking in her breath when he tossed the match and "lipstick" into the nearby ashtray.

"Where are they?" Kurt asked, with no surprise or urgency in his tone.

"They have been with Rolf's parents for the last month. They are in the safest place they can possibly be at the moment."

Elizabeth had thought she was relieved before, but now tears of peace sprang to her eyes. *Thank God!* "But why did you burn the message? How will we know where they live?"

Hans smiled. "I know where the farm is," he said patiently. "It is only about thirty kilometers from the camp. We have stayed there before."

Elizabeth nodded in relief. "Then what happens?" she asked.

"We need to find a way to get Sabrina and Miriam to England," Hans replied. "Then I hope we can meet up with an American unit and liberate the camp."

It was all Elizabeth could do not to let tears of relief spill down her cheeks. Once Sabrina was back home, they could focus fully on Derek. "Why didn't we just hitch a ride with one of the American troops in Rothenberg?" she found herself asking. "It's not like there weren't plenty of them there."

Kurt gave her a gentle smile. "If we had known where Sabrina was at the time, that would have been perfect," he said.

"We could not have done much then anyway, Elizabeth," Hans added. "It was better to wait." He breathed a deep sigh. "The farm is a little more than a day's walk from here. We can do some work along the way, but we need to take a rest."

A long, loud yawn snuck up on her before she could stop it. "Do you guys mind if we stay here?" she asked hopefully. "This bed feels wonderful."

"Okay by me," Hans said. "I can sleep in this chair anyway."

Kurt rose to his feet and grinned at her. "I'll take the floor if I can have the bedspread," he suggested.

Elizabeth giggled. "Be my guest," she said. As she drifted off to sleep a few minutes later, she prayed that everything would work out.

Chapter Forty

ELIZABETH BREATHED A SIGH OF RELIEF when they reached the outskirts of the town where the Siedenstrangs' farm was located. In some ways, the time she had been away from Derek had gone by so slowly, but in other ways it seemed like yesterday when she had left. She prayed that he was alive so he could meet his son or daughter when the child came into the world. By the British accounts of the war, it was only a matter of time before Germany surrendered. They had been able to listen to the BBC at their last contact's house. To her surprise, the Allies had liberated Paris before she had ever been taken to the camp and the Russians were coming closer to Berlin. The weather had finally begun to warm during the day, but it was still chilly at night. The baby's kicking increased and the child seemed to be moving around all the time. The only time she had any peace in that sense was at night. Supposedly, the opposite was more typical, but it wasn't true in her case.

Hans and Kurt had gone to meet a contact, but it wouldn't be long before they returned. Elizabeth was surprised that people's personal business went on as usual, but she waited in an unfrequented spot behind one of the stores.

She began to pace, growing bored as she waited. She walked toward the edge of the building to see whether Hans or Kurt had returned. Breathing a sigh of boredom, she turned back to go behind the building. Before she realized anyone was there, someone stepped in her path.

When familiarity set in and Elizabeth realized that Zarah/Louisa had her Luger pointed straight at her, she froze. *Now is not the time for the "deer in the headlights" stance, Elizabeth. This woman is a psychopath.*

Louisa's dark-blonde hair was styled with a clip at the back of her neck and her navy, calf-length dress matched the dark-blue of her eyes. „*Hallo, mein Freund,*" she greeted, her tone draped in ice. "It has been a long time." She smiled. "I take it from your silence that you know who I am."

Elizabeth remained silent, her mind on Derek's Walther, which she had hidden in the side of her boot. Her fingers itched to be able to retrieve the weapon, but she wouldn't have a chance of beating her enemy.

Louisa chuckled. "How brave you have become, Elizabeth," she said, her voice deceptively bright. "Were you perhaps thinking of using your lover's Walther, which I am sure you carry? Shall I assume the traitor von Vetter has put that brat in your belly as well? It was only a short time before you let him bed you or so Übel has told me."

Elizabeth's heartbeat shot up in dread when her gaze dropped to her tummy. She wouldn't put it past the other woman to harm the baby just to strike back at her. It shocked her that Louisa knew Übel at all, but she refused to comment. It was all she could do not to turn and run away, but her former friend would only shoot her in the back. She had to face her nemesis and fight her or die trying. The worst part was that she hadn't expected to see Louisa again, since it had been so long, although Hans and Kurt had said it was a possibility. "I will not be a puppet for your amusement, Louisa," she found herself saying.

Louisa laughed. "You already amuse me, *Liebling,*" she taunted. She crooked her index finger on her free hand. "Toss your purse onto the ground and come over and turn around. If you do not, I will kill you."

A shudder of alarm rushed over Elizabeth, but she tossed the purse onto the ground. She walked over as instructed and Louisa yanked on her arm to spin her around. Elizabeth wanted to protest at the roughness, but the baby's safety was priority.

"Link your hands on top of your head, Elizabeth. Do not consider moving."

She calmly put her hands on top of her head, but she was shaking, as if someone had poured a bucket of ice water over her head. Louisa began her search and her hands went immediately to her distended tummy. Elizabeth held back a sob, terrified the other woman would harm her baby.

Louisa brought up her hand and searched around her breasts, sending a shudder of disgust through her. Her nemesis chuckled and bent to run her hand down her legs. Elizabeth's heart nearly stopped when a hand came to rest in the spot where the gun lay. Although it was in a false section, the pistol was larger than the designer had anticipated. She was sure the woman would find it, but she fought to breath a sigh of relief when her former friend moved onward.

When Louisa brought her hand back up, she roughly cupped her between her thighs. It was all Elizabeth could do not to shove her away in disgust. She had to find a way to retrieve the Walther. It was a miracle in itself that Louisa had not discovered it.

Louisa rose and chuckled. "I must be sure that you have nothing else on you, Elizabeth," she explained. "I do not want you to harm me."

Elizabeth snorted. "That would be least of what you deserve," she said before she could stop herself.

Louisa slung an arm across Elizabeth's throat and pulled her back against her body. With her free hand, she pointed the muzzle of her pistol against Elizabeth's distended tummy. "Silence!" she snapped. "Keep your mouth shut until I tell you to open it. If not, you are dead."

Elizabeth's heartbeat raced to a new level as her skin became damp with perspiration. She had no doubt that Louisa would kill her, no matter what she did or did not do. It was only a matter of time.

"I would not, if I were you, Louisa," a familiar male voice warned.

When Elizabeth realized that Hans had returned, she released the breath she didn't realize she had been holding.

"If you value the lives of von Vetter's brat and his whore, you will drop the pistol."

Hans' eyes flashed with an emotion Elizabeth couldn't place, but he refused to move. "If you pull the trigger, Louisa, you will die before your next heartbeat," he warned.

Louisa gave a harsh laugh, her arm tightening over her hostage's throat. "Do not be so sure of that," she challenged.

Elizabeth's heart lurched as Hans took a cautious step forward. It amazed her to no end that she had lived with this woman for well over a year and had never realized how cold-blooded she was. What a fool she had been. "I would listen to him, Louisa," she said loudly.

"Shut up, bitch!" Louisa screeched into Elizabeth's ear, the loudness causing her eardrum to numb.

"Put it down, Louisa," Hans warned again. "You will accomplish nothing by killing Elizabeth."

The arm across her throat loosened. "Our New Order will not tolerate those like her," she snarled. "You will conform to our ways or you will die."

Elizabeth couldn't believe the insanity of the statements. It just didn't seem possible that people could be so filled with hate that they would be willing to disregard their consciences and arbitrarily, systematically and completely to wipe the existence of another group of people from the face of the planet. But everything that had been going on within the last several years indicated otherwise.

"You know as well as I do that that the sort of logic you represent cannot go on indefinitely," Hans replied. "The Americans are nearing and it is only a matter of time before they arrive. It is over for your Reich, Louisa."

Louisa burst out laughing, but the sound came out as maniacal cackling. "What a charming man you are," she said with amusement full in her voice. "I would not be surprised if the brat in this woman's belly belongs to you."

Elizabeth's face warmed with a flush at her ex-friend's words. A moment later, Louisa laughed again.

"I see, Lindberg," she taunted, triumph sounding in her voice. "Her face is red with her guilt. I wonder what von Vetter would say if he knew you have been fucking his woman."

"Why did you do it, Louisa?" Elizabeth asked in an attempt to draw away the subject.

"What are you talking about, woman?" her captor snarled as if she were insane.

Elizabeth traded glances with Hans and he narrowed his eyes at her. She let a plea enter her eyes in hopes that he would let her try a different approach. When an understanding light flashed in his eyes, she withheld a smile. "Why did you use me like you did?" she asked, allowing a small amount of hurt to show through the tone. "You were my best friend. I couldn't have loved you more if you were my sister."

"You are a threat to our New Order, albeit a minimal one. You had believed me to be a Jew and you had no compunction in hiding me. If you were willing to do so for me and a handful of others, then how many more would you hide."

"I would hide anyone from your people. Jews have a right to live and be happy like the rest of us. There is no legitimate reason for eliminating them from the face of the earth. That is genocide, Zarah."

"Do not call me that wretched name! Jews are a direct threat to our existence and must be eliminated. There is no other way."

"Then I pity you, Louisa," Elizabeth said, her tone flat. It amazed her to no end how this sort of mentality continued. "How terrified of life you must be."

"How dare you!" Louisa snarled. "I am afraid of nothing." She released the safety and pointed the muzzle against Elizabeth's head.

Elizabeth's heart nearly stopped, but before she could take a breath, something from the corner of her eye caught her attention. And it wasn't Louisa.

"Drop it, Zelig," Kurt ordered calmly from Louisa's right. "This is my only warning."

Louisa let forth a loud growl and shoved her to the ground before Elizabeth realized she had done so. She stared at the muzzle her nemesis had pointed at her and her heart seemed to stop. Before she realized it, several loud popping sounds were erupting from her friends' guns and then the blonde fell to the ground.

As blood seeped from her wounds and her eyes went from cognizant to flat, Elizabeth could tell right away that she was dead. Her blood was making a stain on the ground and her body. She lay at a twisted angle and she possessed an unearthly appearance.

Elizabeth found herself scrambling away, but she did not hear the panicky sobs that spilled from her lips. Violent shudders racked her body when she realized how close to death she had come herself.

Hans pulled her to her feet and into his arms. She clung to him and allowed tears of release to spill down her cheeks. "It's over now, Elizabeth," he assured her gently in English. "It's over."

Kurt nudged Louisa onto her back with his booted foot. He raised an eyebrow as he glanced over at them. "The bitch is history," he said.

Elizabeth chuckled at the American-sounding phrase, but her laughter quickly turned back into sobs as the truth of what had just happened slammed into her.

Chapter Forty-One

A S THEY MADE THEIR WAY TO the Siedenstrangs' farmhouse, Elizabeth's heart pounded wildly in anticipation, since she still found it hard to believe they had finally located Sabrina and Miriam. It seemed as if someone were going to make it all disappear any second. Surreal would have been the word she would have used to describe the scene. The house was very rustic-looking, with brown wood and a full front porch of the same. The roof was a dark maroon, which invited the visitor to feel at home immediately. Tall trees surrounded the house, making it seem as if it were in the middle of a forest. Her attention was drawn from her surroundings when Hans knocked brusquely on the dark-red front door.

After several long moments, a woman of about forty with strawberry hair and a pleasingly slim build cautiously answered. Her dark-blue slacks were a lovely contrast to her hair and a manly red shirt hung on her lush but trim figure without distracting from her beauty. Her aqua eyes brightened when they landed on the two men and she opened the door wider. "Hans! Kurt!" she greeted them warmly. *„Willkommen!"* Her gaze landed on Elizabeth and she gave a nod of greeting. Elizabeth returned the gesture with a smile. *„Herein! Herein!"*

They made their way into the house, where Hans and the woman she assumed was Rolf's mother warmly hugged each other. She then hugged Kurt. Elizabeth couldn't help noticing how similar it was to the inside of Derek's house, but with bolder green, gold and brown and with a few family heirlooms and antique pieces of furniture. It was just as tastefully done, but more unassuming and more family-oriented.

"Mina," Hans said with a smile, motioning toward Elizabeth. "This is Elizabeth Kelley."

Mina turned to her and smiled, grasping her hands. "It is a pleasure to meet you, Elizabeth," she said in nearly accentless English. Elizabeth's heart swelled at the warm greeting and when the older woman briefly dropped her gaze to her pregnant tummy that was outlined by her navy cable sweater. "Congratulations on the baby."

"It's nice to meet you too, Frau Siedenstrang," she returned, instantly liking her. "And thank you."

Rolf's mother chuckled. "Please call me Mina," she offered as she released Elizabeth's hands. "I know you are eager to see Miriam and Sabrina. My husband, Roderich, is working and will not be back for another hour, so we will go to them now."

She led them down the stairs to the basement and into a large room, but it was empty, as far as Elizabeth could tell. Mina walked over to what appeared to be a blank wall and pressed on a small section, which slid away to reveal a hidden room. On the inside, it was surprisingly large and decorated comfortably with a handful of beds, a chaise lounge and an armoire. There were also a small table with two chairs, where the remnants of a card game were laid out. Two women whom she assumed to be Sabrina von Vetter and her companion, Miriam, were rising to their feet.

Elizabeth stood back as Sabrina and Hans exchanged a warm hug. At five eight, Derek's grandmother was taller than she had expected. She had the same smiling green eyes as her grandson and did not look near the age of seventy-five. Elizabeth hoped to be that vibrant if she lived to be her age. Miriam was a couple of inches shorter, with a slender build, and her hair was a shoulder-length brown with pretty red highlights. A smile curved her lips as her gray-eyed gaze went directly to Kurt. Elizabeth was about to say hello to Miriam when she and Kurt introduced themselves to each other. It was clear that they had an instant and mutual attraction, since Kurt's lips curved into a warm smile, which also sparkled in his eyes. Miriam's cheeks were slightly flushed as she gazed back into his, her eyes bright. *There goes Kurt.*

Elizabeth couldn't help but smile as she and Mina exchanged a look of understanding. "I will leave you alone with everyone now," Mina said.

"Thank you, Mina. For everything."

Her new friend squeezed her hand and nodded. A moment later, she made her way out of the room.

Elizabeth turned her attention back to Sabrina and Hans as Sabrina held his hand as if he were her son.

"It is wonderful to see you again, Hans," Sabrina smiled and then winked. "They don't keep us down here, you know."

Hans grinned widely, clearly enjoying the attention Derek's grandmother gave him. "It is good to see you also, Sabrina," he said as he continued to beam.

She chuckled, raising an eyebrow. "You are as charming as ever," she said. "I sure have missed you."

Elizabeth held a smile as they exchanged a hug, although tears filled her eyes and an ache tightened her heart. She only wished Derek was here to be with his grandmother.

"Sabrina, I would like you to meet Elizabeth Kelley," Hans introduced and then turned to Elizabeth. "Elizabeth, this is Sabrina von Vetter, Derek's grandmother."

"It's wonderful to finally meet you," Sabrina greeted her warmly. "Derek has spoken of you often."

Tears sprang to Elizabeth's eyes as the older woman pulled her into her arms and gave her a grandmotherly hug, which reminded her of how much she missed her mother. "I'm so glad to meet you, my lady," she returned.

Sabrina pulled back and let a wide grin curve her lips. She held out her hand. "You may call me Sabrina, my dear," she said warmly. Tears filled her eyes as she glanced down. "I'm thrilled about the baby. Congratulations, dear."

Elizabeth grasped the hand offered. "Thank you," she said. "And I am so glad you are safe. I promised Derek I would look after you."

Sabrina's gaze turned solemn. "How is my grandson?" she asked. "Mina and Roderich have not heard from Rolf since January, so they do not know."

Elizabeth's heart lurched. "I do not know, Sabrina," she said. "We met with a contact a few weeks ago. She said he was alive and in good health when she was there under another pretext, but I do not know how he is now."

"We are to meet with a contact in a few days and will go from there," Hans added. "Our first priority is to get you to relative safety. I promised Derek I would see to that. Then we will try to help him."

"The Americans will be here any day, Hans," Sabrina said. "I am as safe here as I can be anywhere." Hans looked skeptical, but it was clear Sabrina had made up her mind. She grinned. "There's nothing you can do to change my mind."

Hans chuckled. "I am aware of that," he agreed.

"I will wait here until you find out about my grandson's condition and if the worst has happened, I will return to England."

"As you wish."

Sabrina grasped his hands and pressed a kiss against his cheek. "Please let me know what you find."

Hans nodded. "I will," he promised.

Sabrina turned to Elizabeth. "If you or my great-grandchild need anything in the future, please let me know. No matter what happens, I'm here for you. You will always be part of my family."

Elizabeth's heart lurched with emotion and she swallowed hard to keep the tears from welling in her eyes. "I promise," she vowed.

"I know in my heart that my grandson is still alive, but I want you to be aware of your options."

"Thank you, Sabrina. I can never repay you for your kindness."

"You are very welcome, Elizabeth," she said as she pulled Elizabeth back into a hug. "And you already have."

Her tears finally spilled down her cheeks and she silently cried into Sabrina's shoulder.

Later that evening, Mina was kind enough to prepare a decent meal for all of them. It seemed a world away when Elizabeth had eaten hearty food on china and had drunk from crystal glasses. They all shared a laugh as Roderich related many stories of life on the farm and of the family who clearly meant everything to him. The fond memories shone brightly in his gentle aqua eyes and he was never far from a smile.

Rolf mostly resembled his mother, yet his hair coloring was a combination of that of both his parents. It seemed that he took after his mother in personality as well, having a reserved and calm nature. As with her son, Elizabeth suspected there was more to Mina than met the eye.

"Kurt, will you be going with Hans and Elizabeth?" Sabrina asked.

As Kurt and Miriam exchanged a knowing smile, Elizabeth withheld her own. "No," he denied as he grasped Miriam's hand. "I will stay here and assist Miriam in locating her family. She related how you were separated."

Miriam smiled as she turned back to Sabrina and a soft flush darkened her cheeks. "We have already discussed it, Sabrina," she said. "We will be remaining here for a while."

Chapter Forty-Two

AS ANOTHER FIT OF COUGHING WRACKED Derek's body, the ache in his chest intensified. He had been forced to work outside in the cold rain, along with the others and his already pained body screamed out in protest. He had woken up this morning with his body on fire as if he had a raging fever and his camp clothing seemed to burn against his skin. His throat was raw, as if he had had his tonsils removed and the back of his neck hurt so badly that he wanted to do nothing but curl up in a ball and force away his sickness.

Now it was dark and luckily he had been able to get back to the barracks in hopes of sleep. The others stayed away from him for fear of catching his sickness, but he couldn't say he blamed them. Five others in his barracks alone had died from pneumonia in the last week. He hoped that neither he nor anyone else would be the sixth. When he took a deep breath, a thready wheezing came from his lungs. The lack of nourishment and sleep had weakened him and the weight loss he had suffered didn't help. He had never been unhealthy in his life and now he had to admit he didn't like this at all.

Derek had caught a glimpse of himself in a mirror a month ago when Rolf had snuck him into the showers for a bath, which he had not been allowed since just before his outburst against Übel. He had nearly fallen apart emotionally when he realized that he had lost nearly half his body weight. He had been thin as a teenager, but he had still had a healthy face and body. Now he looked ill, as if he had a terminal disease. He hoped that if he ever saw his beloved Elizabeth again, she would not look at him in horror as he did at himself. As it was, the only thing that kept him going was his love for Elizabeth. He wondered if he was at death's door when a sudden warmth enveloped his body. Death would be a welcome visitor.

"This will help warm you," someone said.

He forced himself to open his eyes and turn to the familiar young voice. Rolf was crouched down beside him and had placed a blanket over him. He wore his guard's ensemble, but his rifle now lay flat on the floor. "It is good to see you, my friend," he greeted Rolf with a shaky smile. Derek hadn't seen him for over three weeks, so he suspected the other guards had kept him away.

Worry flashed in the younger man's eyes and he tightened his lips. "I am sorry I have not been able to come sooner," he apologized. "Übel has been having me watched, so I could not get away until now."

"That is fine," Derek whispered, since speaking normally was such an effort. "I am glad you are here now."

Rolf pulled a small box from the inside pouch of his jacket. He opened it and pulled out what appeared to be a small vial of liquid. "I swiped them from Siegfried," he reported. "They'll make you well again."

Derek didn't miss the hope in his friend's voice, but he couldn't dwell on that. "Won't he miss them?" he asked.

Rolf snorted with a chuckle. „*Nein*," he said. "He has been too busy shooting morphine into his bloodstream and would not notice if the Americans were bombing his office. In other words, a typical Wednesday."

Derek couldn't help but laugh. Unfortunately his lungs tightened as a fit of coughing returned. He had suspected that the doctor was addicted to his own medications and his friend's statement confirmed it.

Rolf patted him on the back once he had caught his breath and then grasped hold of his upper arm as he felt for the muscle. "This is only one dose. I must give it to you for several days lest the sickness return. So how are you about taking shots?"

Derek cringed. He didn't like them, but at least he could tolerate them. "Anything is better than this sickness shit," he said honestly. He cringed at the soft piercing of the needle as it slid into his muscle.

"I will be back later with some soup for you," Rolf said as he pulled out the needle.

Derek caught his friend's forearm. "You do not have to do this for me, Rolf," he said. "If anyone finds out about this, they will kill you."

Rolf's eyes went flat. "There is always a chance, Derek, but I will risk it." He shot to his feet at the sound of a couple of guards outside. "That is Übel. When he sees me leave here, he will question me. I must lie to him, so do not believe anything I tell him."

Derek nodded. "Go then," he urged.

Once outside, Rolf caught the angry look Übel flashed him as he walked up. He had decided upon a lie before he had given Derek the antibiotic, so he was prepared for the sergeant's questions.

"What were you doing in von Vetter's barracks?" the other man demanded, his tone laced with suspicion.

"I was checking on our *Kommandant*," he sneered, pretending the chore was anything but what he wanted. Übel's anger turned into a grin and Rolf wanted to gun him down on the spot. It was bad enough that the bastard was forcing himself on Katrine, but what he intended for Derek was unforgivable.

"How is our Jew-lover?"

Rolf forced himself not to react to the slur and grinned at the other man. "He is doing not so well," he said in truth, but his triumphant reaction wasn't. "He is wearing down, as you said. It will not be much longer now before death comes." *For you, Übel, you Totenkopf prick. The Americans are on their way and when they arrive, I will kill you myself for what you have done to Derek, Katrine and the others.*

It was only in the last few weeks that Derek had been physically wearing down. The weight he had maintained after Heinrich had taken over the camp had seemed to suddenly fall off him and he was no longer the healthy individual he had been. Guilt wracked Rolf's conscience and he hated having his health while his closest friend was dying. It reminded him of when he had first came to this camp at the age of nineteen. It had been little more than six months before America had come into the war and when he had realized the horror stories were true, he had forced back his emotional shock.

At the end of his job that day, he had gone into the guards' barracks and fortunately no one was there. Compared to the captives' barracks, theirs was like a four-star hotel. The memories of the captives' gaunt faces, their skeletal bodies and the barracks' general filth had immediately emblazoned themselves on his conscience. He would never forget the nightmare. He had lost the contents of his stomach and afterward had sat on the floor with his head buried in his arms. Shivers of revulsion had wracked his body and the tears had run down his cheeks. His emotions had seemed to be drained and a heavy weight had laid itself upon his soul. He had sworn to do everything he could to help them and to resist every chance he could get.

Part of him understood why people seemed to turn a blind eye to the situations in these camps. They didn't know what was going on in them and they didn't want to. If anyone did speak their mind about the atrocities or attempt to change what was happening, then they would be targeted for elimination as well. It did not justify their silence, but it was understandable. He had his own guilt in turning his back on the truth. It was a shame he would carry around for the rest of his life, regardless of his numerous resistances.

The *Kommandant* in charge at his arrival, Helmut Franz, had been in his late forties with blue eyes and whitening blonde hair. He had had two French mistresses who had been high-priced prostitutes before their internment and he was working his way toward a third, less worldly lover.

Rolf had known nothing of the girl he had been ordered to escort to the *Kommandant*. She had appeared to be barely eighteen years old with soft doe eyes and reddish-brown hair, which had been shaved from her head during the processing.

Herr Franz had raised a hand at him. "I wish to fuck her, Rolf," he had ordered. "Strip her immediately."

Rolf had balked before he realized it. „*Bitte?*" he had asked in confusion, unsure if he had understood correctly.

The *Kommandant* had risen to his feet, his eyes flashing angrily. "You dare question your commanding officer?" he had shouted.

Fear had ignited through Rolf and his cheeks had burned as a flush entered them. He had straightened his back and stared just to the left of the colonel. If he had looked into the *Kommandant's* eyes, he would have pleaded for his life. „*Nein, mein Herr!*" he had emphatically denied.

"Then do as I ordered!"

„*Ja, mein Herr,*" he said. He had turned to the girl and had attempted to convey his apology with his eyes for having to remove the camp uniform. She had refused to look at him and tears had welled in her eyes. His hands had shaken as he had released the buttons of her top. He slid the material off her shoulders and set it down in the chair next to her.

Trying to keep his mind detached from what he was doing, he had forced all thoughts away as he had tugged the bottoms down her legs. He had stepped back from her once she was bare, his cheeks burning with embarrassment.

The colonel had stepped toward her and run his hands over her breasts as if she were a mare he wanted to purchase for breeding. He had slid his hands around her naked body and grasped the cheeks of her buttocks to pull her against him. Thankfully, he had then ordered Rolf to leave.

After that first day, Rolf's emotions had seemed to be numb. Four nights in a row, he had gone into town and had gotten drunk at a nearby *gasthaus*. At sixteen, he had given his virginity to the very young wife of the farmer who had lived on the farm next to his parents, so he hadn't worried about his so-called innocence.

The first night, a beautiful blonde girl had "given him the eye," as Americans said. Even though he had been wearing his uniform, the voluptuous Marlene had been all too willing to allow him to take her to one of the *gasthaus* rooms. In less than two scant minutes, he had had her in bed and had rammed his way inside her. She had reacted wildly in his arms and although he had suspected that she had exaggerated her enjoyment of their sex, he hadn't cared.

After two more nights of torrid, lust-filled sex with two different women who were virtual strangers, he had realized he was heading down the path to self-destruction. There was no doubt that he had wanted to lose himself in the women so he could temporarily forget about the atrocities he had witnessed at the camp. Unfortunately, he hadn't been able to come up with a new way of dealing with his pain.

On the fourth night, he had gone back to the place he had frequented the last few days. Determined not to wind up in the arms of another woman in another bed, he had ignored the smiles and the nonverbal invitations from a dark-haired woman of about twenty. He continued to drink his beer and absently eye the small group of patrons.

„*Hallo*," someone greeted him.

He turned his bored attention to the woman who had been watching him. „*Tschüß*, baby," he had said. "I am not interested."

The woman had sat down next to him and he had forced himself not to push her away. She had slid an arm around his shoulders and had leaned forward so she could gaze into his eyes. He gazed into the depths of her baby-blue eyes and gulped. "I have seen you the last few nights," she had surprised him by saying. "How long have you had the habit of picking up strange women and taking them to bed?"

"Why would you give a damn?" he had snarled. He had been surprised when she let out a chuckle.

"Sometimes hot sex with strangers relieves tension."

"Are you offering your services?" he had found himself asking. He had promised himself that he would not take another woman he did not know, but their talk about the sexual act had caused him to shoot to painful attention.

The woman had smiled, briefly caressing him between his thighs with her palm. "What if I were?" she asked.

Rolf had found himself allowing a smile to curve his lips. "If I take you into a room, I will bed you," he warned. "There will be no changing your mind in the middle of it."

The woman had smiled, the action warming her violet eyes. "I have been warned." She had released him and risen to her feet. "Let us go."

Without another word, he had slid from his seat. Five minutes later, they were in a room.

"My name is Gretchen," she had said. "Your name is …"

"Rolf. Now let us waste no more time with talk." Without another word, he had tugged the navy, short-sleeved shirt over his head and dropped it on the floor. Gretchen watched as he pushed his slacks and regulation boxers down past his hips. He kicked them off, along with his loafers. He stood before her completely bare and raised an eyebrow, his length hardening when she dropped her attention to between his thighs. "Take off your clothes, Gretchen," he had demanded, surprising himself with the abrupt order. "Now."

She had slid off her long skirt first and then began to work on the top. He was glad to see that she wore no bra, but he understood when he eyed her breasts. She was small but well-shaped and he immediately wanted to grasp her breasts in his palms and run his thumbs over her nipples. The curvy plumpness of her hips, thighs and buttocks caught his attention, making them a sensual contrast to her breasts.

They had rushed toward each other and then Rolf had grasped her full buttocks to urge her against his erection. Their tongues had entwined as if they were thirsting for fluid and he had slid his hands from her buttocks to her breasts. He trailed his fingertips over nipples that were swollen and taut in invitation. He had grasped her wrists and held her hands on top of her head before bending his head to her. He had trailed his tongue over and around the heaviness of her breasts, suckling the tips as if trying to pull the nectar from their depths.

Gretchen arched her back against him, allowing groans of pleasure to sound in her throat. A heartbeat later, he had realized what had happened, he had found himself lifting her in his arms and laying her down on the bed. "Open your legs for me, Gretchen," he groaned.

With a coquettish smile, she did so. He grasped a knee and widened the leg more to allow his other hand to part the female lips. He brushed his middle finger over her and into her and brought it back out, urging her to move against it.

"Please," Gretchen begged.

Rolf shared a hot look with her and then bent his head. As soon as he touched her honeyed warmth with the tip of his tongue, his body screamed out for entry into her. She whimpered as he laved her and she slid her fingers through the short strands of his military-cut hair. Crying, whimpering moans burst from her throat and she arched her back in encouragement.

He released her and rolled onto his back so their roles were instantly reversed. A hot groan leapt from within him as she closed her mouth around him. He wasn't sure if it was the beer he had been drinking or how she was making him feel, but his mind quickly drifted into a sea of stars. He nearly groaned in protest when she lifted her head.

As Gretchen lowered herself onto him, he found himself shedding a quick release into her tight warmth. Once he had returned to earth, he leaned back against the headboard and urged her in front of him. He couldn't seem to help himself and began to stroke her breasts slowly, alternately teasing her nipples with his fingers. He grinned when she lifted her arms and linked them behind his neck, releasing a soft mewl of pleasure as he touched her.

He allowed his gaze to fall to her breasts and the outer curves cried out for his attention. She was small, but was she ever sexy. He grinned as the thought popped into his mind. He could get used to this.

Gretchen had tilted her head back to gaze into his eyes. "If you hate being stationed at that damned camp so much, why do you not do something about it?"

"Excuse me?" he balked, shocked that his feelings were so clear to this stranger.

"That is the reason you have been getting drunk and fucking those strange women, yes?" she asked as she moved to face him. "You want to forget about the horrors you see each day?"

Rolf hadn't known if he was more shocked at her words or at the actual truth of what she was saying. She lay back on her forearms and swung her leg out wide then inward again. The damp, dark hair between her thighs tempted him, as well as her very sensual breasts, but he did not want to admit the truth to her. She could be Gestapo for all he knew.

"If you want, I can give you the names of some members of the resistance I belong to. One of them should be able to help you."

He gulped. "It is not wise to broadcast such involvement," he warned. "How do you know I am not trying to infiltrate you in order to turn you in?"

A cold light entered Gretchen's eyes and she arched a dark eyebrow. "My friends will know if you are," she warned in return. "Then I will have them kill you."

Anger briefly rushed through him, but he did understand her point and he took a deep breath to calm it. "I am sorry, Gretchen," he found himself apologizing. "I had to make sure."

It was several days later when he had officially become a member of their resistance and a month later, he had confessed to his parents about what he had been doing. In return, they had surprised him with the fact that they had been hiding Jews, resistants and anyone else who had come seeking their help for several months. Part of him had been hurt at their silence, but logic had taken over. As much as they loved him, he was a guard at the nearby work camp. Since family members had been known to turn against one another, they had to make sure he would not be a threat.

He and Gretchen had continued with their love affair for the next year. They had gone on several campaigns together when Rolf had been able to get away from the camp for the night or when he had been on leave. He had found himself believing he was in love with her and confessing it.

Soon after he had professed his feelings for her, she had been captured and sent to the Ravensbrück concentration camp. She had been brutally attacked by several of the sadistic female guards and afterward had thrown herself against the electrified fence, ending her own life.

Rolf had been devastated by the news, his soul permanently stained. He had sworn never to love another woman and then he had met Katrine. He had known she was his soul mate and the love of his life as soon as he had set eyes on her. They had been able to spend time alone together when Derek was in charge, but for now it was imperative that he not risk her life. He was fully aware of what Übel and Erich were doing to her, but he was not in a position to help her. It brought back memories of what had happened to Gretchen. If he lost Katie, it would destroy him. When Derek had taken command and had requested that Elizabeth be brought to his office, Rolf had assumed he had only wanted her for sex. It hadn't taken him long to realize that Derek would be nothing like the previous *Kommandant* or any other, especially after Elizabeth had confronted him in the laundry. Derek was as sickened by the situation in their part of the world as Rolf was and he had done everything he could to make their captivity bearable.

Now that Derek himself was incarcerated, Rolf swore he would do everything in his power to make sure his friend stayed alive. But he also had to watch his own back, since Übel was making it a point to 'keep tabs' on him, as the American expression went. If he could not help his friend, Derek would surely not live to see the end of the war.

Chapter Forty-Three

HEINRICH TOSSED HIS PERSONAL ITEMS INTO his bag, his mind on his escape. The Americans had begun crossing the Rhine weeks ago and they would be arriving at the camp any day. By then, he planned on being long gone.

His superiors had known for a long while that they were losing the war and the *Führer* had been hiding away in his bunker since mid-January, surrounded by only a select few. No doubt, he would be executed if he were ever caught, but somehow Heinrich doubted it would get that far. His friend would surely end his own life before he allowed himself to be captured.

Heinrich himself had planned to hide away in a village near Caracas, Venezuela, where no one would be able to find him. He hoped to arrive within a week. The door opened and his secretary poked in his head, pulling him from his thoughts.

„Entschuldigen sie bitte, mein Herr?" Anton asked, his lips typically in a moue. "You wish to speak with me?" The little worm always had believed that working in such a place as this was beneath his dignity.

"I will be gone a short while, but if I am not back within the next few days, gather all your paperwork together and burn it. I want no documented evidence to remain for the Americans."

Anton paled at the news, although he gave no other obvious reaction. *„Ja, mein Herr,"* he said.

"I wish to speak with Übel. Find him for me now."

The secretary nodded in understanding. *„Ja, mein Herr,"* he said as he moved from the doorway.

Heinrich tossed the last of his clothing into his bag and latched it. Logically, he had changed into casual civilian clothing consisting of black slacks, sweater and boots. He had hidden his uniform between several pieces of clothing and would dispose of it when the circumstances allowed.

As he finished the thought, Übel strolled into the room. He forwent the required Nazi salute and nodded at him. "You wished to speak with me, Karl," he reminded him.

"Yes, I am leaving as soon as I can arrange it. Gather the evidence of the captives, papers, death warrants that von Vetter had refused to sign while he was in command or anything that documents what has happened here. When that is done and the final liquidation of the prisoners completed, you may do as you wish."

"What should we do about the traitor?"

Heinrich waved his hand, pretending the matter were of no importance. "He will be dead from his sickness by the time I return. He is no longer of any importance to us."

"The Americans will be arriving soon, yes?" Übel said in understanding.

There was no point in denying the information now. They would know soon enough. "Yes, that is for certain," Heinrich admitted. "You may leave when everything has been taken care of."

"Good luck, my friend."

A few days later, Heinrich stood among a crowd of people waiting for his Odessa contact. When a lone man with gleaming brown hair and dark eyes came up to him, he assumed the man was his contact. A small smile curved his thin lips. "Colonel Karl Heinrich?" the man greeted him in high-accented German.

"*Ja*," Heinrich acknowledged.

"Follow me, sir."

Without question, he followed the other man onto the waiting ship. Once inside what appeared to be a supply room, he found himself surrounded by American soldiers with their weapons drawn.

Heinrich forced a falsely jovial chuckle. "Hey, what's going on?" he asked in an attempt to imitate an American accent.

The man he had taken to be his contact raised an eyebrow and stepped back to his left. A blonde-haired woman stepped into view, her gray eyes hard. He had believed her to be a Gestapo agent, whom had come to his camp. Now he knew her for what she was.

Without a word, she held out her identification card and confirmed his thought. It read *War Department, the Adjutant General's Office, Washington DC.* It showed her name to be Adrienne Martin and she identified herself as such. All traces of her German accent were gone. "Colonel Karl Heinrich of the *Leibstandarte SS Adolf Hitler*," she said, her voice as hard as her eyes. "You are under arrest for War Crimes, Crimes Against the Peace and Crimes Against Humanity. You will be coming with us."

Heinrich's head spun and his heart constricted as the truth of the situation sank in. It was now over and there was no escape. He would be executed in his homeland. There was no doubt about it.

Chapter Forty-Four

EREK LAY ALONE IN THE BARRACKS, still weak from narrowly missing pneumonia. He had made several attempts to get up in the last couple of days, but his mind whirled with vertigo each time. He had finally given up and lay on the hard wood until Rolf could come to help him. Rolf had been bringing him small meals, which he had to eat in order to regain his strength. Unfortunately, the idea of putting food into his stomach made him want to retch. There was no way to win.

Heinrich had been gone for the last several days and there was no doubt in Derek's mind that he wouldn't be returning. Even Übel, who had made it his personal goal to break him, now left him alone. He wondered if it was because there had been rumors that they would be liberated by the Americans, who had crossed the Rhine and were now heading in their direction. However, he assumed they were just that; rumors.

The last bit of good news was that Miriam and his grandmothers' last location was the Siedenstrangs' farm and that Kurt then had taken Miriam to find her family, since they had been separated. That gave him some sense of peace, but he still worried about Elizabeth and prayed that she was safe.

He remembered her beautiful, silky locks and the emerald of her eyes. Her smile when she looked at him with love shining on her features. The memory of her soft skin as he held her in his arms after their sensual lovemaking, her scent penetrating his senses as if she were here with him. How she had stood up to him when they first met, how she had told him why she was there and that she was proud of what she had done.

He chuckled to himself in memory of their last, sensual encounter. Elizabeth had been aroused, looking as if she were ready to pass out from pleasure. He found his mind moving to the present as he reached down and cupped his hardening length. "You're a damned horny son of a bitch," he snorted.

At his verbalized thought, someone cleared his throat. His hand shot away from his erection and he took a glance behind him as a flushing Rolf released another cough into his fist.

"I see you are much improved," his friend teased, his aqua eyes sparkling with amusement. "Now it is time to get you on your feet."

Derek groaned, since standing was the last thing he wanted to do. „*Nein*," he said, deliberately adding a whiny note to his voice.

„*Ja*," Rolf returned. "You will only become weaker if you do nothing but lie in that bed. As it is, your lying there is keeping you from recovering."

Derek swore, although he had no doubt his friend was correct. He moved into a sitting position and rested his feet on the cool floor.

"On your feet!" Rolf demanded, his tone reminiscent to that of a superior officer. "Move it! Move it! Move it!"

Derek couldn't help but laugh at the teasing light in his friend's eyes. It was clear he was enjoying giving his superior officer orders. He held up his hand, the palm facing him. "Help me up?" he asked.

Rolf stepped forward and grasped his hand. In a long heartbeat, Derek was on his feet. The room seemed to spin and his heart pounded hard with the effort of remaining upright, but his friend was there to help him. Rolf put his arm around his shoulders and slid his arm around his waist.

„*Danke*," Derek said with a heavy sigh. The spinning had slowed and his heartbeat returned to a more acceptable rhythm.

„*Bitte*," Rolf returned. "Now walk. I promise I will help you."

Derek cautiously took one slow step after another, somewhat embarrassed because of his weakness. He continued to walk, although his legs and arms were still shaky. He expected that would be normal until his strength returned.

„*Gut*," Rolf said after a step and then again after another.

After walking the short distance from the bed to the wooden barracks wall and then back again, Derek's heartbeat began to pound wildly. Rolf helped him back to the bed and he sat down, his body shaking from the exercise. The dizziness had returned and he lay back on the wood, panting as if he had been running. He took a deep breath in order to slow his racing heart. "Thank you, Rolf," he said with heavy emotion in the tone. "I owe you my life."

A boyish grin curved Rolf's lips. "You can repay me by getting better," he said.

"You gotta deal, baby brother," Derek teased in American English, his tone breathless.

Rolf chuckled. "And thanks for helping me with my American, big brother."

Chapter Forty-Five

THERE WERE RUMORS AMONG OTHER RESISTANTS that the Americans were close to Murrbrück, the small city where the camp was located and Elizabeth hoped that that was the case. As voices sounded off in the distance, she and Hans stopped in their tracks. They were too far off to be able to tell what language the group was speaking, but without exchanging glances or words, they made their way into the forest. A moment later, they heard the roaring of what sounded like tanks and some smaller vehicles. Elizabeth's heart raced in dread, as her first thought was that it was a German unit heading their way. She glanced at Hans and caught his nearly undetectable smile.

When he mouthed "Americans," she balked before she could stop herself. *How would you know?* "No way!" she mouthed back.

"You will have to make the first move, Elizabeth," he said, causing her heart to jump. He stepped closer and raised an eyebrow. "I look like the German I am, so you are the logical choice."

She nodded, although her heartbeat raced at the prospect. He was correct. "All right," she agreed with a deep sigh. "But what should I do then? Tell them about you?"

"Do what you need to do to make sure we both go to the camp with them. I owe Derek that much."

As the echo of the unit came closer, she thought she might have finally detected American accents. It didn't quite register in her mind at first, but she was ready in spite of that. "Now?" she asked.

Hans handed her a white sock, using it as he would a handkerchief. "Just in case," he said.

Withholding a smirk at the seemingly clichéd sign of surrender, Elizabeth grabbed it and made her way from the trees. As soon as she stepped into the middle of the road, she noticed the lead men walking with their rifles in hand and wearing the familiar olive of the American army uniform. She nearly chickened out when the enormous tank, transport and several smaller vehicles came into view. She forced herself to wave the sock in the air, albeit feeling a bit silly, since it *was* a sock. It was a moment before anyone noticed her.

"Stop!" she yelled in English. "Please!"

When the lead men stopped in their tracks and pointed their weapons at her, her heart almost stopped beating. She released a deep sigh of relief as they lowered them and motioned with their fists in the air for the troop following them to stop.

She lowered her arms as the lead man came up to her. "My name is Elizabeth Kelley," she said, her tone breathless, but loud enough for him to hear. "I'm an American." *God, it seems weird saying that after so many years.*

"I am Sergeant Douglas Allen," he identified himself in return, his eyebrows crinkled in curiosity. "What are you doing out here by yourself? Is there anyone with you?" Although she, Hans and Kurt sometimes spoke English, the majority of their conversations were in German. The American accent sounded unfamiliar to her since it wasn't something she was used to hearing from strangers. Sometimes it didn't even register. It was amazing in what a short time that had happened. It was something she and her father had noticed right away when they had moved to Germany. Even at her young age, it had taken less than a month.

Elizabeth took a quick glance at the husky, gray-haired gentleman behind the sergeant, who had just stepped from his jeep. A gulp lodged in her throat when she noticed the two general's stars on the front of his helmet. He looked more like she would think someone's grandfather would than an army general. 'Cuddly' would have been the word she would have used to describe him. "I have a member of a resistance group with me," she said to Sergeant Allen. "I must have your promise to guarantee his safety. I owe him my life."

The general stopped next to his sergeant. "You are relieved for the moment, sergeant," he said, his soft tone making his order seem more like a request.

The sergeant saluted his commander and made his way back toward the others.

The general returned his attention to her and held his hand out. "I am General Alan Drake of the United States Army ..." he said and then gave his unit number.

Elizabeth shook his hand in return. "I am Elizabeth Kelley," she returned. She breathed a deep yet silent sigh, but her heart still pounded hard from her nervousness. "General ..." she started. After she had taken a deep breath, she began with the story. "I realize our resistance group is disorganized by your military standards, but my friend is a good man and he has done a great service for the Allies. I must guarantee his safety."

A ghost of a smile curved the general's lips and he nodded. "Is either of you carrying weapons?" he asked.

Elizabeth's heart sank, but she refused to lie. "Yes, sir," she admitted.

General Drake nodded in understanding. "I must ask that you hand them over for the moment, ma'am," he said. "We will return them to you once I have spoken with your friend. If you agree, I will guarantee his safety as well as your own."

Elizabeth nodded, breathing a sigh of relief. "I agree, sir," she said. "Thank you."

Not five minutes later, Elizabeth and Hans were aboard the transport vehicle with the general and some of the other soldiers. Drake must have been satisfied with their answers, since he returned their weapons soon afterward.

Elizabeth watched with a smile as her friend became deep in conversation with the soldiers. It was amazing to see how quickly he made friends and she was somewhat envious. She turned to the general, who sat to her right. She briefly wondered why he didn't ride in his jeep, but she ignored the thought. "Pardon me, sir," she said. "But are we by any chance heading toward the Murrbrück work camp?"

The general crinkled his eyebrow in surprise. "Yes, ma'am," he said, with the same surprise in his tone. "Are you familiar with it?"

She couldn't help but chuckle. "Yes, sir," she said before sobering. "I was there until I escaped in January. Unfortunately, the man I love was unable to and he is still there." Tears welled in her eyes and she took a deep, shaky breath. "I hope he is still alive."

Hans reached from the seat across from her and squeezed her hand, his expression soft. He looked toward the general. "We were hoping that we would be allowed to travel there with you, sir," he said in English. "After searching for her fiancé's grandmother and having located her, we have found that she is safe. However, we have nothing on her fiancé's current condition. We are not aware if allowing us to travel there with you is against your regulations, but please. It is imperative that we find our way there."

"I will allow you to travel with us," the general said, giving no answer as to whether or not Hans' inquiry was true. He turned to her. "I knew there was a reason you looked familiar. I know your father, Daniel. You look very much like him and your mother."

Elizabeth sat back, stunned. The phrase "it's a small world" was truer than she had ever realized. "You know my father?" she asked. "How?"

Drake chuckled. "He interviewed me several years ago," he said. "I knew he had been transferred here on assignment, but I did not realize you were here with him. How is your mother? Is she still here as well?"

"She died shortly before we came here," Elizabeth explained.

The general crinkled his eyebrows. "I'm sorry," he apologized. "I did not know." He paused. "Someday, I would love to discuss in further detail how I knew Daniel."

Her father hadn't contacted her in the last couple of years, but he would be able to now, since she was sure the war was nearly over. "I would like that very much, sir," she said.

It wasn't long before the gray outer wall of the camp with the electrified razor wire along the top came into view. The same cold hand of death trailed itself down the length of her spine just as it had when she had first seen it, but this time was different in another respect. Instead of being a captive along with the others, she was here to liberate them. Her hair stood up on her arms at the knowledge and a warm feeling found its way into her heart, which erased the feeling of dread.

Unfortunately, as they came up on the camp, she realized that the guards had rounded up several of the captives, who included her friend Talia. The captives were very malnourished and their eyes seemed to be sunken into their heads. A general look of hopelessness clouded their features and stark panic shined in the eyes of others. It was then that she realized how little she had gone through when compared to them. Hot tears filled her eyes and it was all she could do not to release the sob that had tightly gripped her heart. Her friends were tied to the whipping posts while guards raised their rifles and aimed at them, ignoring the approaching general and his entourage.

Her heart leaped into her throat at the sound of cocking rifles. Within the next heartbeat, the American soldiers raised their weapons at the tower guards. To her surprise, no one resisted. The guards laid down their weapons and raised their hands in surrender. She nearly jumped when other American soldiers shot off the locks with their rifles. Soon afterward, the unit began storming through the gates. A loud, banging crash of iron and bricks nearly numbed her ears as they slammed to the ground. What surprised her most was that the guards at the posts still did not react to their entry.

The troop stopped once they were inside and the cocking of the weapons echoed as the soldiers aimed them at the guards. General Drake rose to his feet and propped a foot on one of the seats. "I would advise against it, gentlemen," he said, unexpectedly in German. „*Hände hoch!*" Hands up!

The majority slowly lowered their weapons to the ground and raised their hands in surrender, but one daring guard whom Elizabeth recognized sharply turned and aimed his gun at the general. She barely kept a scream from leaping out of her throat when Sergeant Allen shot the younger man, the force knocking him to the ground. Her head swam with relief.

The expressions on the captives' faces went from terror to happiness and they seemed to cry out with relief at the same time. She absently noted a scuffle in the distance, but before she realized that she had moved, she made her way with the others to the captives. At the same time, the able-bodied captives poured out of their barracks and greeted the soldiers. Recognition flashed in Talia's eyes as their glances met a few moments later.

Elizabeth barely realized it when the tears began streaming down her cheeks. As if in a dream, she swiftly untied her friend. Once Talia had been freed, the women shared a welcoming hug. "I've been so worried for everyone," Elizabeth said into her friend's shoulder."

Talia pulled back, the emotion in her dark eyes turning from defeat to relief. "Thank God you are here, Elizabeth," she said with the happiness full in her voice.

Before Elizabeth could answer, others whom she recognized came over to hug her. She hugged everyone she could with equal emotion, but her mind was on Derek. *Oh please, God,* Elizabeth prayed for the umpteenth time, her heart beating wildly. *Let Derek be alive.* She was shaking so hard, she wondered how she was able to remain on her feet.

She turned to Talia and took a deep breath, forcing herself to remain confident. "Is Derek still alive?" she asked without preamble.

"He was a few days ago," Talia said, causing Elizabeth's heart to leap with hope. "But we have been kept apart from the others since Tuesday. It is only today that the guards have allowed us to leave our barracks, but only for them to bring us here." Talia closed her eyes and swallowed hard. "If you were but a few minutes later ..."

Elizabeth squeezed her hand, trying to ignore her sinking heart. "I know," she said.

Talia squeezed hers in return. "Go, my friend," she urged with a smile. "Find the man you love. I will do the same by finding Sam."

Elizabeth made her way inside the confines of the camp and more of the captives she recognized came up to greet her and thank her, including Naomi. It was several minutes before she was able to go on her way. Her emotions hardened as her gaze landed on the guards sitting by the main processing room. Their hands were bound behind their backs and various ranking soldiers were guarding them. Although Rolf wasn't among them, Erich was. It was apparent, from the bruise on his left cheekbone and the blood that had caught at the corner of his lips, that someone had fought with him. She briefly wondered whether some of the captives were responsible and she couldn't say she blamed them if that were the case. Erich returned her brief attention with a deeply black look, but she turned away from him in the hopes of finding the man she loved. Erich wasn't worth her time.

Chapter Forty-Six

ENERAL ALAN DRAKE EYED THE TAWNY-HAIRED guard with the cold, cerulean gaze, withholding a chuckle at the sight of his superficial wounds. A small group of female prisoners had jumped on him and started beating him up as the unit had broken into the camp, but the young man's injuries were minimal. The women's strength had surprised Drake, considering their weakened condition, but Erich Kurtz must have been one of their main aggressors. "I wish to speak with your commanding officer," Drake stated, forcing an authoritative tone that indicated that the guard had better answer.

"The *traitor* is in barracks fourteen," the guard said with heavy contempt in his tone. "He will be wearing a prisoner's uniform."

At the word 'traitor,' Drake wasn't sure what to think. "His surname?" he asked.

"Von Vetter," the guard confirmed. He leaned back against the building, crossing his legs at his ankles as he turned his attention away.

Drake shook his head, not surprised at the young man's attitude. Some of the guards had willingly surrendered, but those such as this man gave nothing away willingly. He found his way over to the barracks labeled fourteen and two men came out into the daylight as he approached. They were as malnourished as the others in the compound and his gut tightened with revulsion. Not at the people themselves, but because it still shocked him that they had been deliberately and cold-bloodedly starved well past the point of emaciation. He was surprised anyone had survived. He rested his foot on the bottom step. "Can either of you men identify Major Lord Derek von Vetter?" he asked.

The older of the two men narrowed his eyes, although a sparkle of an unknown emotion flashed in their depths. "I am Rabbi Samuel Benjamin," he identified himself in American English, nodding sideways toward the other man he supported. "This gentleman is Derek von Vetter."

Drake turned his attention to the younger of the two men. Although he wondered if the rabbi had understood him, it went along with the derogatory term the guard had called him. "I'm sorry," he apologized. "I was looking for the camp *Kommandant* named von Vetter."

The younger man nodded. "I am one and the same, General," he stated in upper crust English. He tugged his dog tags from his now oversized shirt and handed Drake the bottom half.

Drake had heard rumors that the younger man possessed more than one English title in spite of his commission with the German Army. He now knew the rumor to be true, although he would ask for a more detailed explanation later. He handed the section back to him.

"I was *Kommandant* for merely a few months," Derek advised. "Any number of the captives as well as the guards will verify my identification."

"Forgive us, General," the rabbi interrupted. "But Derek has been ill and is recovering. He needs to regain his strength. So if you wish to interrogate my friend, you will have to wait."

The general crinkled his eyebrows, still stunned from the picture before him. Benjamin didn't seem in well enough health himself to support the larger von Vetter and in addition to this, he had referred to Derek as his "friend." Drake had come there with every intention of arresting von Vetter as he had been ordered to do and having him sent to Nürnberg with the others to be tried for Crimes Against Humanity.

He had seen the attempts of other *Kommandants* as well as guards to hide their identity by dressing as a prisoner or civilian, but they were in excellent physical and emotional health, unlike the others. Von Vetter wore the garb of a concentration camp inmate as well, but he was every bit as malnourished and emaciated as the others interned, the polar opposite of those attempting to hide their identities. The clothing was the only similarity between the two. This young man had freely given his name and had that same flat, hopeless look of despair in his eyes as the other captives. The major had given him no indication that this scene was anything but genuine. Although there was clearly more than what met the eye, he would conduct a full investigation. "The interrogation cannot wait," he stated. "However, I will allow your friend to aid you in walking over to the office."

Chapter Forty-Seven

ONCE INSIDE WHAT USED TO BE Derek's office, Samuel helped him down onto the sofa and slid his arm from around him. "Let me know if you need anything, Derek," he offered.

"Thank you, Sam," he said with a slow smile. Although he sometimes needed help to move around, he was slowly regaining his strength. He wasn't as self-sufficient as he had hoped at this point, but at least there was an improvement.

"Thank you, sir," General Drake said.

Sam nodded before turning to Derek. "I will be in the outer office if you need me," he said.

"Thanks."

Sam gave the general a deep look. "Please be kind to him, General," he said. "He's been through hell."

Surprise leaped in Drake's eyes, but he nodded. After Sam had gone, the general sat down in the chair in front of the desk. "I must say offhand that I'm not sure where to start," he seemed to confess. "How did you come to be interned as a prisoner in this camp?"

"Let me start at the beginning," Derek said with a deep sigh. "Miriam Ephram is my grandmother's companion and secretary, and she is a Jew. I had identity documents falsified, stating that Miriam's name is Maria Ehrmann. Somehow, Colonel Karl Heinrich discovered what I had done and I was summoned to Berlin. He informed me that I was to be given the assignment as *Kommandant* of this camp and that if I did not accept it, my grandmother, Miriam and I would be taken into "protective custody." He also stated that the three of us would be eliminated, once there."

Derek went on to tell him about the changes he had made and about his minor involvement in the resistance. He had refused to sign even one death warrant, considering such an action to be flat-out murder. He explained about the colonel discovering his newer secrets and taking over as *Kommandant* of the camp. He explained that all the changes he had made had been dumped by the wayside and that the captives' health had taken a turn for the worse.

He watched the mixture of emotions that crossed the general's face, but he did not stop or soften his descriptions. He told him of his covert attempts at documenting all that had happened since the second day of October. He mentioned Heinrich's withholding of food, about the treatment of the other captives and that Heinrich had had no compunction about meting out the harshest punishment for the smallest infraction.

The general stood up and began pacing the floor with his hands behind his back. "I will interview the captives to verify what you say, Major, but that is a formality. I had come here with the full intent of arresting you and sending you up for indictment, but it will serve no justifiable purpose to do so. Your refusal to sign even one death warrant will go in your favor, as well as your treatment of the captives and your resistance work. I must have your promise that you will testify as a witness against Karl Heinrich in his trial at Nürnberg, along with the other Nazi hierarchy, telling everything you know. Your documentation will help in that as well."

"I will do so, but I have one favor to ask of you, sir."

"Let me know what it is about and I'll see if I can help you."

Derek withheld a sigh. It was better than no answer at all. "I would request asylum and immunity from prosecution for my guard, Corporal Rolf Siedenstrang," he said. "If it were not for him, many of the other captives' lives would have been lost, along with my own. He and his family are active in the Resistance as well and he put me in contact with several of their members. I and many others in this camp are alive because of this young man."

Chapter Forty-Eight

THROUGH THE HORDE OF SOLDIERS AND captives, Derek's heart lurched as he caught a glimpse of Elizabeth in Hans' arms as they shared a brief hug. When they pulled apart, Derek's gaze dropped to her clearly pregnant tummy and he had the fleeting suspicion that Hans was the father of the baby she carried. Almost immediately, logic took over and reminded him that she hadn't been gone long enough for that to be true. Although he wasn't an expert, she appeared to be about five months along.

Elation surged him with the realization that she was really here and it was *his* child she carried. Even with the joy of the fact, he had the inkling of a suspicion that there was more to their relationship than just friendship. He brushed off the thought when she worriedly scanned the crowd of people. Unable to keep a grin from curving his lips, he looked up at one of the American soldiers standing next to him.

As if the soldier realized he was being watched, he glanced down and raised a curious eyebrow. "Can I help you with something, sir?" the young man asked in faltering German.

"Would you be so kind as to help me up, private?" Derek asked in his natural English. "I am still somewhat weak."

Surprise crossed the young man's features, but he nodded and held out his gloved hand in assistance. "Not a problem, sir," he said in English.

Derek hid a smile and returned his attention to Elizabeth. She hadn't seen him yet, but it was only a matter of time. Now that he was on his feet, he could help her accomplish that goal. He noticed from the corner of his eye that the soldier watched him and he turned his attention to the young man.

The private nodded toward Elizabeth. "Who's that?" he asked.

Derek grinned. "Elizabeth," he replied. "She's the mother of my child and she's going to be my wife." A heartbeat later as he turned his attention back to the woman he loved, their eyes met. Hers instantly filled with tears and her jaw dropped. A moment later, she slapped her hand over her mouth, not because she was horrified at seeing him in his present condition, but because he was still alive. Her love for him and the sheer relief of finding him alive shined on her features and in her emerald eyes. Before he realized that either of them had moved, they were bawling in each other's arms. It was all he could do to remain on his feet. The silky red hair she had shaved off now fell softly to just under her ears and he slid his fingers through the lustrous strands. His insides softened at her swollen tummy pressed against him and he wanted to hold her forever. He now had no doubt that he had survived the trauma of his confinement and that they were meant to be together. He knew it in his heart as well as in his soul and the life inside her proved that.

Elizabeth pulled back and gazed deep into his eyes, seeing neither his dramatic weight loss nor his weakened condition. It was clear that she did not smell the stench of his body or the prisoner's uniform, which hung on his emaciated body. The only thing she saw was the man she loved with her entire soul. "I love you, Derek," she said with all her feelings in her voice. "I was terrified I'd never be able to tell you that again. I've missed you so much."

He cupped her cheek with his hand, caressing her soft cheek with his thumb. His eyes filled with tears. "I love you, sweetheart," he returned. "I've missed you so much. A day didn't go by that I didn't think of you."

When she grabbed his hand and placed the palm on her rounded tummy, he had no doubt that he loved her more than life itself. "This is our baby, Derek. I love you so much," she half-wailed. "I just can't tell you enough."

"Marry me, sweetheart," he said, his voice tight with emotion. "Neither of us will settle for anything else. I love you too much ever to be without you."

When tears rushed into her eyes, his heart swelled with love for her.

"Yes, my love," she agreed. "There's nothing I would love more than to be your wife."

As she tugged down his head and opened her mouth to allow his tongue inside to caress hers, he wrapped his arms around her and pulled him fully against him.

Epilogue

ELIZABETH ANNE KELLEY AND DEREK EDWIN von Vetter married by one of the formerly-captive priests the night the camp was liberated. Elizabeth wore her cable sweater and slacks, and Derek wore his camp uniform with the boots from his military uniform. Although German brides weren't "given away," she wasn't German and was thrilled when General Drake offered to do so for her. Samuel Benjamin was unable to officiate the wedding due to their different faiths, but that didn't stop the shouts of *Mazel Tov!* from Jews and Gentiles alike. The ceremony wasn't the prettiest in the world, but it was more than heartfelt. A couple of friendly soldiers snapped a number of photographs, taking them from angles that wouldn't show how bad the condition of the camp was.

Elizabeth caught the smile of happiness and contentment Derek shared with his grandmother. Rolf's parents had attended the wedding with Sabrina, who was now deep in conversation with Hans and Sam. She eyed Kurt as he held Miriam's hand, knowing it wouldn't be much longer until they were married, since their love for each other was unmistakable. As soon as she tossed her bouquet over her shoulder, someone gave a loud squeal of excitement. She turned around as Katrine flung herself into Rolf's arms and pressed kisses along his cheek and jaw.

When Derek slid his arm around Elizabeth's waist and tugged her to his side, she shuddered deliciously at his body warmth. "They'll be married next," he said into her ear. "Funny how that always seems to work."

Elizabeth chuckled, since the prophecy did always seem to come true. She gazed deep into his eyes. "I love you, Derek," she said with her feelings full in her voice. "I don't ever want to be without you again."

He winked and pulled her fully into his arms. "I love you, too," he returned. "Always and forever."

Elizabeth couldn't help but smile as Rolf slid his arm around Katrine's shoulders. "Does that mean you are going to marry me, Katie?" Rolf asked, his love for her clear to anyone who saw them.

Katrine's jaw dropped, but she was unable to utter a word.

"Would you rather discuss this somewhere more private?" Rolf asked. When she nodded in stunned response, he turned to Derek. "Would it be acceptable if we used your quarters, Herr von Vetter?"

Derek laughed. "Yes, Herr Siedenstrang," he teased in return. "It would be acceptable."

As they started to walk by, Rolf took a moment to pause. The men exchanged a conspiratory look before he leered. "Just do not come in there for about an hour. We're going to be busy."

"Rolf!" Katrine protested, her cheeks bright pink.

Elizabeth couldn't help but chuckle. "You'd better get used to it, Katie," she said. "Derek does that to me every chance he gets. You know how alike they are." When the men gave each other a cat-calling, double high-five, they all laughed.

Rolf laughed. "Later, guys," he said.

"You are terrible, Rolf," Katrine drawled. "Is there no shame in you?"

Elizabeth turned to the man she loved and smiled as their friends made their way to the quarters to be together. A weight had been taken from her shoulders and now she could concentrate of the man she loved.

Derek raised an eyebrow, a teasing light shining in his beautiful eyes. "So what's this about 'Derek does this to me all the time'?" he asked.

Elizabeth burst out laughing, but then turned when she noticed General Drake stroll over to them with a bottle of champagne in his grip. He handed it to Derek.

"Enjoy," he said with a smile.

Derek grinned. "Thank you, my good man," he said. "You have

saved all of us and I will be forever grateful. We all have a reason to smile again."

Elizabeth smiled with tears in her eyes. "Thank you again for all you have done, General," she said. She would always have a soft spot for the kind-hearted, older gentleman because of it. "We appreciate it more than we can ever show."

He winked. "Just have a happy life," he said. "You two deserve it."

There was no doubt in Elizabeth's mind that she and Derek would be together for the rest of their lives and that nothing would ever tear them apart again.

About the Author

Valerie Michaels has been writing since just after the birth of her son and writes contemporary as well as historical stories. She has been inspired by her love of history and from being a citizen volunteer at the police department in her city.

She tries to be as realistic and factual in her stories as possible and relies on her enjoyment of history and her volunteering as most of her research.

Her pseudonym is a combination of her children's first names, Valerie and Michael. She lives in a small suburb north of Dallas, Texas, with her husband, Steve.